Kicking

New Beginnings Book 2

ROBIN MERRILL

New Creation Publishing
Madison, Maine

Scripture quotations taken from American Standard Version (ASV).

And when we were all fallen to the earth, I heard a voice saying unto me in the Hebrew language, Saul, Saul, why persecutest thou me? it is hard for thee to kick against the goad.
—Acts 26:1

Prologue

The little girl knelt beside her bed. Her shoulders shook with her sobs.

She had been so excited for this party. She'd invited every girl in her class. Why, God? Why hadn't anyone come? Why didn't anyone like her?

Then her mother had hollered at her for letting her spend so much money on a party that no one was going to come to. The little girl had never been so sad. She'd never felt so alone. "Why, God?" she said aloud. "Why am I like this?"

She tried to start her normal bedtime prayers, but she couldn't. All she could say was, "*Why?*"

Suddenly, someone was kneeling beside her. She knew that if she opened her eyes, she wouldn't be able to see him—but he was there.

She knew that it was Jesus.

His arm slid around her and pulled her toward him. She leaned her wet face into his chest and sobbed. And he held her there.

Her crying gradually slowed, and she grew sleepy.

Kicking

She'd had a horrible birthday. No one had come to her party. Her mother had been embarrassed and had taken it out on her.

But she was still loved.

She still belonged to Jesus.

Chapter 1
Zoe

Zoe's foot struck something hard and unyielding, and she pitched forward into the darkness. She shoved her hands out in front of her to brace herself, but her face still hit the cold ground. She cried out, too loudly, and then froze. She held her breath. Had they heard her? Were they still coming for her?

A flashlight beam swung across the trees in front of her.

Yes. They were still coming.

She pushed herself to her feet and veered off to the left, hoping not to be lit up by their beams. Though her chest burned and she couldn't see more than a few feet in front of her, she started to run again. How far into the darkness could those flashlights shine? Pretty far, she thought.

Just because she'd seen the light didn't mean they were on her trail, she told herself. They might not even be after *her* at all. Several kids had scattered into the same patch of woods.

The cops couldn't catch them all.

She needed to be one of the ones who got away. She didn't know what would happen if they caught her. She didn't know what she'd be charged with. She'd used, but could they prove it? Could they make her take a test? She didn't know. She didn't have anything on her, so they wouldn't think she was selling. She'd just been in the wrong place at the wrong time. Maybe they'd go easy on her. She'd only been arrested twice before, and both of those times were for drinking. This would be her first drug-related offense. Maybe they'd have mercy on her.

Did mercy even exist?

And even if they did take pity on her, that didn't mean that her stepfather would. She had no idea how he might react to a drug charge. He'd called strike two about eight strikes ago. Eight? Or was it nine? She'd lost count. But she didn't know how much more he could take. He hated her, wanted her gone, had been threatening to send her to some "facility" for "at-risk youth." How she hated that phrase! At risk for what? Punching him in the throat, maybe.

Shouting. And the deep bark of a dog. Had that been her imagination? Surely the cops wouldn't bring out the bloodhounds to search the woods for some teens? She had a terrible thought: maybe the teens weren't the only ones in these woods. She slowed down a little, as if that would help her spot others. This was ridiculous. She could stand perfectly still and still not see anything.

She pushed her burning legs to go faster again. The terrain was uphill now. She had no idea where she was or where she was going. She hoped there were other teens in the woods, other kids for the cops to catch. She hoped the hookups weren't in the same woods. She didn't know those guys, but they hadn't looked especially friendly. She didn't want to run into one of them out here. She thought they'd probably string her up to slow the cops down.

She didn't know how much more she could run. She wasn't in particularly good shape, and her lungs really hurt. She couldn't catch her breath. It was all uphill now. Should she turn and go back down? Try to slant away from them? She stopped and turned. She couldn't see anything. No movement. No flashlights. Maybe she was okay. Maybe she'd lost them. Maybe they'd given up.

She changed her course by ninety degrees. She wouldn't go up or down; she would go sideways, give her legs a break. She didn't run. She tried to walk quickly, but she knew there was no quick left in her. She heard another bark, and then her left foot missed the ground. She cried out again as her left foot kept sinking. Where had the ground gone? She flailed her arms for something to grab onto. Her right fingers found the needles of an evergreen tree, but as she grasped at them, they came off in her hands, and then she was falling ... falling ... sure this was it ... she was going to die this time.

And all she could think about was her mother.

Chapter 2
Esther

"It's hard not to be discouraged," Dawn lamented.

Esther tried to ignore her.

"Are you kidding?" Rachel looked around the sanctuary in wonder. "God has given us this beautiful building and beautiful people to love on. What's discouraging about that?"

"He didn't *give* us the building," Vicky broke in. "Cathy bought it."

"I had lots of help," Cathy said quickly. "And I never would have been able to chip in if it weren't for God's provision."

"A little less talk and a little more action, ladies." The furnace wasn't working, and they were running around trying to find outlets that worked so they could plug the space heaters into them. But Esther was doing most of the running around.

"It'll be fine, Esther," Rachel said. "It's October, not January. No one is going to freeze to death."

Esther bristled. "I want them to be comfortable."

"Who?" Dawn cried. "Who do you want to be comfortable? That's the discouraging part!

We've been at this for months, and still no one has come!"

"That's not true—" Rachel tried, but Dawn interrupted her.

"I know, I know. The Puddys. And they're wonderful. But when they walked in that first Sunday, didn't you all think that they were a sign of things to come? I certainly did. But they weren't. They were it. No one else is coming."

"People will come." Esther tried not to grind her teeth. "Would you all please help me?"

Rachel picked up a heater and moved toward the altar outlet. "It's only been a few months. And we haven't done much outreach yet."

"Outreach?" Dawn cried. "We've fed nearly a hundred people! And Tonya gave away nearly everything she owned!"

Esther really needed Dawn to be quiet. Esther wasn't discouraged, but Dawn's attitude was contagious. Trouble was, she didn't know how to make Dawn stop talking.

The old door creaked open. Esther glanced at the clock. It wasn't even ten yet. Someone was early.

A man with long, greasy hair stepped into their sanctuary. His clothes were torn. He was filthy. Vicky audibly gasped.

"Good morning!" Esther hurried to say. "Welcome to New Beginnings!"

"It's getting kind of cold out there," the man said slowly. "I was wondering if I could warm up a bit in here."

"Of course!" Esther said before Vicky or Dawn could say otherwise. "Make yourself at home."

Vicky headed her way, and Esther picked up the last space heater and scurried in the other direction.

Vicky caught her anyway. "I don't think that's such a good idea."

"I know you don't. But this is a church, and we don't turn people away."

"But he's not here to go to *church*."

"How do you know?" Esther snapped and then felt guilty. She bent down to plug in the heater. Nothing happened, and she moved on to the next outlet. "We know nothing about him, but he can do no harm to us just sitting there."

As if she'd directly challenged him to cause trouble, he started to sing. Vicky gave her a knowing look that she didn't appreciate. His voice grew louder and more confident, and his song—which Esther was fairly confident she hadn't heard before—featured a few expletives.

"We've got to get him out of here," Vicky said without moving her mouth, "before the children arrive." She looked like an amateur ventriloquist, and Esther didn't know why she'd bothered. He was singing too loudly to hear anything.

"He's fine. We told him to make himself at home. He is."

"*We* told him no such thing," Vicky argued. "That was all you."

The newcomer tipped his head back and howled at the ceiling.

"For all we know, that could be Christ himself."

Vicky gave her a sardonic look. "Christ doesn't howl."

Esther hadn't enjoyed his singing, but when he stopped howling and returned to singing, she was grateful. She headed in his direction. *Don't get too close.* No, get as close as you can. He is a child of God. "Would you like some coffee?" She forced a smile.

He looked stunned by her offering. "Sure! Thank you!"

See? Quite polite! "Cream and sugar?"

He looked confused. "Sure," he said again, after a pause.

She went to the back of the sanctuary, where their coffee pot was set up. Her friends gathered around her to bicker. They were all talking very quietly and very quickly, but it was still easy to get the gist of what they were saying. Half of them wanted him gone. Half were excited he was there. Vera remained quiet on the subject. There was a chance she hadn't heard the howling.

Esther stirred the coffee and then turned to leave her friends behind. She took long strides across the sanctuary, trying to look confident. "Here you go."

"Thank you." He took the coffee from her outstretched hand.

She forced herself to edge closer. "I'm Esther."

He took a sip of coffee that had to have been too hot to drink. He didn't say anything.

"What do people call you?"

The door opened, and Fiona came in, struggling to carry a bag heavy with her sheet music.

The man whirled toward her, dropping his coffee on the carpet.

Esther suppressed her cry.

Vicky did not.

"Who are you?" he said to Fiona, who had stopped walking and stood staring at the newcomer.

"Who are you?" she fired back. This made Esther very proud of their organist.

The visitor wasn't amused, though, and whipped a small knife out of his pocket.

Esther reflexively took a step back, but then she tried to be objective. It was a small knife. There were eight of them. Granted, they were all over seventy, but still—eight against one. And he hadn't moved. He simply stood there looking at Fiona, holding the knife menacingly.

Fiona backed up a step.

Esther feared that if Fiona left the building, she'd never come back. She couldn't let that happen. "What's wrong?" She tried to step into his peripheral vision.

He ignored her.

"If you tell me what's wrong, we'll try to help."

He continued to ignore her. The arm that held the knife was shaking, and his lower lip trembled.

Keeping her eyes on their newcomer, she tried to keep her voice even as she said, "Rachel, call Roderick."

Chapter 3
Zoe

Had she broken her skull? That was the only explanation Zoe could come up with that would explain this level of pain. She tentatively reached one hand up to the side of her head, afraid of what she might find. Her hair was sticky with blood, but her skull felt intact. No dents, cracks, or holes. She breathed a sigh of relief and tried to open her eyes.

The sun felt unreasonably bright. How much had she drunk last night? She blinked and looked around.

The woods.

It all came rushing back to her, a wave that made her ill. She *had* drank and she *had* used, but that was the least of her problems. She was somewhere in the woods, far from home. Why? Why had she done this? Why had she come to a party in hillbillyville? Now she was lost in the Ozarks, and even if she could find her way back to the party house, she didn't know if it was safe. There could be cops there. Or worse.

She closed her eyes and lay there. Why couldn't she have died in the fall? Maybe if she lay there long enough, she would die.

Maybe a mountain lion would get her. That would be fun. Or a bear. Or a coyote. Or maybe they could all work together to make her demise swift and painless.

She wouldn't be that lucky. She was never lucky.

She tried to sit up, and the pain in her head magnified, making her brain swim. She pushed her hand into the ground to steady herself. Finally, sitting up, she looked around, squinting in the daylight. She squinted up at an overcast sky. How was the sun so bright with all those clouds?

Her eyes landed on a ledge above. Had she fallen from *there*? She looked around, but saw no other explanation. But it was so high! How was she still alive?

She felt her body over, looking for blood or breaks, but she couldn't find anything amiss except for her head. Slowly, she got to her feet. The dizziness came again, and she almost toppled over, but she spread her feet apart and gave herself time to adjust, breathing slowly. Her mouth was full of cotton. She needed water.

The dizziness passed, and she scanned the forest. She didn't know what direction to walk in. She couldn't tell where the sun was.

Again, she wished the fall had killed her. And she didn't know how it hadn't.

She listened for cars, listened for water, listened for anything that might help orient her, but there was nothing but the wind. She knew she'd come from the ledge, but she wasn't about to try climbing back up there. She made eye contact with a black bird. It seemed to be judging her. She couldn't stand it, so she turned her back on the uppity creature and headed away.

Her head pounded. She didn't know where she was going. But she put one foot in front of the other. She couldn't think of any other option.

Chapter 4
Esther

Roderick Puddy flew through the door and headed straight for the knife-wielding stranger. As if he did such feats every day, he rounded on the man and from behind, dropped a firm arm over the knife arm. Stunned, their visitor dropped the knife and tried to wheel around to face his attacker, but Roderick wouldn't allow it. He pinned the man's left arm behind him at a painful angle.

The nameless man wrestled against Roderick's grasp, whimpering.

"Could one of you ladies grab that knife?"

At first no one moved. They all looked at one another, waiting for someone else to do it. But then Rachel, though she was the farthest away from the action, stepped into the fray to retrieve the small weapon.

Once she was back to her spot, Roderick calmly but firmly said, "If you stop working against me, I'll let go."

Instantly the man's body went rigid, and he nodded.

Slowly, Roderick released his grip. "Did you call the police before you called me or after?" He didn't look at any of them when he asked but kept his eyes on the newcomer.

The women exchanged another wordless look.

Roderick finally looked at Esther for an answer.

"Police?" She felt foolish. "We didn't call the police."

Roderick snickered. "Well, I'm honored to be your first resort, but you should call them now."

Esther wasn't so sure.

"I'll do it," Rachel said.

"Thank you," Roderick said.

"Wait!" Cathy held an arm out toward Rachel. "Is that really necessary?"

"He threatened me with a knife!" Fiona cried. Though the circumstances weren't ideal, Esther still thought it was nice to hear her voice. She rarely spoke to any of them.

"He didn't, though," Cathy said. "Not really."

Esther knew where this was going. Someone had finally come through their doors, someone who obviously needed help. Cathy wanted to help him, not throw him back outside. But if Cathy didn't acknowledge Fiona's thoughts on the matter, they would lose her instead. And Esther didn't think this guy could play the pipe organ. "Fiona's right," Esther said quickly. "We need to call the police."

Cathy looked surprised. People didn't usually argue with her. But she was usually right and therefore didn't need to be argued with.

Esther didn't know who was right in this situation, but she wanted to protect Fiona. "It doesn't mean they'll even arrest him." Esther nodded at Rachel. "Please call." Then she turned her attention to their visitor. "You are welcome here, sir. But church needs to be a safe place. We can't have you threatening people."

He looked confused. "I wasn't threatening anyone." He pointed at Fiona. "She was trying to sneak up on me."

Fiona barked out a laugh. "Oh, that's believable."

The man started babbling nonsensically as Rachel spoke into her phone.

"Would you like another cup of coffee?" Esther asked.

The man looked down at his hand and seemed surprised and confused to not find coffee there.

"You dropped yours," Esther explained.

The man looked up at her and gave her a smile so warm and so friendly that it almost knocked her back a step. "That would be lovely."

"We still didn't catch your name," Esther said.

It took him a few seconds to come up with it, and she wondered if he was going to make one up. "Derek."

"Good to meet you, Derek."

On shaky legs, Esther returned to the coffee pot. They really should be attacking the stain that his previous serving was forming on the carpet, but he was straddling it. She returned with a half-full cup and, keeping a pew between herself and the men, stretched the offering out toward Roderick.

He smiled, took it, and handed it to Derek.

Derek looked down at the pew. "Can I sit?"

Roderick nodded. "Sure." Then Roderick sat beside him. "Where are you from, Derek?"

He shrugged. "Nowhere."

"Do you live around here?"

He looked down at his coffee and shook his head. "Don't live anywhere. Used to live in Thorndike. Then I was in the shelter in Belfast. But they kicked me out."

Vicky wobbled on her feet and grabbed a pew to steady herself.

They heard a siren. Oh great. Now everyone in town would look out their windows to see the police pulling up to New Beginnings Church.

Fiona stepped closer. "Why'd they kick you out?"

He shrugged. "I was dating someone. We broke up, so they gave me the boot."

This didn't make any sense.

"Did you pull a knife on her?" Fiona mumbled.

At first it appeared Derek didn't understand her quip, but then understanding dawned on his face, and he looked at Roderick. "Can I have my knife back?" he asked, as if he'd just remembered he'd ever had a knife.

"I'll give it to the police," Rachel said.

Esther was proud of the kindness in her voice. This wasn't exactly a scenario they'd been expecting, but she thought they were handling it well enough. No one had been stabbed.

The door opened, and a policewoman stepped inside. Esther didn't know her personally but had seen her around town. Carver Harbor didn't have very many police officers.

"Ah, Derek. I thought it might be you." She strode toward him but cast her eyes at the ceiling. She whistled. "Wow, look at this place. This is gorgeous."

"Thank you," Esther said because she didn't know what else to say.

The policewoman told Derek to stand and then looked him over. "Where's the weapon?"

"Here." Rachel hurried to give it to her.

She looked at it, seemingly surprised by the diminutive nature of it, and then looked at Derek. "Really? What were you thinking?"

He pointed at Fiona. "She was sneaking up on me! She was going—"

"Come on." She spun him around, but he kept talking. "You know the drill."

"What will happen to him?" Barbara asked.

"That depends on a lot of factors," the policewoman said evasively. Then she looked at Fiona. "Are you the one he threatened?"

Almost imperceptibly, Fiona nodded.

"Let me get him into the car, and then I'll come back and get your statement." She pulled Derek into the aisle.

"I'd rather not."

She stopped. "I'm sorry?"

"I don't want to give a statement. I don't want to get any more involved with any of this."

Fiona was fraying at the edges. Esther was scared she was going to run away and not come back.

"If you choose not to press charges, then the DA probably won't proceed with this."

Fiona waved a hand dismissively. "I don't care. I'm going to my organ."

Chapter 5
Esther

One week after Esther met Derek, she found him sitting on the front steps of the church. She'd left home early to unlock the building and get some heat going, and there he was. She stopped on the sidewalk, unsure of how to proceed. Should she turn around and go back home until the other ladies arrived? Then they could all deal with him together?

She didn't want to call Roderick Puddy again. They couldn't be bothering that poor man every time one of them got a splinter.

Derek spotted her. Oh no. Too late to turn around. He lifted his arm in a genial wave, and she tried to make her return wave just as friendly.

She got her feet moving again. "Good morning, Derek! How are you today?" The closer she got, the more nervous she got. She still wasn't sure what she was going to do when she got there.

"I'm all right." He studied her. "Don't worry. I won't follow you inside until others get here. I don't want to make you nervous."

Should this self-awareness comfort her? Or frighten her further? "I'm actually not going inside just yet." She forced a smile. "It's still early."

"Then what are you doing here?"

She looked around the yard, trying to come up with a lie. Why had she come to church so early if she wasn't going to go inside? She could claim she'd come to rake the leaves, but there was no rake. She could pretend to check the mail, but he was sitting inches from the mailbox. She could say she was going for her morning walk, but then ... "Actually, Derek, I was going to go inside, but now I've changed my mind. I'll think I'll wait for the others." She braced herself, waiting for him to be offended.

He nodded understandingly. "Sorry. I didn't mean to scare you." He stood up. "I was just eager is all, and I've got nowhere else to go. But I'll go for a walk. You go on inside and get things ready. I'll come back later." He smiled, but his eyes were sad. He came down the steps toward her.

She felt guilty. Maybe she shouldn't be so nervous. God would protect her. "Nah, it's all right. You can come in."

He watched his feet as he walked. He shook his head. "Nope. You were right the first time." He kicked at the leaves. "I'll go try to find a rake."

She watched him go and then, realizing how cold she'd gotten with all her indecisiveness, hurried inside. She locked the door behind her and then went to turn the heat up. Barbara's son Kyle had finally gotten the furnace working, and they'd even managed to squirt a bit of oil into the tank, so they wouldn't have to mess with the space heaters today. Those had worked well enough, but they'd flipped two circuits in the process. She didn't need to be trudging up and down the stairs during the service to flip circuits.

With the pastries out and the coffee on, she sat in the front pew to catch her breath. All the windows were installed now, and the soft morning sunlight streamed through the windows and lit up the old wooden cross over the altar. Thank God for Kyle. He'd done a lot of work on the place already. It still looked like a work in progress, but it no longer looked like an abandoned building.

Her pocketbook started to vibrate and she pulled it closer to her and dug out her phone. She assumed it was one of the ladies calling to say they were feeling under the weather. It was getting to be that time of year. But her heart leapt when she saw the caller ID. It was her daughter!

"Christy! Good morning!" She made no attempt to keep the glee out of her voice.

"Mom ..." That's all she said, but Esther could hear the pain.

"What is it? Are you all right? Is it Zoe? Or Danielle?"

Christy swallowed hard. "We're all okay. Sorry, didn't mean to scare you. But ..." Her voice cracked. "But I am scared. It's Zoe. I don't know what to do, Mom. She won't listen to me. She won't stop."

Chapter 6
Esther

Esther didn't know what she meant. Stop what? What was Zoe doing? "Back up a little, honey. What's going on?"

"Oh, you know. The drinking, the pot. She stays out all night. I never know where she is. She's skipping school and hanging out with criminals." She said all of this as if Esther had already known it.

But she hadn't. She had no idea it had gotten this bad. Was Christy exaggerating? Surely Zoe wouldn't smoke pot.

"Last weekend she came home with a giant gash in her head, and she wouldn't tell me what had happened. She wouldn't let me take her to the hospital, and I know it needed stitches ..."

Esther's breath caught. What was going on? If a child needs stitches, you *get* them to the hospital. You don't let them have a say in the matter! She realized Christy was still talking and made herself focus. "Trace is done. He says he's going to send her to Reboot, but I can't—"

"Reboot?" What was Reboot?

"It's here in Missouri. It's a residential facility for at-risk youth. And I don't think she should go there. I don't think she belongs there. She's not some abused, mentally ill criminal or something. But Trace says that she's *exactly* the kind of kid that Reboot is for. But it would be like jail, and we would never see her. It's three hours away from here. She would live there and go to school there—"

"Is it juvenile detention?"

"No," Christy said quickly. "That would almost be easier."

A chill raced over Esther. Had her daughter really just said that?

"This is a private facility. It's more like a rehab, but for teens, and they go to school while they're there." She laughed bitterly. "I guess you could call it a private school, even. It costs a fortune to go there."

How could they afford it then?

"But Trace will pay anything to get her out of his hair." She sobbed. "Mom, I don't know what to do. He says it's not safe for Danielle. I *know* Zoe would never hurt Danielle, but eventually she'll just be a bad influence ..."

Esther's chest tightened in defense of the granddaughter she hadn't seen in four years.

"And the people she's hanging around with. I can't let those people around Danielle!"

"But you don't want them around Zoe, either, do you?"

Christy stopped talking. "What? What's that supposed to mean?"

Esther groaned. She heard someone's key in the lock. "Sorry. I really didn't mean to be critical." But she'd felt critical, hadn't she? Why was Christy acting like Danielle was the only one who needed protecting? "I only meant that we need to get Zoe away from them too."

"But I *can't*. Mom, I've tried everything. We've tried rewards. We've tried punishment. We've tried tough love and talking about her feelings."

Had they tried Jesus?

"I'm out of options. And I know you can't fix it. I'm not expecting you to come up with some magic wand, but I was hoping you had some advice. You were such a great mother to us. But I know I never put you through what Zoe is doing to me."

Rachel sat beside Esther on the pew. After one glance at Esther's face, her smile slid away, and she put a hand on Esther's shoulder.

"You're not out of options."

"I'm not?" Her voice was laced with hope, but then it vanished. "Mom, do *not* say get her into Jesus, because that's not going to work. She would never step foot in a church or a youth group or anything."

"I wasn't going to say that." She was thinking it, but she wasn't going to say it. She knew better than to ask a teenager to go to church when her own mother refused to.

"Then what were you going to say? What option do I supposedly have?"

Esther looked at Rachel as she said, "Send her here. That's your option. Send her to me."

Chapter 7
Rachel

Rachel watched her longtime friend hang up the phone. "Send who to you? What's going on?"

"Zoe. My granddaughter. She's in trouble, I think." Esther sounded scared. This wasn't like her. If she was ever fearful, she hid it well.

"How old is she now?" She added the word "now" as if she had any idea how old the child was. Time flew so fast, the kid could be thirty for all she knew.

"Sixteen."

Rachel whistled. "That's a tough one."

Esther looked defensive. "That's a bunch of malarkey. The teen numbers are the same as any other number. A human doesn't get to lose their mind when they're thirteen."

"I didn't say that—"

"It's like our world convinces teenagers that they have a right, no more than that, a *duty* to be a punk until they turn twenty. But that's a lie. Back in my day, teenagers were respectful, responsible young adults."

Rachel held up one hand to stop the sermon. "I'm on your side, Esther. I wasn't arguing with you. Nor was I trying to speak some sort of chaos over Zoe's life."

Esther closed her eyes. "I'm sorry. I'm a little overwhelmed right now. I found Derek sitting on the front steps. He should be back any minute."

Rachel didn't want to be done talking about the girl. "Forget the big lie that teens are automatically punks. I'm trying to make a separate point. I'm saying that since the Lord invented hormones, being a teenage girl isn't easy."

Esther laughed. "I guess I've forgotten. But menopause was no picnic."

Rachel joined her in her laughter. "True. But back to Zoe. So her parents get divorced, and then her mother moves her halfway across the country." She held up a hand to stave off another defensive tirade. "I'm not blaming Christy for anything. I'm only recounting the facts. So Zoe is in a new place with a new stepfather and a new baby sister, and she just started a new school year. There could be jerks in her class. Or maybe she's all gaga over some boy. Probably some boy broke her heart. So she's acting out. What did Christy say, exactly?" Was that prying? "If you don't mind me asking."

Esther took a deep breath. "I think it's more than that, unless Christy is exaggerating. She's drinking—"

"Which could very well be due to the boys."

"And maybe using drugs."

Uh-oh. That wasn't good.

"And she's skipping school—"

"Which fits perfectly with my theory."

Esther scowled at her. "And according to Christy, she's hanging out with criminals."

Double uh-oh. "I see. So you have invited her to come here?"

Esther looked around the sanctuary. "I panicked. They are thinking about sending her to some home for wayward juveniles."

A pain stabbed Rachel's chest. Esther was right. She had to interfere. "Will your building let her stay with you?"

"I think so. Why wouldn't they? It's not a nursing home."

Oops, Rachel hadn't meant to offend.

Esther gave her a crooked smile that told her she wasn't hurt. "Just because it's a building full of lonely old people doesn't mean it doesn't allow teenagers." She chuckled dryly.

"And can you afford to take care of her? Food? Clothing? Stuff she'll need for school?"

Esther slowly shook her head. "I don't know. I don't think so."

Rachel patted her knee. "Don't worry. We'll help you with that."

Esther snickered. "We bought a church! Now we're all broke!"

Rachel laughed too. "I know, I know. But we'll figure it out. Neither of you will go hungry." She leaned back against the pew and looked up at the wooden cross. "You were right. At first I thought you were a little crazy to be making the offer, but I don't see as you had any other choice. And this will probably be the opportunity of a lifetime."

"I hope so. I want what's best for Zoe."

"Well, yeah. That too. But I meant the opportunity of a lifetime for *you*."

A hopeful smile spread across Esther's face, and the sight of it made Rachel's heart warm.

The church door opened, and they both turned to look.

Vicky stepped into the sanctuary. "Why is that criminal camped out on our front steps, and who raked the lawn?"

Chapter 8
Zoe

Zoe hurried down the gangway, away from the obnoxious babysitter her mother had hired to escort her through the airport. Really? She was sixteen. Did she really need the unaccompanied minor service? Like she couldn't figure out how to get on and off a plane? Typical of her mother. Ask her to act like an adult but treat her like a child.

That babysitter had been stuck to her since the check-in desk, where her mother, sobbing like an Oscar-nominee, had hugged her goodbye. Trace had stood by the doorway, holding Danielle in his arms. This had made Zoe even madder. She would have liked to have a moment to say goodbye to Danielle. But Trace always acted like Zoe posed some sort of danger to his little angel, so she didn't know why she was surprised.

She found her seat and flung her backpack into the overhead bin. Then she plopped down in the window seat. She buckled herself in, put in her earbuds, and looked out the small window. Ah, Missouri. She'd hated to leave Maine and move to Missouri, and now she didn't want to make the reverse trip. It wasn't that she particularly loved Missouri, but she knew Maine wouldn't be any better. Would life suddenly be fair in Maine? Would she suddenly become likable? She didn't think so. And she wasn't even going back to South Portland, where she'd grown up. She was going to the boonies, to Carver Harbor, where her *mother* had grown up.

Apparently, her mother hadn't gotten into *any* trouble in her entire childhood, and she hoped Carver Harbor would have the same effect on her daughter. What a load of bull. Zoe closed her eyes and tried to relax. She still couldn't believe this was happening. When she'd first been told the plan, she had promptly decided to torture her grandmother until she sent her home.

Now she wasn't so sure. That plan made her feel guilty. None of this was Gramma's fault. She was a very nice woman. Gramma had tried to see her as much as possible when they'd lived in Maine, even though she'd lived three hours away. They'd been so busy that it hadn't always been easy to get together, but Gramma had always made the effort. She'd come to her stupid school plays. She'd always been around for Thanksgiving and Christmas. And she'd taken them to the beach a few times each summer. Maybe this wouldn't be so bad. Maybe she would just stay in Maine. Maybe she would just stay with Gramma. That would protect her from Reboot, at least.

A man stopped in the aisle and checked his boarding pass. Then he flipped open the bin and heaved his bag up into it. He pushed and shoved and swore. Then he reached in and reefed on her bag, yanking it over to the side of the bin. It slammed into the wall, and she gave him a dirty look, which he didn't see. He went back to pushing and shoving and swearing. Finally, he got the bin door shut. She was glad she hadn't put anything breakable in her backpack.

He sat down, perching on the edge of his seat as if she were contagious. Really? Had he never been on an airplane before? The seats were kind of close together. She hoped the drink cart ripped off his kneecap. She slammed the window shut, turned up the Pearl Jam, closed her eyes, and rested her head on the hard plastic wall.

She didn't know what she wanted. All she knew was what she didn't want. She didn't want to move to small-town Maine to live with an old lady. She didn't want to leave Missouri. She didn't want to go to Reboot. But what did she *want*?

Pearl Jam sang her to sleep, and suddenly she was driving a car really fast on a shoulderless road on the side of a mountain. To her right, a wall of rock. To her left, nothing. If she looked straight down, she saw exactly zero earth below her, as if the mountain was just floating in the sky. She realized the car was about to careen around a corner. The road was impossibly narrow, so she yanked the wheel to bring the car as close to the right side of the road as she could. But the wheel didn't do anything. Did she have no control over the vehicle? She pressed her foot to the brake.

Nothing.

She was in the driver's seat, but she wasn't driving. She glanced around to make sure she was alone in the car. She was. That was good. If she crashed and her car flew off this mountain, she would be the only one to die. No great loss.

The car rounded the corner to reveal that she was about to leave the mountain behind. A bridge stretched out in front of her. It had no guardrails. It was a narrow road across the sky, heading toward another mountain in the distance. As her car flew out onto the bridge, she cried out and brought her hands up over her face. She felt sick to her stomach. But the not being able to see where she was going was worse than the seeing, so she dropped her arms to see that she was fast gaining on this new mountain, and the road went straight up it. Her stomach rolled. What was this? She had to get out of this car!

The car lurched, and gravity pressed her into her seat as she drove toward the sky, nearly perpendicular to the bridge she'd just left. She strained to look out the windshield. What if the road tipped a few more degrees, and the car fell over backward, plummeting roof-first into nothingness? She'd seen dirt bikes defy gravity. She didn't think she could pull it off. She started crying. No, no, no, please let me get to the top of this mountain. I don't want to die. I don't want to fall. She didn't think she'd ever been so scared and didn't know if she could bear this kind of fear. And then she saw it.

The crest of the mountain.

But what came after? It was a mountaintop. There was no evidence that the road leveled off. She couldn't see any more road at all. Either it dropped down over the hill or it simply stopped. If it stopped, she was dead. The car was going *so* fast. Even if the road pitched down, at this speed she might go flying straight ahead, leaving the relative safety of this insane road beneath her. She stomped on the brake again, crying. She was almost to the top. She closed her eyes, and her stomach dropped out of her as the car crested the mountain and headed straight down. Was she still on the road? Or was she only falling? She didn't know, and she didn't dare open her eyes to find out.

Chapter 9
Zoe

Zoe disembarked her second plane to find yet another babysitter waiting for her in the jet bridge. She shivered in the unheated space as the woman flashed her a giant fake smile. "Welcome to Portland!" Her teeth were far too white.

Zoe didn't respond. If you have nothing nice to say, say nothing at all.

"Right this way." Her plastic smile fixed, she turned and headed up the gangway.

Zoe hefted her backpack onto her shoulder and followed. The tunnel was freezing cold. Welcome to Portland, indeed. It was only October. Why was it so cold already? And she knew Carver Harbor would be even colder than Portland.

They spilled out into the gate area.

"Follow me for baggage claim." Still smiling.

The smell of burgers hit Zoe's nose, and her mouth watered. There was no hope, though. Even if she didn't have a taskmaster-escort, she couldn't afford a twenty-dollar burger. She hoped her grandmother would feed her on the way home. She didn't think she'd last all the way to Carver Harbor.

The baggage claim area, which was also freezing cold, smelled horrible, and her hunger dissipated—a little. Even though she knew it would make no difference, she said to her babysitter, "I think I can take it from here."

The smile returned. "I'm sure you can. But I can't leave your side until I verify your ..." She looked at the piece of paper in her hand. "Until I check your grandmother's ID."

Zoe almost snickered. Who on earth would impersonate her grandmother in order to kidnap Zoe? If anyone kidnapped her, they would give her back—pronto. Her parents would probably demand the kidnapper pay *them* a ransom before they'd take her back.

The suitcases finally started appearing on the belt and made their slow trek around the oval. People crowded around the beginning of the belt. Everyone was in a terrible hurry, apparently. Why were all these people even coming to Maine in October? People flew to Maine in July, not October, didn't they? What were these people thinking?

"Let me know when you see your luggage."

Zoe rolled her eyes. Or she could just go grab it herself.

People greedily grabbed for their luggage and then flooded toward the revolving door.

Zoe watched the belt closely, knowing they must be coming to the end of the luggage. There hadn't been *that* many people on the plane. She watched the rude man from the seat beside her retrieve his lighthouse-covered suitcase and then roll it toward the door with two perfectly healthy kneecaps. Nothing ever went her way.

The bags stopped coming. She waited, trying not to freak out.

Her babysitter shifted her weight, looking uncomfortable. "Will you come with me, please?"

Zoe followed her to a door near the belt. She opened the door and then stuck her head into it. What a predicament. She couldn't leave Zoe behind, and Zoe wasn't allowed behind the secret door. Zoe smirked.

She hollered into the void. She was annoyed and trying to hide it. She waited a minute and then hollered again.

Eventually, a male's voice hollered back.

She propped the door open with her foot so she could wave him over. When he appeared, he looked reluctant. He was also wearing a lot of clothes for October. Her babysitter spoke in hushed tones, and he held his hands out and shrugged.

There was no more luggage.

Would he please double-check?

Sure, but there was no more luggage. He walked away, and she let the door swing shut.

Zoe was doubtful that man was going to check anything, and she thought her babysitter knew that too. For the first time, she felt sorry for her escort, who was no longer smiling.

"Bear with me one minute. I'm going to call for assistance." She took her cell out of her pocket and turned away from Zoe.

Why was this process so secretive? They had lost her luggage. Did they think she didn't know that yet?

She spun back around, her smile back in place. "They're going to do some investigating, and they'll call right back. Don't you worry. Lost luggage is very rare these days."

Of course it was. And of course she'd be the one to interrupt their winning streak.

Chapter 10
Esther

"You just missed the exit," Vicky crowed. "That's why I didn't want to take the turnpike!"

"Route One would have taken forever," Rachel said from the back. "And the next exit will work just fine, Esther."

Esther was grateful for Rachel's presence. Esther wasn't comfortable driving around Portland and hadn't even done it since her daughter had moved away.

"No, it won't! If you take the next exit, there's no way to get across the bay!"

"Yes, there is! Westbrook Street," Rachel said. "Now stop distracting the driver!"

"Westbrook Street is *so* far out of the way. You're going to be late. Now your granddaughter is going to be standing alone out in the cold wondering why you forgot about her."

"Enough!" Rachel said, sounding uncharacteristically stern. "Stop, Vicky!"

Vicky folded her arms across her chest. "I'm only trying to help."

Esther knew her well enough to know that this was true. She also knew she often didn't need or want Vicky's help. "I'm taking the next exit." She turned her blinker on.

Vicky opened her mouth, and Esther knew she was about to comment on how early she'd signaled, but she thought twice and snapped her mouth shut. It was a miracle.

Once on the off-ramp, she said, "Tell me where to go, Rachel."

Rachel groaned. "It seems they've done some construction since I was here last. Changed the layout. Don't worry, though. We'll figure it out. Go that way." She pointed. "South on Route One."

"Mm-hmm. Could have taken Route One after all."

The miracle was over.

"Ignore her … Good job … now take a right at the light." She leaned back into her seat, and Esther missed her already. "Right onto Broadway."

"I'm so glad I don't live in Portland," Vicky mused, looking out the window.

That was something they could agree on. She turned onto Broadway. "Now what?"

"Now go to the end of Broadway."

Esther glanced at the clock. Vicky was right. They were going to be late. But Esther didn't think it was her fault. Rachel had been so kind to offer to accompany her, saying it was for moral support, but Esther suspected

Rachel was worried that Esther couldn't get to the jetport and back. But Rachel had made the grave mistake of making her offer within earshot of Vicky, who had then inserted herself into the road trip. It had been Vicky who hadn't been ready when they'd pulled into her driveway, and it had been Vicky who had demanded a restroom break in Gardiner.

Maybe Zoe's flight would be delayed. Wasn't that usually the case?

"Okay, now right on Westbrook."

Someone lay on their horn, and Esther jumped. Her heart started thumping. "What? What did I do?"

"It probably wasn't about you," Rachel said.

But she somehow knew that it was.

"You're doing great. Just keep going."

Esther tried to relax her grip on the wheel, but it wasn't easy. There were so many cars! She couldn't wait to get back to Carver Harbor, where she enjoyed tooling around. Rachel had offered to drive, but Esther didn't want Zoe's first impression of her to be that her grandmother was some kind of invalid who couldn't drive in the city.

"There it is!" Vicky cried, seeming shocked that they'd made it after all.

"There it is," Esther repeated. Her anxiety about driving disappeared, swiftly replaced by an excitement to see Zoe. She was nervous to take in a young woman after all these years, but her love for the child easily trumped those nerves.

"Nope!" Rachel cried, pointing. "That way!"

Esther swerved onto the right road, only thinking to check the mirrors afterward. There was someone behind her, but she was thankful that he was not the horn-honking type. Blessed are the merciful. She started to pull up in front of the sidewalk in front of baggage claim.

"She hasn't texted you yet, has she?" Rachel asked.

Oh shoot. That was right. She was going to text when she got in. "I have no idea."

"Well, check the phone!" Vicky cried. "We can't just sit idling at the curb like we own the place."

Esther started to dig through her purse.

"No, you drive," Rachel said. "I'll get it."

"Drive where? You want me to leave the airport?"

"No, the road loops right around." Rachel fiddled with Esther's phone as she pulled back out into traffic.

Esther hoped that Zoe would stay forever. This airport navigation was strictly for the birds.

"No, nothing yet. Sorry."

Esther followed the cars in front of her, avoiding the enticing tunnel into the parking garage, and then when she saw a road labeled "Exit," she took the other option. Soon she recognized where she was and took a moment to be proud of herself for getting there without Rachel. "So should we park in the garage or do another drive-by?"

Rachel chuckled. "We should probably swallow the fee and park in the garage." The phone chirped. "Oh, wait! She's here! Oh, praise God! She's here!"

Esther was touched by the sincerity of Rachel's enthusiasm.

"So, yes, just pull back up to the curb like you own the place." Her excitement was contagious.

Several people peppered the sidewalk, and Esther scanned them eagerly. But she didn't see Zoe, or any kids for that matter.

"Is that her?" Vicky pointed.

Esther started to say "No" but stopped. It *was* her. She was so tall! Taller than she'd been four years ago, but also just *really tall*. She towered over the woman beside her. The shorter woman was dressed like a flight attendant, and Esther assumed it was the minor accompaniment person. She pulled her car into the small space.

"Well done!" Rachel said, and only then did Esther realize what a tight space she'd squeezed into. Miracle number two, she thought, but then she realized that God had likely executed a hundred miracles for her that day that she was entirely unaware of.

She climbed out of the car, which wasn't easy after being folded up for so long. She rounded the front of the car, surprised at how nervous she was. This was her granddaughter, for crying out loud! Why was she so nervous? "Zoe!" She spread her arms wide. "You look so beautiful!"

Zoe flinched at the words, and Esther had a pretty good idea as to why. She *wasn't* beautiful in the traditional sense. She was a big girl. Tall, thick, with a little extra fluff. Her face was round and pale and inflicted with acne. Didn't they have sun in Missouri? And her short, disheveled hair wasn't doing her any favors. It was dyed a black so black it looked like ink. Her lip was pierced. But yet, Esther had meant the compliment. She *was* beautiful. She was a strong, tall, healthy young woman with her grandfather's eyes—and she was Esther's grandbaby, her baby's baby. She wrapped her arms around Zoe, who half-heartedly returned the embrace.

Esther squeezed her as tightly as she could and then let go so she could get another look at her. She held her arms as she stepped back. She knew she was beaming. She probably looked ridiculous, but she didn't care. "It's so good to see you, honey."

"Ma'am?"

Esther turned to look at Zoe's escort.

"I'll need some photo ID."

"Oh yes, it's in the car. Let me get it." She turned toward the car, but Rachel got there faster.

"I'll get it!"

Esther turned back to Zoe.

"We are so sorry to say that there's been a luggage mix-up."

"Oh?"

"Yes, it seems the agent in St. Louis got her airport codes mixed up. Instead of sending it to Portland, Maine, she sent it to Portland, Oregon."

"Oh my!" Esther said. That was a long trip for a suitcase.

"We'll locate it and have it delivered to your address as soon as we can."

Esther nodded. "All right. Do you need my address?"

"We already have it."

"How long is that going to take?"

This was the first time Esther had heard Zoe's voice in a while, and it stole some of her joy. Her voice was deep and sharp. She sounded angry, aggressive.

"Shouldn't be more than twenty-four hours," the woman answered, but Esther could hear in her voice that it might well be longer than that. The look on Zoe's face suggested she had heard that too.

Rachel handed Esther's ID over.

"No matter. We'll make sure you have everything you need. Come on, go ahead and get in the car."

Zoe picked up her backpack, stepped toward the car, and then looked down at Vicky, who was still sitting in the front seat. "Who's that?"

Chapter 11
Zoe

The highway rolled by as her dismay grew. What had she gotten herself into? She couldn't *believe* they'd lost her stuff, and now she was trapped in this car with three weird old biddies. Why had her grandmother brought friends? Was she afraid to be alone with her? What had her mother told her?

The one in the front—Vicky—was especially mean. And the one beside Zoe—Rachel, the one wearing a ridiculous, giant, floppy, pink hat—was overly friendly. Zoe looked out the window and tried to avoid conversation, and eventually, Rachel stopped trying.

Zoe was desperate for food, but didn't want to go to a restaurant with these three. She'd rather starve. She shifted in her seat. She knew she wouldn't be able to get comfortable in the back seat of a small car, but she was trying to get less *un*comfortable. Her long legs were folded up like an accordion, her knees nearly touching the ceiling. She was losing feeling in her feet. She realized the woman beside her was watching her and stopped squirming. That woman was no elf. She was fairly tall herself, so much so that the top of her goofy hat was smashed into the ceiling. Zoe couldn't imagine why a woman would wear a hat like that, but even if she deemed it necessary, why didn't she take it off in the car? Did she have a bald spot or something? Zoe glanced at the woman's legs, which were nearly as jackknifed as her own. Why on earth had her grandmother given the front to the small, mean one?

"I think Zoe needs a pit stop," Rachel said. "There's not much room back here, and her legs are falling asleep."

How could she possibly know that? Were her legs asleep too?

"Sorry, honey!" Gramma said, sounding truly sorry. "I should have thought of that. And you must be hungry too! Do you want to get some food?"

She decided it was worth the pain. "Sure. Thanks."

"Of course! Now, where is the nearest grub?"

Zoe looked out the window. She couldn't imagine. Based on the solid line of forest as far as the eye could see, they were nowhere near any "grub."

"Freeport has lots of options," Rachel said.

"Everything in Freeport is so expensive," Vicky said. "I can't imagine why they would name the town *Free*port and then make everything the opposite of free!"

Zoe decided then that she really hated the woman in the front.

Gramma wrenched the rearview mirror to the right so she could look at her. "What kind of food would you like?"

She shrugged. "Any fast food."

Gramma grimaced. "Oh, no, we need to get you something healthy."

And there it was. It had begun. Zoe dropped her eyes, hoping no one would see her reaction. She wasn't always so easily hurt, but that one had stung. She hadn't imagined it coming from her grandmother, especially so early, especially in front of other people. Yes, she was too fat, but Gramma wasn't exactly a wafer. Maybe she'd gotten her genes. Her mother had no trouble being tiny and skinny and perfect. But Zoe sure did. Zoe was an amazon, and she hated every inch of herself.

She felt Rachel's eyes on her.

"Why don't we let her get fast food this once? You can start nurturing her with home-cooked meals when you get home. Let her have a treat after her long day of traveling."

"Fine," Gramma said, and didn't sound the least bit upset to relent.

"Besides, I doubt Freeport will have many healthy options."

Zoe was grateful for Rachel's interference, but she didn't meet her eyes; she didn't want Rachel to see her tears.

"So, what is your favorite fast food?" Gramma asked.

Zoe swallowed hard, not wanting her voice to betray her crying.

As if she'd read her mind, Rachel answered for her. "I think the only fast food in Freeport is McDonald's. There are a lot more choices if we wait till Topsham, but I doubt Zoe's legs want to wait that long. Isn't that right, Zoe?"

Without looking at her, Zoe nodded.

"She says that's right. McDonald's it is, then!"

"Good. I have to use a restroom!" Vicky added.

McDonald's wasn't her favorite, but she was still *very* excited to go there. She looked out the window and tried to get control of her emotions. She didn't need to get caught crying in the McDonald's parking lot.

Chapter 12
Rachel

Rachel couldn't decide whether to interfere. She had seen the whole thing so clearly from her cramped spot, but she knew both her dear friend and her dear friend's granddaughter had misinterpreted the moment entirely. If she didn't speak directly to Zoe about it, then she had to speak to Esther, and she knew that Esther would be embarrassed. She wanted to avoid that.

As they waited for their food, Rachel tugged on Zoe's arm. "Come take a look at this." She gently pulled her toward the free-toy display, and Zoe looked at her as though she were mad. Once they were out of earshot, she said, "I know you're sixteen and don't care about these toys. I also know that you misinterpreted what your grandmother said to you about healthy food."

Zoe's eyes snapped up, finally meeting hers. She looked defensive. Ready to fight.

"It's not your fault," Rachel said quickly. "She wasn't clear, but I know her well enough to know what she really meant. And she wasn't commenting on *anyone's* weight. I don't think she'd ever do that. Esther loves food, and she loves to nurture people with food. So when she said *healthy*, she didn't mean salad. She meant *real* food. Food prepared by human hands with human love."

Zoe's face finally relaxed.

"Your grandmother thinks *blueberry pie* is healthy."

The corners of Zoe's mouth flickered up in the briefest of smiles.

"I saw that you were hurt, so I wanted to tell you that she didn't mean what you thought she meant." She waited for her to say something. "So, forgive her?"

She shrugged and nodded. "I wasn't holding a grudge or anything."

Aha! She'd gotten her to speak. "Good. And forgive yourself too. There's nothing wrong with being a little thick in the hips. It even has its benefits."

Zoe looked uncomfortable, as if she was thinking about how to escape the conversation. But she was saved by the order number being shouted across the lobby. She turned and headed away from Rachel, but then paused and turned back. "Thanks," she said quietly, in that deep rumbling voice of hers. Rachel wondered if she could sing contralto.

She watched her walk away. There was something about this young woman. Rachel had expected to care about her because she cared so deeply about her grandmother. But now there was something more than that. Now, somehow, the child had endeared herself to Rachel, and Rachel had no idea why. She'd never been particularly drawn to teenagers, but there was something special about this one. Rachel could practically feel the pain radiating off her skin. She was hurting. But Rachel thought it was more than just compassion that was affecting her.

Maybe it was the long legs. Maybe it was the bold hairdo. Maybe Zoe reminded Rachel of someone. Maybe Zoe reminded Rachel of herself.

Chapter 13
Zoe

Zoe looked around the small, dimly lit apartment in dismay. This was it?

Gramma slowly lowered herself onto the couch, as if she was afraid it wasn't going to hold her. "I'd give you a tour, but I'm too exhausted." She waved her arm around. "But feel free to wander around. Make yourself at home."

Her wandering didn't take long and increased her trepidations. This was a *tiny* apartment. And there was only one bedroom. "Where will I sleep?"

Esther patted the couch. "This folds out, though we may find that it's not worth the hassle. I find the couch more comfy than the hide-a-bed. I have sheets and real pillows for you, of course." She read something on Zoe's face. "I'm sorry, honey. I wish I had more for you. But I promise to keep you warm and fed and loved here."

Zoe swallowed hard. She didn't want to hurt Gramma's feelings, but this was ridiculous. And because her luggage was lost, she didn't even have anything to sleep in. She didn't really want to sleep on the couch in her underwear. "When will we be able to go shopping for clothes and stuff?"

Esther waved her arm dismissively, and Zoe's chest tightened. "Let's see if the luggage gets here tomorrow. If it doesn't, we'll make a special trip to Ellsworth." She said the word *Ellsworth* as if it was some exciting shopping destination. What stores would Ellsworth have? Did Gramma expect her to wear cheap box-store clothes? Like she wasn't going to have enough trouble starting at a new school without that added bonus.

Gramma looked at her carefully. "I bought a bunch of snacks I thought a youngster might like, but if you want to make a list of foods you like, we can do some grocery shopping too." Something in her voice suggested she didn't really want to do this.

The couch was the only furniture in the tiny living room, so she sat down beside her grandmother. The couch was short, like her grandmother. If she tried to sleep on it, no way would her legs fit. She looked at the TV. "What are we watching?"

"Not sure. Whatever is on. Here." She handed her the remote. "You can change it. I get about twelve stations."

Twelve? Boy, a regular mother lode. She started to flip through, but of course, nothing was interesting. When she got back to where she'd started, she stopped surfing. "Do you have Netflix or Hulu?"

Gramma's face fell, and Zoe felt bad for asking. "Those take the Internet, don't they?"

"Yeah. It's okay." She took out her phone. "Watch whatever. I'm good." She was also going to live without the Internet, apparently. How long would her data plan last, roaming in Maine with no Wi-Fi? What had she gotten herself into?

"All right." Gramma sounded sad. "I'm going to go lie down for a bit. Then we'll have something good for supper."

The word supper warmed Zoe's heart a little. She hadn't heard it in ages, but she remembered that when she was little, her parents had used the word supper. Her mom didn't anymore. Now it was always called dinner—a much chillier word. *Supper* sounded like thick beef stew and biscuits, or lobster stew and blueberry muffins. *Dinner* sounded like baked fish and rice. She watched her grandmother hobble away, and her heart swelled for her. "Gramma?"

She turned back. "Yes?"

"Thank you for all this."

She nodded. "Of course, honey. I love you."

She smiled, and the act felt foreign to her face. If Gramma hadn't been watching her, she might've touched her cheeks to see if they'd cracked. She hadn't smiled in a while. "I love you too." She meant it.

Gramma smiled and turned for the bedroom.

When was the last time someone had told her that they loved her? It had been months, maybe years. When was the last time she'd said it to someone else? Or even felt it for someone else?

Forever.

Her Gramma loved her. Maybe this wouldn't be so bad after all. She could live without Netflix if it meant being loved, right? She flipped through the channels till she found a sitcom and then fiddled with her phone. She'd expected her Missouri friends to be texting her with questions. Had she gotten there yet? What was it like? But they hadn't texted anything. Apparently they'd already forgotten about her. This didn't really surprise her. Some part of her had known all along that those people didn't really care about her. Party buddies, yes. Friends? Maybe not.

Zoe glanced into the kitchen, wondering what her grandmother had meant by snacks. Maybe she should go forage.

But she decided she was too tired. Maybe Gramma had the right idea. Maybe it was time for a good nap. She stretched out on the couch. Yes, it *was* comfy. Her feet dangled off the edge, but this wasn't as bothersome as she'd thought it would be.

Chapter 14
Zoe

Zoe managed to wait until noon before reminding Gramma about the luggage. When Zoe finally mentioned it, it was clear that it had entirely slipped her grandmother's mind. Unbelievable. Zoe was wearing the same clothes she had on yesterday, and had no deodorant or toothbrush, so her missing luggage was very much on *her* mind.

"Let me call the airport."

Zoe wasn't sure this would be helpful, but she sat down to wait. Slowly, Gramma looked up the number to the airport, and Zoe wished she'd done that part for her. But eventually, she was on the phone, listening to an automated menu. Gramma scrunched up her face in annoyance, and it was adorable.

"I want to talk to a real human."

Good luck.

She pressed a button.

"Wait, what number did you just push?"

"Zero."

"Why? What does zero do?"

"No idea"—she stabbed at the phone—"but I pressed it again." She held the phone up to her ear for about two seconds and then stabbed at the screen again. "Zero! Zero!

Zero!" she cried, reminding Zoe of her little half-sister demanding more Cheetos. She couldn't quite say, "Cheetos," so she would chant "Eee-o! Eee-o! Eee-o!" in a frustrated but eerily effective tone.

"It's ringing!" she said, sounding quite pleased with herself.

Zoe couldn't believe it. So, when frustrated with a robo-menu, the thing to do was to pound on the zero?

Apparently, yes, because on the third ring, a human answered the phone.

Gramma explained the situation, and the voice kindly asked for permission to put her on hold. What choice did she have? She agreed.

The seconds ticked by and turned into minutes, and if it wasn't for the obnoxious music playing through the speaker, Zoe might have thought the airline had hung up on her. Gramma sank back into the couch cushion and pointed her chin at the TV. "Find something good. We might be here a while."

Zoe tried to hide her annoyance. She didn't want to spend the whole day on hold. Couldn't they go shopping whether or not the luggage arrived? What was the worst that could happen? She'd have an extra toothbrush, which she would use eventually. She picked up the remote. The first channel was soccer. Gramma winced. The second channel was football. Maintaining the original wince, Gramma shook her head emphatically. How had Zoe not noticed before how much Gramma looked like a baby? Or maybe she just looked like Danielle? Or maybe Danielle looked like her, rather.

The third channel was PBS, and Gramma nodded emphatically.

Awesome.

But Zoe managed to get lost in the episode of *This Old House.* A young couple had purchased an old Victorian that the previous owners had tried to make look modern—and had failed. The new owners wanted to go back to the Victorian look. It was surprisingly riveting, so much so that she didn't notice at first when someone finally came onto the phone line. But then her grandmother spoke.

"Yes ..."

Zoe could hear the other person talking, but couldn't make out the words.

"Oh dear ..."

That wasn't good.

"Are you sure? ... Oh, okay." There was a long pause. "Yes ..." She gave them her name and address, though they should have already had it. "Yes, I'll have her get that to you right away. How will she get back in touch with you without being put on hold? Oh okay." Gramma started waving her arm around, acting as though Zoe should know what that meant. Zoe looked at her blankly, trying to figure it out. "A pen! A pen!"

Zoe whipped out her phone. "What?"

"I need to write down an email address."

"Okay, tell it to me."

Gramma looked at her, a bit panicky, as if she didn't believe such a thing could work. But she started to recite the email. Zoe easily typed it into her memo app and then leaned toward Gramma's phone and loudly recited it back to airline headquarters.

The woman declared the transfer correct, and Gramma's face finally relaxed. "All right. Thank you very much for your help." They exchanged pleasantries, and then Gramma hung up.

"Well?" Zoe's knee bounced up and down with impatience.

"Well, they can't find your bag."

She wasn't surprised, but she was still disappointed.

"But she needs you to email her a list of all the possessions in your bag, and the airport will write you a check for the value."

Zoe snorted. "None of it was *valuable*, except for the fact that it was everything I owned, and now I own nothing."

It appeared Gramma didn't understand.

"My favorite jeans are probably worth fifty cents, but it would cost a hundred dollars to replace them, if that's even poss—"

"A hundred dollars? Where has your mother been buying your jeans?"

Zoe thought her grandmother's horror was a bit over the top. "We got them used. Don't worry. Mom would never spend that much on me."

Gramma flinched.

Oops. She'd said too much. Gramma probably didn't want to hear complaints about her daughter.

"Money has been tight for most of your mom's life."

Whatever. Money wasn't too tight for the new crib, the new stroller, or the new car seat that looked like something one might strap into before embarking on a Mars mission.

Gramma reached over and patted her on the knee. "You get started on that email. I'm going to find some money so we can go shopping."

Find money? Had she hidden it somewhere?

Still carrying her phone, Esther headed toward her bedroom, but then turned back. "Can you send an email from your phone?"

Duh. "Sure can."

She smiled. "Great. Go ahead and send it when you can. I'll be right back."

Chapter 15
Zoe

Zoe looked down at the phone in her hand. She'd already listed the things that were in her bag. Now she was thinking about what else she could add. A leather jacket? Real jewelry? Did people even put jewelry in their checked bags? Or how about a name-brand purse? She almost snickered at that one. She'd never carried a purse.

They wouldn't know that. She added it to the list. Then she stared at the brand she'd chosen. Maybe that was too obvious. Maybe she should pick a less expensive, less famous brand. She deleted it and tried to think of a replacement, but she couldn't. Fine, focus on the leather jacket. She added that to the list. Then she added diamond earrings. Wait, no one would believe that. And this whole ruse would fail if she got caught in the lie.

This idea made her think about her grandmother. If she did get caught, would this lie reflect back on Gramma? She didn't want that to happen. She didn't know if committing fraud against an airline was a real crime, but if it was, she didn't want to get Gramma in trouble. So she erased the leather jacket from the list. Fine. She would just tell the truth and get a puny check. Why had she thought she could do anything different?

Before she could talk herself out of her honesty, she sent the email. Then she looked toward her grandmother's closed bedroom door. What was she doing in there? Zoe got up off the couch and walked softly across the carpet.

She could hear Gramma on the phone, but it was obvious that she was trying to speak in a hushed voice. Zoe couldn't understand what she was saying. She got closer to the door, terrified that at any second it was going to fly open and reveal the spy behind it.

She could hear words now ... "no" ... or had that been *know*? "Yes" ... something, something ... "a hundred?" A hundred? A hundred what? "Thanks ... no ... Zoe ... appreciate ..." Wait, what was she being accused of appreciating? Or maybe Gramma was appreciating something. Had she even said appreciate? Maybe she'd said, "At least she ate." She must be talking to her mother. This made Zoe's heart ache. She couldn't believe it, but she missed her mother. Homesickness washed over her. Home wasn't perfect. Not even close. But it was home. This was something else. *Was* her grandmother talking to her mother? Or course. Who else would she be discussing Zoe's eating schedule with?

She knocked on the door.

Her grandmother stopped talking, and she heard footsteps. Still holding the phone, her grandmother opened the door, looking a bit ashen. "Are you okay?"

"Yes. I sent the email. Is that my mom?"

Gramma looked down at the phone as if she didn't quite know the answer to Zoe's question. "No. It's Cathy."

Cathy? Who was Cathy?

"She's my friend. One of the church ladies." She said this as if Zoe should know that she had church ladies. Of course, now that she thought about it, this made sense. But she hadn't thought about it. She hadn't given an ounce of thought to anything about her grandmother's life.

"I'll be one more minute." Then her grandmother was closing the bedroom door in her face.

What on earth? What could be so important? Was there a church bake sale emergency?

Zoe wondered if she would have to go to church. Her grandmother might make her. She would try to get out of it, naturally, but it wouldn't be easy tomorrow. She didn't have any time to get busy or to find something else to do. Eventually, there would be homework and tests to lie about studying for, but she didn't have any of that yet.

Zoe had gone to church when she was little, when she'd still lived in Maine. She'd been quite the little church mouse back then. Always right on time in her little dresses and tights. She'd liked Sunday school and loved junior church. The teacher who had led junior church had been the best. She'd made it fun, but she hadn't treated them as if they were stupid. She'd talked to them as though they were intelligent, albeit short, human beings.

Zoe had really bought into all the Jesus stuff back then, mostly because of that junior church leader, but things had changed when her father had left and her mother had moved her to the Midwest. Her mother had met a new man, and he didn't go to church. They'd never found a church in Missouri. They'd tried a few when they'd first moved, but her mother didn't like either of them. Now, if Zoe mentioned church, she knew her mom would get flustered and say, "I don't have time!"

The door opened to show Zoe still standing there. "Sorry," she rushed to say, "I was daydreaming."

"That's all right." Gramma shooed her out of the way. "We can get going now. I found some money."

Zoe stepped back. "What do you mean, you found some money?"

Gramma grabbed a light coat off a hook on the wall. "I don't have any cash, and won't for a few weeks, but we have a fund at church set up for people in need—"

"I'm not in need!" Zoe was horrified. "We're going to take money from a *church* to buy me a toothbrush?"

Gramma smiled and pushed her out of the way again so she could get at her shoes. "We're not taking money from anywhere." She held onto Zoe's right arm as she slid her left foot into its shoe. "We all tithe to God, and we've set aside some funds for when people need money, and this is one of those times." With her left foot secured, she went to work on her right.

"I still feel bad."

"Well, don't." With both shoes on, Gramma let go of her and looked up into her eyes. "And you're going to need more than a toothbrush."

Chapter 16
Zoe

They went to a box store. Zoe couldn't believe they'd driven nearly an hour and had only arrived at a box store. She'd been afraid to ask, but she'd hoped they were heading toward Portland or Augusta, some town with real clothes.

But no.

Was she really going to start at a new school with box store clothes?

Her grandmother must have sensed her discontent. "I've got another check coming soon, and then we can go somewhere more exciting. I just wanted to get you the basics today."

Zoe's stomach rolled with guilt. They'd already stopped at the world's oldest church to get money. She didn't want to have a second shopping trip. Why had the stupid airport lost her stupid bag? All of this could have been avoided.

"This is fine, Gramma. Thank you." She tried to remain positive as she looked at the offerings.

There was nothing to be positive about. So she gave up and started tossing things into the cart. A package of basic underwear. Two basic sports bras. She didn't want to take the time to try on box store jeans, so she grabbed two pairs of sweatpants and threw them into the cart. Yes, she was going to wear sweatpants to a new school. It was okay. She was starting to think she wouldn't be at this new school for very long. She was reaching for a plain T-shirt when Gramma asked, "Honey, are you okay?"

"Yes," she said quickly, feeling guilty. "I just hate shopping." This wasn't a lie. She *did* hate shopping. Nothing ever fit right, and she often ended up crying in the dressing room. She tried to force a smile. "I think that's enough clothes. Let's go get that toothbrush."

The sincere concern on her grandmother's face deepened her guilt. "What about socks?"

Oh yeah. Socks. She looked around for a sock rack, found it, and pushed the cart in that direction. Then she tossed a package of nondescript socks into the cart. She turned to look at her grandmother and realized she'd accidentally left her behind. She hurried back.

Gramma grabbed the cart and leaned on it. "You know, we can do better than this." She glanced distastefully at the sweatpants balled up in the end of the cart. "You can get some real pants."

When Zoe didn't respond, Gramma took a deep breath. "I'm sorry. I shouldn't have told you about the money thing. I'm sure it seems odd for you because you're not used to it. But we really didn't take money from a church. *God* himself has given us this money so that I, your grandmother, can provide what you, my granddaughter, needs. He delights in providing for us. It's part of who he is. But if you don't let me get you what you want, there's far less delight in that." She forced eye contact. "Please, Zoe, don't think about the money and where it came from. Just let me get you what you want."

How could she tell her grandmother that she didn't want anything from a cheesy box store? That she was going to get made fun of at school if she showed up in off-brand clothing?

She couldn't. She couldn't tell her. She looked around, trying to come up with a lie. Her eyes landed on a hideous sweatshirt. "I kind of like that one." She pointed with her chin.

Gramma's face lit up. "Terrific! Let's go get one of those!"

Zoe grabbed a 2XL off the rack.

"That looks awfully big. Maybe you should try it on."

Awesome. First she forced her to buy something. Now she was going to micromanage the purchase? Zoe shook her head. "It's good. I like my clothes baggy." This wasn't a lie either. The baggier, the better.

"All right, dear. Let's go get you some school supplies."

Zoe suppressed a groan. She couldn't believe she had gotten herself into this. She was going to have to go to school. In Maine. *Small town*, Maine. Alone.

Chapter 17
Zoe

Zoe didn't want to go to church, and she tried to make that clear to her grandmother without actually saying the words. But Gramma was oblivious. She was bustling around the apartment like she just couldn't wait to get where she was going. Then, hours before church was supposed to start, she announced that she was leaving.

"What?"

She stopped at the door, purse and Bible in hand. "I'm sorry. I thought I told you. I have to get there early to set up."

"So what do I do?"

She paused. "It starts at ten-thirty. Just come over any time before that." She pointed behind her at the wall. "It's right there."

She wanted her to walk into church *alone*? As if this situation wasn't bad enough as it was?

Gramma must have read her mind. "Do you want me to come back and get you?"

Now she felt like a baby. "No, it's okay."

Her body relaxed, and a warm smile spread across her face. "Great. I'll see you soon. Can't wait for you to see the inside of the place." She stepped toward her, grabbed her by the shoulder to pull her in, and then kissed her on the cheek. "Love you, honey." She turned then and left with more energy than Zoe could ever remember having.

Love. Did Gramma really love her? She hardly knew her, so how could she love her? But she certainly acted like she loved her. Did grandmothers have some sort of default love setting for their grandkids, something that caused them to love them even if they went for years without seeing them?

She sank into the couch and found the remote. She didn't want to go to church. It would have been one thing if it had been *her* church, the one she'd gone to with her mom when she'd lived in South Portland. It would be cool to see the old place and to see some of her old friends, though she didn't think any of them would recognize her, and she certainly wouldn't go out of her way to speak to them. She didn't want them to see that she'd turned into a Goliath. She flipped through the channels, but there was nothing on, which shouldn't have surprised her. Gramma only had twelve channels, and it was Sunday morning.

Leaving the TV on for the noise, she got up and went to the kitchen to root around for a snack. She'd only been there two days, and already Gramma was running low on good food. She had plenty of *her* kind of food: pot roast, meatloaf, frozen peas, and lots of potatoes. But there weren't any snacks.

She found some bread, toasted it, slathered it with jam, and then sat down in front of the nameless TV show. What would happen if she didn't go to church? If she just didn't show up? How mad would her grandmother be? Would there be consequences?

She didn't think so. But as she was mulling the option over, it occurred to her that her grandmother might be *hurt* if she didn't show up, and she didn't want to do that. Then, as she forced herself to get dressed and run a brush through her hair, it occurred to her that her grandmother might be *embarrassed* if she didn't show up. She didn't want to do that either.

Shoot. She had to go to church.

Keeping a close eye on the time, she played on her phone until quarter past ten. Then she stepped out of the safety of the tiny apartment and into the hallway, which smelled like mothballs. She passed a few tenants on the way to the stairs, and they looked at her curiously. She avoided their eyes.

Then she was outside, blinking in the bright sunshine. There weren't many trees along Providence Avenue, but those that were there had turned a glorious shade of orange. It nearly took her breath away. Were trees that pretty in Missouri? She couldn't remember. They probably were. She'd probably been too miserable to notice.

A bunch of people were clustered on the front lawn. She was going to ignore them, but then she saw that Gramma was one of the people. She was almost to them when the church bells rang, and she nearly jumped out of her skin.

It was official. She hated church.

Chapter 18
Esther

Esther saw her granddaughter coming across the lawn and tried to get to her before she saw what was written on the church sign, but there were so many people between her and Zoe that she couldn't quite manage it. She watched Zoe's eyes grow wide and her mouth fall open.

"Everyone!" Esther said, desperate to distract them from the filth that had been left on their lawn. "This is my lovely granddaughter Zoe!"

Zoe flinched at her words, and Esther wished she hadn't used the word *lovely.* Of course Zoe was lovely in her eyes, but she could see why Zoe might not believe it. She was tall and strong, and, with the way she was currently presenting herself, not very feminine.

Esther put her arm around Zoe's waist and turned to face her family. "This group here is the Puddy family. And that there is Walter Rainwater." Her voice faltered a little on his name, embarrassing her. She hurried to add, "And of course, you already know Rachel. And this is Emma." It occurred to Esther that Zoe and Emma could be friends. Emma was quite a bit younger than her, but stranger things had happened.

"What happened to your sign?"

Esther let out a long breath. "This sign is brand-new, and we don't know what happened to it. I mean, I think it's pretty obvious what happened to it. Someone profaned it, but we don't know who."

Emma mumbled something under her breath, but Mary Sue elbowed her.

Oh yeah, Mary Sue might be another friend for Zoe! Esther tried to stop herself. Zoe might not want a bunch of eighth-grade friends.

"Who did it?" Zoe asked.

Hadn't she just said they didn't know?

Zoe was looking at Emma. "You said you know who did it, so why you holdin' back?" There was something different in Zoe's voice—a toughness, but it didn't sound convincing to Esther.

Emma looked scared. "It's only a theory."

"We have no proof," Mary Sue hurried to say. "But there is one girl in town who likes to do stuff like this, that's all."

"Who?" Zoe pushed.

Still, the girls hesitated.

"Who?" Esther repeated.

Emma looked at the dead grass by her toes. "Isabelle Martin."

"Ohh," Lauren Puddy said thoughtfully. "That *is* a possibility." She looked at Esther. "Should we call the police?"

"Again?" Mary Sue said.

"What?" Zoe said, looking at Esther. "How often do you call the po-po around here?"

Emma snickered, probably at Zoe's use of the word *po-po*.

"No, let's not call the police just yet," Rachel said. "We can start with Isabelle's mother. And right now, we need to get to worshipping the Lord. That's what we came here to do."

Esther wasn't sure, but she thought Zoe groaned. She smiled at her granddaughter. "Right this way." She swept an arm toward the church steps, proud as punch that her granddaughter was about to walk into the building with her.

Rachel fell into step behind them. "You look nice, Zoe."

Again, Zoe flinched.

"The color of your T-shirt looks great with your hair."

"Thank you," Zoe mumbled.

Esther stood on her tiptoes to get closer to Zoe's ear. "You have no idea how beautiful you are, but I'm going to try to convince you."

Chapter 19
Zoe

It was the weirdest church Zoe had ever seen. Granted, she'd only been in a few churches, but still. This one didn't even look finished. Some of the walls had fresh paint, but some had hideous peeling wallpaper. Half the light fixtures were missing. In their place, bare wires dangled out of the ceiling.

On one side of the sanctuary, pews had been pushed up against each other to make room for the pallets and pallets of food stacked along the wall. Zoe had never seen so much food in one place. Had Gramma and her friends robbed a Walmart? And if so, why? Were they preparing for the apocalypse? Were Gramma's friends preppers? "What's with all the canned okra?"

"We've been asking for donations from grocery stores," Gramma explained. "We take whatever they're willing to give, including okra. And then we give it out to people in need."

They would have to be in *real* need to eat canned okra. "That's nice of you," she said noncommittally. She did think it was nice, but she didn't want to sound too impressed.

"It's not us," Gramma said quickly. "It's all God."

That was going to get annoying. She'd tried to give her a compliment, and she'd pointed to God. Fine, she wouldn't give her any more compliments.

A giant hydraulic lift sat folded up along a different wall. This made sense, as she didn't know how else these people were going to reach that sky-scraping ceiling—which, incidentally, was also only half-painted.

And there appeared to be a homeless man sitting in the back pew. He sat all alone singing to himself.

A few rows in front of him sat an absolutely gorgeous guy who looked about her age. She ripped her eyes away from him as the room filled with music. Her eyes followed the sound to an enormous pipe organ. Her mouth dropped open a little. She didn't know an organ could sound like that. The beauty of it gave her a chill.

"Are you cold, dear?" Gramma asked.

"No," she said quickly. "I'm fine."

"There are doughnuts and coffee back there." Gramma pointed. "All different flavors. The doughnuts, not the coffees. Only one flavor of coffee, Folgers. Help yourself if you'd like some."

Doughnuts of any flavor sounded spectacular, but she didn't want to be wandering around the church alone.

"Want me to get you some?" a young voice asked.

Zoe scanned her surroundings to find it. It had come from the girl with two names. Bobby Jo? Bobby Sue? Something like that. She wasn't sure how to answer that. "A doughnut would be good."

"Great!" The girl whirled away from her.

Zoe followed Esther toward the front, hoping they weren't going all the way to the first pew. She needn't have feared, as they slid into the second pew. Awesome.

"Let me introduce you to some of my other friends. This is Cathy."

A well-dressed, put-together woman offered her a handshake. This was the woman who'd bought her the ugly T-shirt she was currently wearing. Awesome. She shook her hand.

"And this is Barbara, and this is Vera."

It seemed Vera hadn't heard Gramma and ignored them both. This was fine with Zoe.

"And of course, you know Vicky."

Ah yes, of course. Vicky, the petite woman who'd needed the front seat so the two women over six feet could sit in the back.

Doughnut Girl materialized beside her with a chocolate doughnut wrapped in a napkin.

"Wow, thanks," Zoe said and meant it.

"No problem! Let me know if you need anything else! And welcome to our church!" She zipped away.

Zoe looked at her grandmother. "That girl sure does have a lot of energy."

"Yes. The whole family is like that. I think it's all the goat milk."

What? Goat milk? Gross!

Cathy stepped up to the pulpit and cleared her throat. "Good morning! Welcome, welcome, welcome! We are so excited you are here! As most of you know, we have been praying mightily for a pastor, but he's not here yet, so you're stuck with me again."

Some people behind Zoe tittered.

Zoe was glad they didn't have a pastor yet. She liked the looks of Cathy. First, she reminded her of Zoe's old junior church teacher. And second, if Zoe was going to have to listen to someone blather on about the Bible, she'd rather it be this woman than some stuffy suit.

"But first! Let's sing a few songs. Rachel will be leading us." She swept an arm toward the woman Zoe had shared a back seat with. Today, Rachel had on a gold-colored dress and an enormous, and enormously hideous, orange hat. It reminded Zoe of the vests that hunters wore. Maybe Rachel was going hunting after church. As if her ensemble wasn't bad enough, a thick strand of chunky gold beads wrapped multiple times around her neck. It looked heavy. Zoe was surprised she could stand up straight under all that bling.

"Let's start with one of my favorites!" Rachel was unnecessarily excited. "Joyful, Joyful, We Adore Thee." She turned and nodded toward the organ, but that woman wasn't even looking at her. Nevertheless, she started to play, and people scrambled to find the song in their hymnals.

"Why didn't she tell us the number?" Zoe mumbled, her mouth still full of chocolate doughnut.

"Can't," Esther explained, flipping madly. "We've got about ten different hymnals here."

Zoe closed her eyes. This was the weirdest church in the world.

Chapter 20
Esther

Esther tried to watch Zoe listen to the sermon without letting Zoe know she was being watched. She didn't know where Zoe was spiritually, but she didn't think it was a good situation, based on all the trouble she'd been in. Esther wasn't worried, though. Lots of people get into trouble, but then when they feel Jesus' love, they choose to hunker down inside of it instead of running around looking for distractions.

Cathy was doing a good job. She had a knack for sharing the Word without sounding preachy. She used examples from her own life or from the lives of people she knew personally, so everything was relatable.

Esther caught herself eying Walter and yanked her eyes away before he caught her too.

"Do you have a crush on him or something?" Zoe whispered.

Esther's cheeks got hot.

"I'm sorry?"

"You keep staring at him."

No, this was the first time she'd looked at Walter since the service had started. Before that, she'd been staring at *Zoe*, but she couldn't exactly tell her that. "No, I am too old for crushes."

Zoe looked skeptical. "I don't think anyone is too old for crushes."

"Shh." Esther wanted her listening to the sermon, not thinking about her grandmother's crushes, but when she shushed her, Zoe looked injured, and Esther regretted the shushing. She slid an arm around her shoulders and pulled her closer. Then she tried to catch up with what Cathy was saying.

"My niece could have preached at that woman until she was blue in the face, and I don't think it would have made any difference. But the woman said, 'I am saved because you touched me.' You see, no one had gotten close to her in a very long time. How can you convince someone you love them if you keep them at arm's length? This woman was a pariah, a castaway, an undesirable. But my niece, filled with the love of Jesus, reached out to her—not in the metaphorical sense! She didn't send her an email! She didn't have flowers delivered. She used her actual hands, and she touched the woman. And this seemingly small act changed the moment! It changed the way this woman saw herself. Suddenly, she wasn't alone! Suddenly, she wasn't contagious. Suddenly, she was a normal person, just like everyone else, something she hadn't been in a very long time."

Esther wasn't certain, but she thought Zoe's body stiffened at these words.

"So this act changed the moment, changed this woman's life, and changed eternity! It changed the kingdom of God because this woman came to know Jesus, and then she shared Jesus with her husband, and then he shared Jesus with their three children. We don't know yet how many people those three kids will affect in their lifetime, but think about it! It all started with one touch!

"It wasn't even a big deal! She didn't pull her off a cliff or give her a kidney. She just touched her hand! Imagine! We don't know what people need. But if we are willing to get close to them and just give them basic Christian kindness, we might well meet that need. And in doing so, we might change a moment. We might change a life. We might change a family. We might change eternity! Imagine!"

Cathy took a deep breath. Esther imagined that she was exhausted. "Next time God plops a person down in front of you who makes you uncomfortable, ask for his direction before you back away. Of course, and this is especially for the women, make sure you are safe. I'm not suggesting you go wandering into a dark alley to touch a homeless man."

Esther fought the urge to look at Derek. Was he still sitting back there?

To her credit, Cathy didn't look at him either.

"Lots of dark alleys in Carver Harbor," Zoe muttered.

At least she was listening.

"But if you are in a safe situation, and God presents you with someone, I don't care how dirty or sick or stinky he is! You show him the love of Jesus! Not because I'm telling you to, but because someday, when you are hanging out in heaven, God might show you all that might have happened if you *had* gotten close to that person. And you don't want to regret your decision then." Cathy leaned back from the pulpit and rubbed her hands together as if they were cold. "That's all I have for you today." She brought one hand down on top of the pulpit as if she were playing Slap Jack. "Let's pray!" Cathy sure did get excited about prayer.

"Wait!" a voice called out.

Chapter 21
Zoe

Someone had had the gall to interrupt Cathy. Zoe bristled at this offense. She followed the sound to see a petite lady in the front row struggling to come to a stand and felt less aggressive. It was difficult to be annoyed with a woman this frail.

Zoe sneaked a peek at Gramma to see if she knew what this interruption was about. It was clear that she didn't. Whatever was happening, Gramma didn't know about it and didn't look enthused. Zoe shifted uncomfortably on the hard seat. She'd come to church, she'd sat still and listened, and now she was ready to go home.

The woman slowly turned to face the small congregation. Then she took a shaky breath. "For those of you who don't know me, the name is Vera. The Lord's been nagging at me this whole service." She took an unnecessarily long pause, and Zoe wondered if she'd forgotten what she was going to say. "Someone in here knows Jesus, but has forgotten about him."

Zoe quickly looked at the floor.

"I've been asking God who it is, so I could just go to them privately instead of making a scene. Anyway, I'm here to tell you that he hasn't forgotten about you. In fact, he's been waiting for you to come home to him for a while now. And I'm here to tell you that it is time." She stopped. "I know some people wait until they are on their deathbed"—

Oh good, she *wasn't* talking to Zoe because Zoe wouldn't be on her deathbed for quite some time.

—"but Jesus is about more than going to heaven when you die. I got saved when I was just a little girl, and I have known him every step of the way, and I can tell you that life is better with him. So don't wait until you are dying and afraid of hell. Reach out to him right now, because this life is worth living well, and you can't live it well without him."

Zoe's cheeks grew hot. She had known Jesus, hadn't she? When she was little, in that southern Maine church. But she didn't know him now. Was this woman talking to her?

Chapter 22
Zoe

Zoe really didn't want to ride to school with her grandmother. She wanted to walk before it got too cold to walk. Even then, when it was too cold to walk, she'd probably want to walk, not be driven around like some third-grader. But Gramma insisted. She had to do a bunch of paperwork anyway, she said. Might as well go in together.

Awesome.

It wouldn't be bad enough being her and walking into a new school, one that was so small that a new kid was big news. It wouldn't be bad enough watching them all stare and whisper when they saw the new behemoth with the black hair and ugly sweatshirt. She would also get to walk in with an old lady.

She loved her grandmother, but walking in with her made it clear that she didn't have any parents. Or at least, none that wanted her. At her Missouri school, kids only lived with their grandparents when their parents were drug addicts, in prison, or both.

Awesome.

They pulled into a smallish parking lot of an oddly shaped brick building. It looked like a lollipop with a too-thick stick. One long rectangular chunk led to a giant round dome. The architecture was odd, but the building was larger than Zoe had expected, and this gave her some hope. Maybe this wasn't such a small town after all.

Gramma opened the front door and gave her a wide smile. Could it be that she was actually excited about this? They stepped inside to the smell of carpet shampoo. Carpet? This school had carpeted hallways? She'd never heard of such a thing.

They were early enough that these carpeted hallways were empty. Gramma looked around, confused.

"The layout is different."

Since when? Since she'd gone there? Of course it was. Chances were good they'd remodeled sometime in the last fifty years. Zoe pointed at a giant plexiglass window that was obviously the office. "I think we're supposed to go in there."

"Ah yes." She toddled toward the window, and Zoe couldn't help but smile. She was adorable.

Zoe looked around to make sure no one was laughing at them, suddenly feeling fiercely defensive of her grandmother. She was doing the best she could.

The window slid open to reveal a grumpy looking woman in a too-tight sweater. She had bright red lipstick on her teeth.

"Good morning. We need to sign up for school."

The woman looked Zoe up and down and then tilted her head toward a closed door. "Come on in."

Zoe followed her grandmother into the office, which was surprisingly small. A tall counter stretched the length of it. The office woman ignored them for a minute but then came to the counter and laid a stack of multi-colored paperwork in front of them. "Fill these out, and then we'll send her ..." She hesitated and checked Zoe as if to confirm that she was, in fact, a *her*. Deciding that this was her best guess, she continued, "to the guidance counselor to set up a schedule." She looked at the clock. "When she gets in." She was annoyed, but Zoe didn't know if she was annoyed that the guidance counselor was late or that Zoe was early. Or maybe she was annoyed because her sweater was too tight.

Gramma nodded, still looking excited. "Thank you." She picked up a pen and started on the top page. The counter was so high, or

Gramma was so short, that it looked uncomfortable.

Zoe was annoyed that they hadn't given her a chair and table to work at. This stack of paperwork was *thick*. She dropped her backpack at her feet. "Do you want me to fill out some of them?"

Gramma readily handed over half the stack. "Yes, please." She made a weird clicking sound with her tongue. "I don't even know your social security number."

"That's all right. I do." Ten minutes later, when she'd written said number a dozen times, she added, "I don't understand how this is the most efficient way to do this."

"What do you mean?" Gramma didn't look up from her task.

"I mean, do we really need to tell them my name, address, and social security number twenty-seven times? Couldn't they do that part electronically?"

Her grandmother didn't respond. Maybe she wasn't annoyed by it. But Zoe certainly was. With all the technology in the world, the institution charged with preparing her for said world didn't have the technology available to simplify this process? Her phone auto-filled her Five Guys order and her mother's credit card number while playing her favorite songs, but her *school* was making her handwrite her mailing address ad nauseam?

That made no sense.

She rubbed her cramping hand and then kept going, intent on protecting her grandmother from the brunt of the ridiculous paperwork load.

Her grandmother finished while Zoe was listing her sibling for the third time. Why a podunk school in Maine needed to know the name of her baby sister in Missouri was beyond her.

"I don't have your shot records either."

Zoe shrugged. "Call Mom. I'm sure she'd be thrilled to send them."

"Hey!" a voice said from behind. "Didn't I see you in church?"

She cringed and slowly turned, glad there were no other kids nearby to hear about her church attendance.

The hot guy from church grinned broadly, and Zoe's stomach somersaulted. "Hi, Esther!" He held out his hand toward Zoe. "I'm Jason." He looked at the woman behind the counter. "Good morning, Linda!"

Wait. Podunk students called school secretaries by their first name? She didn't even *know* the name of any of the secretaries at her old school.

The woman's expression softened at the sound of Jason's voice.

"When she's ready, I'm happy to give her a tour."

"That's very nice of you, Jason." The secretary wasn't annoyed anymore.

Chapter 23
Zoe

Too-hot-for-words Jason spread his arms wide. "This is my home away from home."

He'd started his tour of her new school in the gym, which was a considerable distance from the main office. But he'd said he would start at the best spot and then work his way back to the English classrooms. She looked around the dark gym. It looked cavernous.

"Actually"—he dropped his arms— "I prefer this home to my other one."

She looked at him quickly.

"Not that I'm an abused child or anything. I'm not." He laughed uncomfortably. "My home is fine. I just like it here better."

Zoe didn't. She had no use for gyms and was ready to continue the tour.

"You don't play basketball?"

She shook her head.

"You should. You're so tall."

People had been saying this since she popped out of the womb, and every time she heard it, it increased her resolve to never touch a basketball. She shrugged. "Don't really like sports."

He stepped closer to her, looking appalled. "We should fix that." He studied her, and she was glad to notice she was only a hair taller than him. She wished she wasn't taller at all, but at least she didn't tower over him. "Was your last school big?"

She shrugged again. "Medium. Couple thousand kids."

He snorted. "Couple *thousand?* Only a couple hundred here."

Oh boy.

"And most of them play sports." He put his hands on his hips and looked around. "It's all right. I have a month or so to convince you." He looked at her and winked. "You could be a star."

Yeah right. She pointed her chin to a dark hallway on the other side of the gym. "What's over there?"

He wrinkled up his nose. "Nothing much. Just locker rooms. Come on, I'll show you the weight room."

Awesome.

She followed him up some stairs and into another carpeted room. This one didn't smell like carpet cleaner. It smelled much, much worse. She stepped through the doorway and jumped, surprised to see two more kids. They wore gym clothes and were all sweaty.

"Hey! This is Zoe. She's new. Zoe, this is Chevon and Hype."

She glanced at Jason to see if he was joking. Those were the weirdest names she'd ever heard. Didn't the word Chevon mean goat meat? "Hype?" she asked, not wanting to be rude to the girl.

The boy named Hype laughed too loudly. "Yeah, as in, is that guy really worth all the hype?"

She raised an eyebrow. "There's a lot of hype about you?"

Jason laughed. "Not really. Because he wasn't worth it."

"You didn't wash off the bench." Chevon wrinkled up her nose. "I had to do it."

"I did it!" Jason protested.

"No, you didn't." Chevon put her hands on her hips. "It was all wet."

"Okay, sorry." He opened the door behind them and then held it open for her.

She had to duck under his arm to get out, and the action felt oddly intimate. It wasn't lost on her that she'd met a guy who could reach over her shoulder. She stepped out into the hallway and took a long breath. "It was really stinky in there."

He laughed. "Yes, yes, it is."

They started walking. "Is that why you're here so early?"

"Yep. Mondays, Wednesdays, and Fridays, I'm here at about six. You're welcome to join us anytime."

"I can't believe they just let you in here unsupervised."

He looked at her, surprised. "Why wouldn't they?"

She heard voices and the banging of lockers, and her stomach tightened. This was getting real.

He pointed toward another door. "That's the special ed room." He kept walking and they came into another oversized room. "This is the cafeteria."

"It's huge."

"Yeah. I have no idea why it's so big. I think this whole place was built with the idea that the paper mill would never go out of business, and papermakers would keep making babies."

She snickered. She followed him through the cafeteria and back into the carpeted hallways, where they ran into a couple holding hands.

Jason stopped and introduced them. This couple was less friendly.

"You don't have to introduce me to everyone," she said when they were out of earshot. "I'm kind of antisocial."

He laughed. "All right." He stopped in front of a lit trophy case. "Here is our pride display."

The case was packed full of trophies, plaques, gold basketballs, and framed photos. One of the most prominent ones featured Jason himself with a basketball net around his neck. "Is that you?"

"Yeah. When me and Hype were freshmen. We were Class C state champs."

"So Hype is pretty good at basketball?" She didn't care, but she liked it when Jason talked.

"Yeah, he's good, but maybe not as good as he thinks he is."

Out of nowhere, a giant kid jumped on Jason from behind. "DeGrave! What's up?" The kid was really loud.

Zoe stepped away from him and saw that he was being trailed by a dainty little snot who was looking Zoe up and down. The girl wore a shirt Zoe had seen in Ellsworth, and Zoe realized that every kid she'd seen had been wearing box store clothes—even Jason.

"Who's this, DeGrave?" The tiny girl sounded like a chew toy.

Jason stepped closer to her. The gesture felt almost protective. Or was that her imagination? "This is my friend Zoe. She's new here."

Totally ignoring this, the big kid once again invaded Jason's personal space. He lowered his voice. "Hey, full moon tonight. We're all going to the Cove. You in?"

Jason inched back. "Maybe."

"Maybe?" he cried. He looked at his girl. "That's probably a no." Then he looked back to Jason. "Come on, man, it'll be awesome. How often is there a full moon?"

"Every twenty-nine and a half days," Jason muttered, but they didn't seem to hear him.

"She can come too," the girl said, making it clear she didn't want that to happen.

The boy shoved Jason in the chest and swore. "Come on, DeGrave. Don't be such a—"

"Fine!" Jason gently guided Zoe around them. "Maybe." He kept walking, and Zoe was grateful. Those two had been obnoxious.

"That was Nelson and June. They're not as bad as they seem."

Zoe doubted that. She thought they were probably even worse than they'd seemed.

The hallway was filling up now, and Zoe's anxiety worsened.

"This is the library." His tone suggested he had no use for the library. "And obviously, these are the classrooms. When you get your schedule, I can show you where your classes are." He stopped walking and looked at her. "What year are you?"

"Junior."

"Me too. Cool. We'll probably be in some classes together."

This was getting to be too much. Why was he being so nice to her? Was this some elaborate hoax? Was she being punked? No way was the too-hot-for-words junior basketball star *this* friendly. Something was up.

"Mrs. Chesney is probably here by now. I'll show you her office."

Zoe didn't know who Mrs. Chesney was.

"The guidance counselor."

"Oh. Yeah. Thanks."

A blond girl came running down the hallway, and Zoe braced herself for what she knew was coming. This girl was gorgeous. She had perfect, long, wavy locks. She was petite yet athletic-looking. This was her. This was Miss Jason.

For a second, Zoe thought she might have been wrong. It appeared that the alleged Miss Jason was going to go screaming right past them, but she caught Jason's arm on the fly and swung to a stop, a giant, entirely-too-peppy grin on her face.

"Who's this?"

"This is Zoe. She's new."

The girl tightened her grip on Jason's arm and leaned into him. "Is this the girl from church?" She spoke the word *church* as if it tasted bad in her mouth, and she spoke it entirely too loudly.

"Yes."

Miss Jason turned her eyes on Zoe. Her smile stayed in place, but there was absolute menace in her eyes. "Jason has been *so* weird since all this Jesus stuff. He's bringing home strays all the time now."

"Alita!" Jason said. His smile was gone. He looked angry and even more than that, embarrassed.

She ignored his reproof and started tugging on his arm. "Come on, we're going to be late." She dragged out the word *late*, making it an obnoxious three syllables.

Jason yanked his arm out of her grasp. "I have to show Zoe where Mrs. Chesney's office is."

"Oh, I'll go with you." She tried to grab his arm again, but he pulled it away—more subtly this time.

"I'll meet you in homeroom." He looked at Zoe. "Come on. We're almost there." He turned and walked away.

Avoiding looking at Alita—what kind of a name was Alita, and why did everyone in this school have a weird name—she followed him.

He reached an open doorway and turned to wait for her.

"She seemed nice," Zoe said. Jason flinched, and Zoe felt awful. "Sorry. I didn't mean to—"

"No, it's fine." But it was clear that it wasn't. He swung his arm through the open doorway. "This is guidance. Let me know if you want help finding anything." He started to leave.

"Thanks, Jason," she called after him, but he didn't reply. She wanted to kick herself. Why had she been sarcastic with him? Why was she always doing that?

Chapter 24
Zoe

Zoe walked into first period English about ten minutes late. She handed her late slip to the teacher and then looked for an empty desk. The only one was right up front, and this was really bad news. She hated sitting up front and knew it would allow everyone to stare at her. Still, she had no choice, so she folded herself up and slid into the desk. Her belly rubbed against the top of the desk and her knees hit the bottom.

Awesome.

The teacher introduced her, and there was the requisite snickering.

"Where are you from?"

She knew the teacher was trying to be nice, but he was really bad at it. "Missouri," she said and though she hadn't meant for it to happen, the word dripped with a southern accent.

More snickering.

"Missouri? I've never been to Missouri!"

No kidding.

"Well, welcome to Carver Harbor." He walked to a bookshelf, pulled out a worn paperback, and returned to her. He handed it to her. Gatsby. Awesome. She'd read this when she was a freshman. He read her mind. "Have you read it?"

She shook her head.

"Great. We're on chapter four. You've got some catching up to do!" He said this as if it were an exciting prospect.

There was more murmuring behind her. She couldn't make out the words, but clear as day, she heard Jason say, "That's enough!"

She endured the discussion of the fourth chapter of the great American novel. The list of party attendees reminded Zoe of those Old Testament genealogies, and she couldn't believe that anything had reminded her of any part of the Bible. Sure, she'd spent a great deal of her childhood in Sunday school and junior church, and she'd memorized her fair share of Bible verses so she could get the stickers, but that had all been a very long time ago. She certainly couldn't remember any of them now.

Finally, mercifully, the bell rang, and she turned her body to extricate herself from the desk. Before she could do that, Jason was in front of her. He picked her schedule up off her desk and studied it. Alita hung nearby, obviously displeased.

"This is great. You have the same exact schedule as me."

Alita's face grew red. Obviously, she *didn't* have the same exact schedule as Jason.

He handed Zoe the schedule. "So it'll be easy. You can follow me around."

Zoe nodded, not sure what to say. It appeared he had forgiven her for her earlier offense, and she didn't want to offend him again.

They stood there awkwardly. She was willing to follow him, but was he going to move?

"Aren't you going to walk me to math?"

Jason sighed. "Yeah." He looked at Zoe. "Small detour. Let's go."

Zoe grudgingly followed Jason and Alita to her math class, turned away uncomfortably as Jason kissed her goodbye, and then followed him down the hall.

"Is she a junior too?"

He nodded. "Yeah. But she's in the dumb math."

Zoe suppressed a snicker.

They entered a starkly appointed white-walled room. An ashen-faced man in a short-sleeved white dress shirt stood and headed toward the front of the room. Blank marker boards hung on every wall. The English classroom had sported a smart board. This guy was old school.

Thanks to the Alita detour, they were late, and again Zoe found herself in the front row. But at least this time, she had Jason beside her.

The girl behind Jason leaned forward. "Are you going to the Cove tonight?" she whispered. "Jameson got a keg. There's going to be a lot of people there."

Jason gave an almost imperceptible nod. "Maybe." He looked at Zoe out of the corner of his eye.

"What's the Cove?"

"It's a little beach on the backside of the peninsula, kind of away from everything. Kids hang out there a lot."

"People in Carver Harbor get drunk on a Monday?"

He shrugged. "It's a full moon."

She laughed. "Are you going to go?"

He looked discouraged. "Probably. Probably Alita will make me."

Chapter 25
Zoe

Zoe played on her phone until she was certain Gramma was asleep. Then she slid out from under her blanket and carried her shoes to the door. She paused with her hand on the doorknob, listening for any stirring from the bedroom behind her.

There wasn't any.

She slipped out into an empty hallway, softly shut the door behind her, and then slid her shoes on. Then she was down the stairs and out the door.

The cold night air felt fantastically refreshing. She loved her grandmother, but she hadn't had a moment alone since she'd gotten to Maine. It felt good to be outside, alone, in motion.

But she had no idea where the Cove was. It was on the ocean, but Carver Harbor was on a peninsula. She couldn't just head toward the water because she was surrounded by water.

She stepped onto Main Street's sidewalk and looked both ways. Two gas stations. Only one with lights on. And it wasn't even ten o'clock yet. She headed toward the lights.

There was no one there but a clerk.

"Can you tell me where the Cove is?"

He frowned. "Why?"

Why? What kind of a question was that? Why not?

"Um, because I'm new here, and my friend told me to meet him there, but I don't know how to get there."

He gave her a lewd smile. "Ah, I see." He straightened up and looked out the window. "You on foot?"

She didn't answer.

She didn't have to. "It's a long walk."

She sighed. "Are you going to tell me where it is or not?"

He held up a hand. "Easy! All right, I'll tell you. It's all the way on the other side of the peninsula. The easiest, shortest way is to cut through the woods." He looked her up and down. "But I'm guessing you don't want to do that."

It was clear this was an insult, though Zoe didn't know how that was insulting. Why should she *want* to take an unknown shortcut through the woods, alone, at night?

"But if you keep going this way"—he pointed back the way she'd come—"until you see Battle Ave on your right, you can take that and follow it until it ends. It's quite a ways, but it will come out on Hill Street. Then turn right onto Hill Street and go down the hill. The beach is right at the bottom. The road keeps going, curves off toward the right, but you'll see the beach."

"Thanks." She turned away, eager to get away from his leering.

"Have fun!" he called after her, and she suddenly wanted a shower. She walked briskly, motivated to put some distance between that guy and herself, and soon she was back beside her grandmother's building. She strongly considered ducking back inside, abandoning this whole idea.

But Jason.

If he was there, she wanted to be there. And it had sounded as though he would be there, maybe even against his will. She should be there, then, to keep him company, to cheer him up. Oh, who was she kidding? She shouldn't be entertaining thoughts about Jason. That was insane. He would never be interested in her. She knew that. And yet, she still wanted to spend time with him.

As she walked down Battle Ave, Main Street's streetlights faded behind her, but it was still light enough to see, thanks to the moon. She patted her back pocket to check for her phone just in case.

The road narrowed, the sidewalks stopped, and the houses thinned out. How long was this road? Maybe she *should* have cut through the woods. Nah. The last time she'd gone off into the woods it had taken her an entire day to find her way back out. She cringed at the memory. She was still very embarrassed. Lots of kids had run into the woods that night, but she was the only one who had spent the night there. She was the only one who had fallen off a cliff and then spent the night passed out in the dirt.

Her stomach churned. No wonder her mother wanted to get rid of her. She was an embarrassment.

A stop sign came into view. Thank God. Battle Ave *did* have an end. She didn't know how long she'd been walking, but much longer and the party would be over. If it even was a party. She couldn't believe these people partied on a Monday. They were hardcore. She turned right on Hill Street and saw the ocean. The water was smooth and calm, and the moonlight reflected off it beautifully. The ocean really was something. She'd missed it.

She started down the hill, hoping she wouldn't have to walk back up it. Maybe

Jason would give her a ride home. Jason *and Alita*, she corrected her thinking.

She heard them before she saw them. Sounded like the whole school.

But it wasn't. It looked like only a few dozen kids, but they were *loud*. Six pickups sat backed in with their tailgates down. Kids sat on the tailgates, their legs swinging, holding red solo cups or beer cans. She didn't see a keg.

Nor did she see Jason. She stopped at the edge of the sand, scanning the crowd nervously. Where was he? At this point she would even be excited to see Alita.

"Hey!" someone cried, and then a round kid was coming toward her.

Nelson.

He tried to throw his arm around her neck, failed because it was too high, staggered back a bit and laughed while simultaneously trying to take another drink from his plastic cup. He choked, coughed, and then lowered the cup to give her an excited smile. "Whass you name again?" he slurred.

"Zoe."

He tried to fling his arm around her neck again, and this time she lowered her shoulders so he could do it, though she didn't know why she'd done this. She was afraid of disappointing Nelson, apparently. "Hey, everybody!" he hollered, his spittle hitting her face. "Look! It's Zoe!" He lowered his voice. "Less get you a drinkie-drink."

He dragged her toward the second pickup, and someone shoved a cup into her hand.

"What is it?" she asked, and they all laughed.

He removed his arm, and she straightened up and sniffed what was in the cup.

Smelled like straight whiskey. She took a sip. Yup. If there was a mixer in there, there wasn't much of it. It tasted like fire and burned her throat going down. It was so warm it was almost hot, and she put her hand over her mouth, afraid she was going to throw it right back up.

But the feeling passed, and soon the familiar relaxing warmth filled her, and she started to breathe again. Nelson introduced each of them by name, but his slurring and the loud music made it hard to hear anything. It didn't matter. It wasn't like she was going to remember any of their names, and even if she did, she wouldn't be able to attach those names to any faces once she saw these people in the fluorescent lights of Carver Harbor High.

When Nelson finished with his lengthy introductions, Zoe said, "I can't believe the cops let you drink here."

One of the girls let out a high-pitched squeal. "They don't! They could come bust us up any second."

This made Zoe nervous. She did *not* need to be running from the cops again. "So why haven't they?"

Nelson shrugged. "Lazy," he said, and all the girls laughed.

Zoe noticed Nelson's girlfriend wasn't there. What had her name been? Someone took the cup out of her hand.

"So what's Missouri like?" one girl asked.

Zoe didn't want to talk about Missouri. It made her sad. "Where's your girlfriend?" she asked Nelson.

Nelson tipped his head back and barked a laugh. "Girlfriend?" he cried. "What girlfriend?"

The anonymous server slid the cup back into her hand. It was even fuller this time. "Thank you." She took another swig. It was going down easier now, and she was feeling much better—so relaxed, so blissfully numb. "I don't know. That girl you were with this morning."

"June?" he cried. Then he laughed again. "June's my cousin!"

The small circle erupted into hysterical laughter. "And she's over there." He waved an arm at the ocean.

Embarrassed, Zoe decided to stop talking and just listen. She took another drink and leaned back against the pickup. She tried to follow their conversation, but she didn't know any of the people they were talking about. She found herself gazing out at the ocean. It was so beautiful. The reflection of the moon stretched all the way to the land, making it look like a giant wide path of moonlight that one could walk on. She headed that way, leaving the loud chaos behind her.

She reached the water's edge. Now that she'd walked away from the music, shouting, and laughing, she could hear the water lapping at the shore. The moon-path started only inches from her feet. She wanted to step out onto it. It wouldn't hold her, of course. She knew this. She couldn't walk on water. But still, she wanted to try.

As she contemplated, Nelson appeared beside her. This time, he slid his beefy arm around her waist. No boy had ever done this to her before, and despite Nelson's profound unattractiveness, she liked the feel of his arm around her.

He stood on his tiptoes to press his lips to her ear. "Let's you and me go for a walk." His breath was hot and wet on her ear, and she jerked away from it, but his arm was strong around her hips. He stepped around to face her, and he was uncomfortably close. "Come on, don't be like that." He laughed and stepped closer. "Don't play shy."

Chapter 26
Zoe

Nelson was grotesque. Zoe knew what he wanted, and the thought made her sick. And yet she was still considering it. Would it be so bad, going off into the woods with Nelson? At least *someone* wanted to go into the woods with her. She'd never kissed anyone. The curiosity was powerful. If things went horribly wrong, she could just move back to Missouri.

She stepped back and tried to take another drink of courage, but her cup was empty. He was still leering at her. "Does anyone have some weed?" She didn't necessarily want pot in that moment, but she wanted to distract him, and a little pot wouldn't be so bad. She'd always preferred it to booze anyway, and her swimming head made it clear to her she shouldn't have any more whiskey.

"Weed?" he cried and barked out another laugh. "Only stoners smoke pot! Are you a stoner?" He was being really loud now—and aggressive. Either he'd just had a mighty mood swing, or she had entirely misinterpreted the situation.

She backed away slowly, tripped, almost fell, and then turned toward the road. She could feel eyes on her. She kept her head down and headed for the road. She needed to get out of there. Suddenly, she was afraid of Nelson, and she picked up speed. She heard a burst of laughter behind her and was certain that she was the butt of the joke. She stopped at the road and looked both ways. Which way was she supposed to go?

Oh yeah. Uphill. She needed to go uphill. She turned right and scanned the crowd for Jason. Nearly every single person there faced her, stared at her. Jason wasn't there. She looked away and started up the hill, but walking was hard. Now that she was moving, she realized she'd drunk far too much. Fear gripped her. What had she drunk? How did she know there hadn't been something awful in that cup? Something *more* awful than warm, cheap whiskey? She tried to pick up speed. She had to get back to Gramma's. She would be fine once she was there. She would be safe. And she could get something to eat, which would sober her up.

She started up the hill. The walk ahead of her seemed impossibly long and the hill impossibly steep. Just get to the top of the hill, she told herself, and then the rest will be easy. She craved the lights of Main Street. She turned to look back at the ocean, to glimpse that beautiful moonlight one more time, but this swing of her head threw her off balance, and she fell forward, slamming her right knee into the tar.

She was far from the crowd now, but still she thought she heard them laughing. She got herself to her feet and looked down at her knee. Her sweatpants had ripped, but it was too dark to see if there was much damage to the skin. It didn't hurt, but she knew she'd drunk enough to cover the pain. She started upward again, keeping her head down, concentrating. She didn't care if she lived or died, but she didn't want those people to see her dead body as they drove by on their way home. She didn't want to give them that pleasure.

She realized she was still holding the plastic cup and threw it into the ditch in disgust. Then she trudged upward.

This was the tallest hill in the world. She hoped that all this physical exertion would sober her up, but as she finally crested the hill, she almost fell over sideways. She stopped, bent over, and put her hands on her knees, trying to catch her breath. She started crying.

She realized she was in danger of passing out, and she forced herself to stand up straight. She turned to look for Battle Ave, but there were only trees. Oh no, where was the street? She looked both ways and saw that she'd walked past it. "You've got to be kidding me," she said aloud to herself. "You idiot." Slowly, she went back down the hill until it met Battle, and then she turned right.

She'd wasted precious walking time. She couldn't wait to slide back into the safety of Gramma's apartment and then her comfy couch. She was never leaving that apartment again. Still breathing hard, with her hands on her hips, she started down Battle.

Then the sickness came.

This was a good thing. She knew that if she could throw up, she'd feel better.

But she didn't throw up. Her stomach churned and threatened, but nothing came up.

She started walking again, but the nausea was overwhelming. She looked around for a spot to rest. She just needed a break, and she knew it would pass. Her eyes landed on a tiny church building. A light lit the small porch. It was the cutest little thing. There was no sign to indicate what kind of church it was, but it looked very old. She crossed the street and sat down on the front steps.

Though she knew she shouldn't, she tipped over and laid her cheek on the white boards. You're not going to pass out here, she told herself. We're just taking a little break.

Her eyes slid shut. Out of nowhere, words drifted through her mind like lost song lyrics: *All we like sheep have gone astray; we have turned every one to his own way.*

What was that? What did that mean? She remembered a sticker. A big pink heart with a cross in the middle of it. *Oh wow, I am so drunk.* Heart stickers and sheep—she needed to get some sleep—

"Zoe."

She didn't open her eyes. She knew no one was there.

"Zoe," the voice spoke again.

She tried to ignore it.

She couldn't. "What?" She sat up and looked around.

"You know better than this."

She didn't say anything. She knew no one was there, but she still peered into the darkness.

"This is not who you are."

"How do you know who I am?" The anger in her own voice surprised her. She didn't even know who she was. How dare this invisible man claim to?

"Get up."

"No."

"Get up. This is not where you're supposed to be."

She tipped her head back and then couldn't stop herself. Her body flopped backward, and her head hit the porch hard enough to hurt, even through all the alcohol.

She felt a warm hand in hers, and then she was being lifted.

"I can't," she whispered. Tears spilled out of her closed eyes and rolled down her cheeks.

"I know," he whispered back. She'd never heard a voice so gentle.

She knew she was crazy. She knew no one was there. Yet It sounded as if this voice loved her. And wasn't there something familiar about it as well? And now she was floating. Back to the street. She opened her eyes and saw that her feet weren't on the ground. She was being carried. She was in someone's arms. The fact that this someone was invisible wasn't even the unbelievable part. The unbelievable part was that anyone was *strong* enough to carry her.

In an instant, she was on her feet in front of her grandmother's house. Her stomach had calmed down. She was still very, very drunk, but she was almost to that couch.

"Remember." His voice was deep and magnetic. She didn't want him to leave. "You know better than this." And then he was gone. She didn't see him leave; she hadn't seen him at all. But she knew he was gone. And the loneliness of his absence was crushing. She leaned against the door and wept.

Chapter 27
Esther

Esther sat in the darkness, staring at the windows of the common room. She wasn't sure Zoe would come in through one of these windows, but she didn't know how else she would do it. The windows in the hallway were locked—Esther had made sure of it—and she hoped Zoe wouldn't break into some poor individual's apartment.

Maybe she would. What did Esther know? She hadn't thought she'd sneak out on a Monday night either. She hadn't thought she'd be gone for hours and not answer her phone.

Esther squeezed her phone in her hand. Every few minutes, she tried Zoe's number again. And every few minutes, she considered calling the cops. She wasn't sure how that would play out. Esther didn't want her granddaughter thrown in jail. She wanted her home safe and sound. She'd considered calling Christy to ask for advice, but she didn't want to admit to her daughter that she'd managed to lose Zoe in less than a week.

So she simply sat there. Crying. Praying. Shaking with alternating fear and fury.

And then she heard her.

Zoe was crying.

Most of her wanted to run toward the sound, let her inside, make sure she was all right, but a small part of Esther forced her to stay put and wait. She shouldn't make this easy on Zoe. Zoe should have to struggle to get back inside.

She saw her. Zoe cupped her hands against the window and looked inside. Esther didn't think she could see anything, as the streetlight over her head was mightily bright compared to the darkness inside the common room. Esther took a deep breath and tried to be patient.

And then Zoe was pushing the window open. Esther had left it unlocked for this purpose. Esther relaxed as she watched her struggle to climb through the relatively small window. She looked healthy. She was all right.

Zoe got the window open and then stuck her head inside. Then she pulled herself in so that she looked like a seesaw, her belly the fulcrum. She stayed like this for a moment, and Esther wondered what her plan was, but then she lost her balance and spilled inside, head first. She smashed into a hard wooden chair, which skidded out of the way, and then her head hit the floor. Good thing for the chair;

it had broken her fall. Still, she cried out at the contact.

Esther almost got up and went to help her. Hadn't Christy said that Zoe had only recently suffered a head injury? How many head injuries could a teenager get before there was real damage done?

Zoe had stopped moving. Had she knocked herself unconscious, or had she simply fallen asleep? Her head, shoulders, and arms were on the floor, and her feet still stuck out through the window.

Esther was just about to get up when Zoe rolled over, and her feet slid inside. Again, she lay still, and Esther thought maybe she planned to sleep there.

But slowly, Zoe got up, looked at the corner of the room, and screamed.

Apparently, she'd seen Milton.

"Hi, there," Milton said, unbothered by the scream.

Without saying anything to Milton, Zoe tiptoed toward the door. Esther found this tiptoeing especially annoying. She'd made a huge crash, then screamed, and now she was going to tiptoe?

"Zoe," Esther said, flicking on the light.

Zoe screamed again and spun toward her. She wobbled on one heel and then found her footing.

Esther gasped at the sight of her. She was filthy, and her right knee was a bloody mess.

"What are you guys doing?" Zoe asked.

Esther took a breath, trying not to lose her cool. "It is four o'clock in the morning, and you have the gall to ask *us* what *we're* doing?"

Milton got up, tightened his bathrobe, and then stepped forward and stuck out the hand that wasn't holding onto his cane. "I'm Milton."

Zoe, looking confused, accepted his handshake.

"I live across the hall. Felt bad for your Gramma here having to wait for you, so I joined her. I don't sleep much." He looked at Esther. "Good night, friend." Then he looked at Zoe. "Good night, youngster. Glad you are all right."

Zoe watched him go, open-mouthed.

"I've been sitting here for hours, Zoe. Milton was worried about me, so he joined me in worrying about you."

Her head fell. "I'm sorry."

"I'm sure you are." She paused, wondering what she should do next. "What happened to your knee?"

As if she hadn't realized she had knees, Zoe looked down at hers. "Oh. I have no idea."

Esther exhaled slowly and then, with difficulty, got herself out of her rocking chair. "Let's go upstairs and get you cleaned up."

Chapter 28
Esther

Zoe's knee wasn't as bad as it had looked at first glance. The pants were ruined, and it was a mighty scrape, but it had bled enough that it seemed pretty clean, and it was already starting to scab over.

"I swear to God I won't do it again."

"Don't swear to God." Esther poured iodine over the wound. It probably didn't need it, but she wanted it to sting.

Zoe didn't even flinch.

So much for that plan. She found a large square of gauze and gently placed it on her knee.

"I'm sorry. It was awful. I thought Jason was going to be there. I only went to see him, because his girlfriend is stupid and ..."

Jason? As in Jason DeGrave? Esther didn't know where Zoe had gone, but based on the evidence in front of her, she didn't think it was the type of event that Jason would attend.

"I thought Jason was going to be there," she said again, her words slowing down. "But he wasn't, and his stupid girlfriend wasn't, and everyone laughed at me."

Esther's anger faded. "Why did they laugh at you?"

Zoe shrugged. "Dunno," she said softly.

Esther thought about what to say next as she wrapped and taped the knee. But when she looked at her granddaughter, she had fallen asleep, her head resting on her own shoulder.

Gently, Esther helped her to lie down. She pulled her shoes off and then pulled her heavy legs up onto the couch. They didn't quite fit. She gently bent Zoe's knees and tucked her feet onto the cushion. Then she pulled the blanket up over her. It was almost too small. She had to get her a bigger blanket. And maybe a bigger couch. Earlier that evening she'd been contemplating sending her back to Missouri. Now she wanted to keep her forever.

She straightened up and looked down at her granddaughter. How had that little girl Zoe turned into this young woman? This big, strong young woman. How had *her* granddaughter become a person who made such terrible decisions? Christy hadn't been like this when she was young. And Esther certainly hadn't. If she had, she would have spent her entire adolescence in the woodshed.

She bent over and kissed Zoe on her forehead. Then she turned the light off and went to her bedroom. She should have had her drink some water, but it was too late now. Besides, maybe a horrible hangover would do her some good.

Esther was exhausted. She knew she could sleep till noon, but she had to get up in a few hours to get Zoe to school. And Zoe would sure as Sunday be going to school in the morning, hungover or not. Esther kicked off her slippers, turned off her light, and then knelt beside her bed.

And she prayed for her granddaughter.

Chapter 29
Rachel

Something woke Rachel from a dead sleep. Her eyes popped open, and she looked around her dark bedroom. All was still and peaceful. Had she heard something? She strained her eyes and ears.

There was nothing.

Had she had a nightmare? Her mind raced, trying to get her bearings. She took a deep breath and closed her eyes, trying to calm down.

Zoe.

Looming in her mind's eye, a picture of that young woman, staring at her. That empty stare she'd worn in church—why had that affected Rachel so strongly? "What is it about that girl, Father?" she whispered.

He didn't answer.

She looked at the clock. Four in the morning. Way too early to get up. Probably too late to go back to sleep. And though she was still tired—she was always tired nowadays—she was no longer sleepy. She didn't know what had awoken her, but it had done its job efficiently.

She sat up and swung her long legs out of bed. Might as well make some coffee. But she didn't. She couldn't get that image of Zoe out of her head.

"Father," she said again, this time with more zeal, "you have put this child on my heart for a reason. I think it's time you let me at her. I don't know how you're going to do it, because I don't want to step on Esther's toes." She loved Esther so deeply. Like a sister. "I don't want to do anything to make Esther think that I'm criticizing her parenting or her grandparenting, but I really think I can help, Lord. There's no reason for a child that strong to be that sad. No reason for a child that *loved* to be that sad. Please, Father, let me at her." She paused, thinking of what else she needed to ask.

Nothing came to mind.

"As always, I ask for good health. Give me a good day. And please, let me at her. Orchestrate it. Get it done. Give me a chance."

She opened her eyes. There was no answer. No audible answer. No visual answer. No answer in her heart. And yet, she had a strange peace about it. If God wanted her to help Zoe, he would make it happen.

Smiling, she slid her slippered feet toward the coffee pot. She couldn't wait for that first sip to hit her taste buds. She knew she needed to quit the caffeine, but today was not that day.

Chapter 30
Esther

Esther was so tired she couldn't believe her feet were working. But they were. They were carrying her, with their normal steadfast efficiency, across the church lawn.

She'd gotten Zoe dropped off at school, and though Zoe stunk like a brewery, she hadn't mentioned a hangover, and Esther hadn't asked. The child had hit the orange juice with an eagerness that bordered on desperation, but she hadn't asked for any ibuprofen. Maybe she'd brought some of her own.

Now it was time for ladies' prayer. They'd been meeting every Tuesday to pray, and she was so tired, she'd thought about skipping it this time. She knew they could handle it without her, and she knew they wouldn't be offended by her absence, especially when they learned she'd spent all night sitting in the common room with Milton.

But she didn't *want* to skip it. She needed to ask these ladies to pray for Zoe. And though she could call in the request, she knew it wouldn't carry the same sense of urgency.

Barbara was already there and had the coffee on. Gratefully, Esther poured herself a cup.

"Let's go to the upper room," Vicky said when she arrived. "It's warmer up there."

Esther gave Barbara a chance to claim the comfiest chair, and when she didn't, Esther settled in. Then, listening to Barbara and Vicky make small talk, she nearly drifted off to sleep. Vicky had been right. It was warm in that room, warm and cozy. With her head laid back and her eyes closed, she rested, close to sleep but not quite there. Almost listening to what her friends were saying, but not quite.

A touch on her hand roused her. Rachel had sat in the chair beside her. The ceiling slanted over that seat, and Rachel had to duck to keep her hat from hitting the ceiling.

"How is Zoe?" Rachel asked softly.

"You can pull the chair away from that wall."

Rachel turned to look at the ceiling as if she hadn't realized it was there.

"Just trade with me," Vicky ordered.

"In a second." Rachel's eyes were focused on Esther. "I need an update first."

All eyes were on Esther now. She straightened up in her chair. "Go ahead and trade seats. I might as well share the update with everyone."

As Rachel and Vicky swapped, Esther took attendance with her eyes. "Should we wait for Vera?"

"I don't think she's coming," Vicky said. "She's not feeling well."

"Oh no," Cathy said.

Vera was the oldest among them, and anytime she didn't feel well, the rest of them panicked a little. Vera never panicked. She often said she was ready whenever God was.

"I don't think it's anything serious," Vicky said. She sat back and looked at Esther. "All right, what's going on with the wild child?"

Esther didn't like Vicky calling Zoe this, but she let it slide. "I'm really worried. We had a rough night. She snuck out of the apartment after I fell asleep. I don't know where she went—"

"Did you ask her?" Vicky interrupted.

"No, not yet."

"Well, that might be a good first step in figuring out where she was."

"Let her talk," Rachel ordered, and Vicky's mouth snapped shut.

"I'm not sure it matters where she went. Wherever it was, she said she went there because she thought Jason would be there—"

"*Our* Jason?" Cathy cried.

"Don't worry, he wasn't there. So, I'm assuming she went to a party—"

"On a Monday night?" Barbara cried.

"Let her talk!" Rachel said with even more authority.

"Sorry," Cathy said and swung her arm in a gesture that said, continue.

"Yes, on a Monday. She came back very drunk. She could hardly walk. The building was locked, of course, but I unlocked the windows to the common room and then I just waited for her to come home. Which she did, eventually. At about four o'clock this morning."

Rachel gasped.

"She tried to climb in through the window and managed to fall inside. She hit her head, which made me think I should have just left the door unlocked, but there was nowhere for me to sit and watch the door unless I dragged a chair out into the hallway ..." She put her head in her hand. She was so tired.

"You did great," Rachel said. "Absolutely great."

"I'm really tired. I didn't sleep much after we got her into bed, either. I should probably go take a nap, but I wanted to ask you to pray for her, and I wanted to pray with you." She didn't know for sure that it meant a big difference to God, but she often felt a sense of power when a team of them asked God for the same thing at the same time.

"Yes, of course," Rachel said. "Did she go to school?"

Esther nodded.

"Great. Let's pray for her right now."

"Hang on," Vicky said. "We'll definitely pray for her, but there's something else we need to discuss before Esther falls asleep on us."

Esther looked at her, feeling more awake now that she was so annoyed with Vicky.

"We need a pastor. I know we've discussed it, but we haven't done anything to make it happen, and we need to stop horsing around. We don't have many parishioners, but I'm afraid those we have won't be around much longer if we don't get a real leader. I don't want it to just be us and Derek on Sunday mornings."

Cathy took a long breath, and it was obvious, to Esther anyway, that Cathy was also annoyed with Vicky. "Don't tell me we haven't *done anything* to make it happen. We have. I've been praying fervently, and I know others have too. But we can't ask a pastor to work for free, and we don't have any money. That's what the holdup is, Vicky. It's not that we don't want a pastor. We do, of course. But we can't advertise a job opening if there's no money."

"Maybe it's time to ask for volunteers," Vicky said, her tone uppity.

"We've already discussed that too," Cathy snapped. "Who is going to volunteer to pastor a church for free?"

"We've all been in church long enough," Esther said, feeling almost too weak to speak, "to know that you get what you pay for. We open this up to volunteers, we'll likely get someone no one else would hire. I agree with Vicky, though. To an extent. We can ask for this particular thing with more fervency. I've grown quite complacent about this piece of the puzzle. I'm quite content with the seven us running things. But Vicky is right. We should have a proper pastor. We need someone who is skilled at preaching and teaching, and the day may come when we have a crisis we can't handle."

"And that day is the day that God really gets to shine through," Barbara said.

"True." Esther closed her eyes again. "I really think I need to go home and rest. But first, Barbara, are you saying that you *don't* think we should ask God for a pastor?"

"No," she said quickly. "I think we should ask him. But I don't think we should be panicking over the fact that we don't have one yet."

Esther nodded. "All right. I thought I could, but I can't do this. I need to go to bed." She pushed herself out of the chair. "Please pray for Zoe." She started across the room.

"I'll walk you out," Rachel said.

"That's not necessary," Esther said, but Rachel ignored her and followed her down the stairs.

Once they were on the porch, Rachel grabbed Esther's elbow. "I have an idea." The door swung shut behind them.

Esther hoped she wasn't about to nominate a volunteer pastor. She didn't have the energy to care about that right now.

"About Zoe," Rachel clarified. "I want to help."

Esther bristled a little. What could Rachel do that she, the grandmother, couldn't? "What did you have in mind?"

Rachel scanned the property. "Actions have consequences, right? Well, you tell her that the consequence for her behavior is ten hours of community service, which she will serve at the church."

Esther followed her eyes. "What do you think she'd be able to do?" She didn't think Zoe could rewire the kitchen, and she wasn't sure it was safe to put her up on the lift to paint the ceiling.

"We still need to clean out the basement," Rachel said. Then she nodded toward the sign. "But we can start by repainting that."

Oh yeah, the defaced sign. Esther's stomach turned at the sight of it. "Did anybody call that girl's mother? The one that Emma and Mary Sue think did it?"

"Yes. Vicky took it upon herself. And the girl's mother swore up and down that her daughter had nothing to do with it."

Esther sighed. "All right. So, you want me to force Zoe to serve here?"

"It's not really about the service," Rachel said quickly. "I mean, that's part of it, but really, we're tricking her into spending time with me." Rachel stepped closer. "Esther, you don't know much about the days of my youth, but they were *rough*."

Esther did know a little, enough to believe this claim.

"I think that, if I share some of my story with her, it might help."

Esther wasn't so sure.

"Give me a chance. Ten hours. That's all I'm asking."

Esther shrugged. "Might as well. It can't hurt. And we'll get the sign fixed, anyway."

Chapter 31
Zoe

"You okay?" Jason settled into the desk beside her. "You don't look so good."

She wasn't good. Far from it. Her head hurt so much that she was worried she had done some real damage. She'd already thrown up in the bathroom. That had helped some, but then the lights in the math classroom, which were made worse by the white walls, were making it almost impossible to keep her eyes open.

She sank even lower into her chair. "I'm fine. Why, what did you hear?" She wasn't sure what exactly had happened to her the night before. Her mind held still shots, and a few short video clips, but none of them went together, and she knew there were giant gaps in her recall—gaps which could have been uneventful standing around or could have been much worse.

"I didn't hear anything." He actually looked concerned. "Why, what happened?"

She didn't answer him. She didn't want to answer him. He was obviously a goody-two-shoes, and she didn't want him to think she was a loser.

"Well, if you need to talk about it, let me know."

Why was he so nice to her?

"In the meantime, I wanted to invite you to our Bible study."

She would've laughed if she weren't so horrified.

"We meet on Thursday mornings at Emma Mendell's house. It's the big yellow farmhouse right beside the elementary school."

"Thursdays?" she said because she didn't know what else to say.

"Yes, at six-thirty. We used to meet on Mondays, but we had to change it because of weightlifting."

A Bible study and weightlifting conflict. This guy wasn't a goody-two-shoes. He was something much worse.

And he was waiting for her to answer.

"I don't think so. My grandmother might make me go to church on Sunday mornings, but I'm not really a Bible girl."

His smile faltered a little. He almost looked hurt. "Okay. Well, let me know if you change your mind." Then, even though he'd already gotten his books out and opened them, as if he'd planned to sit there for the entire class, he grabbed his bag and books and got up, moved to the back of the room, and sat down in another desk.

Yep. She'd managed to hurt his feelings.

Her only friend.

Awesome.

She couldn't do this. She was too sick. She had to find somewhere to lie down. Slowly, trying not to attract attention, she shoved her math book back into her backpack and stood up. The teacher looked right at her. "I have to go to the bathroom," she mumbled, which didn't explain why she was taking her backpack, but she couldn't come up with anything better. Keeping her head down, she scuttled out of the room.

The bell rang, and it felt like a hundred knives to her brain. She wanted to cry but she thought she was too dehydrated for tears. She had to get out of there. She didn't care what that meant. She didn't care what happened to her. She just had to get out of there. She had to lie down.

The front door was in sight of the main office, so she couldn't go that way. The hallways were emptying. Most everyone was in class now. She had to get out of sight, or someone would stop her. She headed toward the back door, but a giant sign informed her that an alarm would sound if she opened it.

She didn't want to think about how much that alarm would hurt her head.

She turned away from the doors. Shoot. Where was she going to go? She tried to think, but her head was muddy. Where would she go if she were in her old school? She would simply slip out one of the many back doors. They had made it too easy. This school was so much smaller, so every move she made was so much more noticeable.

She didn't know of any other back doors, and even if there was one, would it also be booby-trapped with an alarm?

The gym. The gym had doors leading outside. But the gym was *so far* away. She raised her backpack strap higher on her shoulder and headed that way, keeping her head down, trying to be invisible, trying to look like she had somewhere to be and had to get there—somewhere she was *supposed* to be.

She didn't want to get caught and get in trouble, but more than that, she simply didn't want to be seen. She didn't want to have to interact with someone. She didn't want to have to *be*, to even exist. She knew this feeling was temporary. She'd been hungover before. She knew how it went. Tomorrow, she'd be good as new. She just had to get through the day.

She entered the cavernous cafeteria. She could sense there were people to her left, but she didn't look up.

"Hey, stoner," a male voice said, and the sound of it made her skin crawl. Her skin knew before her brain did who that voice belonged to. When the others at the table tee-heed at the joke, her brain caught up.

Nelson.

She started walking faster.

"What's the matter, stoner? Got a headache?"

Her eyes burned with tears. That guy was gross. A total loser. She knew that now. And she'd hung out with him. People had *seen* her hanging out with him. Thank God she hadn't gone into the woods with him—

Wait.

She hadn't, had she?

Now she wasn't sure. With the back of her hand, she wiped at her mouth. She was going to throw up again. She rounded the corner into the gym, which, thank God, was empty. She saw the door that led to the outside, but right across from it was an open room full of people. If she tried to go outside, they would see her.

Whether they would care, she didn't know, but she didn't want to take the chance.

She ducked into the locker room, which was blessedly cool and also empty. It smelled bad, but she didn't care. She hurried to the closest toilet and bent over, waiting.

But nothing happened.

She was empty.

She searched the room for a light switch. She had to turn the lights off. She couldn't find one. So she gave up and went to the back of the room, where she lay down on the cold, filthy tiled floor. She stuck the backpack under her head for a pillow and closed her eyes. The lights were still too bright so she sat up, took off her sweatshirt, and then laid it over her face.

She lay back down, facing the wall, curled up in the fetal position. There. She'd made it. She would just rest here until the end of the day or until she died, whichever came first. She was almost asleep when she sensed the lights going off. Oh, of course. They'd been on motion sensors. They'd blinked on when she'd come into the room. How had she forgotten that?

She was so stupid.

Chapter 32
Zoe

A high-pitched scream woke Zoe from a fitful sleep. She started to sit up, but her head got tangled in her sweatshirt, and this caused such panic that she lay back down to disentangle herself.

"What are you doing?" the screamer cried. "I thought you were dead!"

Footsteps. Lots of footsteps.

Zoe struggled to her feet.

"What is it?"

"I don't know. The new girl was passed out on the floor."

Why did she have to be so *loud*?

"I thought she was dead."

The laughter started then.

"Sorry," Zoe mumbled. She bent over to get her backpack and became so dizzy so suddenly that she almost couldn't stand up again. But she managed and then turned to leave the room.

Except that she couldn't, because the girls' soccer team was stretched across the room in front of her. Most of them had already changed and wore cleats and shin guards, or she might have thought it was a phys ed class. But it wasn't a phys ed class. It was the soccer team, which meant school was over, which meant that she had been there a long time.

As she stood there stupidly, the laughter grew louder.

How many bells had she slept through? Was she going to be okay? Had she gone too far this time? Did she have alcohol poisoning? Had she given herself brain damage? She didn't know how much she'd drunk. She didn't know *what* she'd drunk. Maybe someone had put something extra into her drink.

This made sense. She'd never been this sick before from drinking alone.

And besides, there was another partial memory floating around in her head. Again, it was more a collection of feelings and images than it was a memory, but no matter what order she put them in, none of them seemed realistic. That's why she'd been trying not to think about that part of her evening.

She must have been tripping.

She had to get out of this stupid building.

"Excuse me," she said, and walked toward the crowd, knowing they would move, knowing they thought she was disgusting and wouldn't want to get too close to her.

As expected, they parted, and she slunk through them, then out of the locker room, and then outside. Then she looked around, disoriented. Which way was Gramma's house again?

She found a landmark and got herself pointed in the right direction. Then she started walking. It wasn't far. She could do this. The walking would be good for her hangover.

Except that, the closer she got to Gramma's building, the less she wanted to go there. She knew now that she'd still been drunk in the morning, when she had talked with Gramma, but now that she was mostly sober, how could she face her? What would she say? Her grandmother must be so angry, so disappointed, so ashamed of her. Why had she done that? It was one thing to go to the stupid party, but why had she allowed herself to get so drunk?

Gramma's building came in sight, and she slowed. She couldn't go there.

Her eyes floated to the church sign. Still vandalized. Someone should fix that. It looked horrible. Made the church look ghetto. A small part of her felt indignant about this, but most of her didn't care. Most of her was completely absorbed with what she was going to do *right now*. How was she going to survive this moment? She couldn't face her grandmother. She needed to apologize, even *wanted* to apologize, but she knew her messed up brain couldn't come up with the right words right now.

One of the church's basement windows was open. She stepped closer. No, not open. Broken. Had someone broken the church's window? It looked old. Maybe it had been broken for a long time. The church had been abandoned, right? Maybe they hadn't gotten around to fixing that particular blemish yet, like the wires dangling out of the ceiling. It didn't matter. What mattered was whether she could fit through it. A weird old church on a Tuesday afternoon was the perfect place to hide out. Quiet, comfy, and unpopulated. She scanned her surroundings. A woman walked her dog while looking at her phone. Another woman sat on her front stoop smoking a cigarette while looking at her phone. Zoe was pretty sure, thanks to cell phones, that she could break into this church. Still, she made no sudden movements. First, she acted as if she was curious about the sign, and crept closer to it. Then, when still no one was looking at her, she backed up to the wall of the church and then sat down and spun on her butt toward the window. Her head was killing her, so she wasn't going in headfirst. She kicked fragments of broken glass out of the way and then dropped her backpack through the window, listening closely to see how much of a drop there was. It made a terrific bang, but the drop was nonexistent, apparently.

After making sure her cell was secure in her back pocket, she slithered in through the hole, holding her breath as if that would make her smaller.

She needn't have worried. Fitting through the window was the easy part. Doing an uncomfortable backbend, she felt around with her feet, trying to find the floor.

There it was. She put her weight on it and pulled the rest of herself through the hole—except it wasn't the floor. Unless the floor was wobbly. All the way inside the church now, she quickly reached for her cell phone so she could light the place up and see what she was standing on, but that sudden motion caused whatever she was on to topple, and she lost her balance. Flailing her arms for something to grab, she fell, hitting something hard with her right hip and then finally landing on the cool, hard floor. She whimpered and turned on her light. She'd stepped onto the world's smallest table. What had that held in its day, a miniature vase of tiny flowers? It only had one leg—it was a wonder she hadn't fallen sooner. She swung the light to her left. On her way down, she'd hit a bunch of folding tables, which were leaned against the wall. They looked ancient. She felt her hip to make sure there was no scrape. She didn't know if she needed a tetanus shot. How much noise had she made? Enough. Slowly, she stood up, taking inventory of her body parts. When all were present and accounted for, she picked up her bag and swung the flashlight around the room, looking for stairs.

Holy moly what a mess. This basement was wall-to-wall junk. How had a church collected this much junk?

There. Straight ahead. Stairs. She weaved her way through the piles and then trudged upstairs. Never had she been so excited to find herself a pew.

Chapter 33
Esther

"Well, that's interesting," Esther said.

"What?" Christy asked. She'd finally called to check on Zoe.

Figuring—and hoping—that the call would take a while, Esther had headed outside to sit on a bench in the sun and wait for Zoe's return. "I just stepped outside, and I saw Zoe slide …" She stopped. "I saw Zoe *go* into the church."

No need to tell her daughter that Zoe had just broken a window to break into a church. Had the child completely lost her mind? The craziest part was the door was unlocked!

"Why would she go into the church on a Tuesday afternoon? Do you guys drink wine for communion?"

Esther rolled her eyes. "We do not. Maybe she's looking for a quiet place to study." She knew this was bogus.

Christy knew it too. "So you're telling me that she hasn't given you *any* trouble since she arrived?"

No, Esther had *not* told her that. Neither had she told her that she *had* given her trouble. She didn't think that omission was lying, under the circumstances. "Don't worry.

She's doing great here. It's good for her to be away from the people she was hanging out with at home."

Christy gasped.

"No, no," she hurried to say. "I'm not criticizing anyone. I'm just saying a change of scenery can be good. And she's already made a friend. He's in her grade, I think. He goes to our church. And he's *very* cute."

"Cute?" Christy laughed derisively. "Then they must be only friends. That poor girl has not attracted any cute ones in her life."

Esther bristled in Zoe's defense. "I hope you don't let her hear you say things like that."

"You know what? I'm sorry, Mom. I have to go."

Esther had only just sat down. "I'm sorry, Christy. I don't want to fight with you."

But she was already gone. Esther hung up the phone and started to get up, but then she saw something else interesting. Jason was walking down the street. A car was parked behind him, and it appeared that's where he'd come from, but where was he going?

Apparently, he was going straight across the church lawn, and then, without even looking around to see if he was being watched—the child would make a terrible criminal—he stuck his feet through the broken window and disappeared into the church basement.

Esther sighed. *Guys, the door is unlocked.*

Chapter 34
Zoe

With her backpack under her head and her sweatshirt for a too-small blanket, Zoe was right on the verge of falling asleep in a pew when she heard something. She tried to ignore it. She wanted to go back to sleep. She wanted to sleep forever. *It's just a mouse*, she told herself. There had to be mouse in that basement. Or maybe it was a cat going after the mouse. A cat could easily go in and out thanks to the broken window. Someone should really fix that.

She was almost asleep again when she heard her name. It occurred to her that it was God, and she panicked a little. She turned her head and opened one eye to see the gorgeous Jason DeGrave looking down at her curiously.

Awesome.

She sat up. "What are you doing?" she managed.

"Me? What are *you* doing? I was driving down the street and I saw you break into a church!" He sounded horrified.

"I didn't *break* in. Don't be so dramatic." She wanted him to leave, though now that her heart was pounding this hard, she knew she wasn't getting back to sleep anytime soon.

"If you break a basement window and then go inside to squat, that's considered breaking in."

She was incredulous. "I didn't break the window! Who do you think I am?" As soon as she asked the question, she knew the answer. He had no idea who she was. How could he know? "And I'm not squatting."

"Sorry." It sounded like he meant it. "I hadn't noticed it was broken. I don't think it has been for long." He sat down in the pew behind her. "Anyway, are you okay? I heard about what happened last night."

She tried to exhale but her lungs were empty. "What happened?"

He raised an eyebrow. "You don't remember?"

She shrugged, trying to play it cool. "I don't know. You tell me what happened, and I'll tell you if I remember it."

He looked amused.

She lay back down and closed her eyes. "I take it you don't drink."

He hesitated. "No, sorry."

"Of course not. Jesus freaks don't drink." She sensed his displeasure at her words.

"Sorry, didn't mean it as an insult." Hadn't she, though? She didn't know.

"I haven't been a Jesus freak for long." She could tell by the way he spoke the words that the phrase was new to him. "But even before I knew Jesus, I had self-respect. And I'm an athlete, so I can't really afford to just be an idiot and trash my body."

She didn't know if she'd ever heard a more condescending tone, and at first it rankled her mightily, but then a thought occurred to her. Surely the good kids—the athletes and the scholars—in her old school had thought the same thing. Maybe even said it out of earshot. But they'd never said it *to* her. They'd never cared enough to. She dragged herself back to a seated position.

"Sorry, that was kind of harsh."

"No," she said quickly. "It really wasn't. I appreciate people who say what they're thinking."

He chuckled. "That's usually not me."

She raised an eyebrow. "So I just bring it out of you?"

He seemed to be considering it. "I don't know. Or maybe I'm just changing. Anyway, I wanted to tell you, though you might already have figured it out, Nelson is kind of a dirt bag."

"I sensed it. You said he wasn't so bad."

"I was trying to give you a good impression of Carver Harbor. Sorry. So, anyway, apparently you showed up at the Cove, no big deal, but then you drank a *lot* of moonshine, and—"

"Moonshine?" she cried. *Moonshine?* People still made moonshine? Why would they do that when stores on every corner offered an endless supply of booze? "Are you serious?"

He nodded. "Nelson's family makes it. It's awful. I don't think he even drinks it, but he brings it to parties to dare people to drink it. And apparently, you accepted the dare."

"I didn't accept anything. I didn't know what it was. I thought it was whiskey."

"It wasn't whiskey."

She closed her eyes and exhaled. "Thanks."

"Or maybe it was. I have no idea. But apparently you drank a lot of it. And then you got mad and left."

"Mad? I don't think I was mad." Had she been? She couldn't remember.

"Well, they said you started to leave but then turned and told them all off."

She opened her eyes. Jason looked uncomfortable. With her eyes, she asked him to elaborate.

"You hollered, you swore, told them they were all white trash losers."

She wouldn't have done that. She didn't do that. They were lying.

"It didn't go over well."

She looked down at her legs. "I've never been good at popularity contests."

He leaned toward her a little. "Just stay away from them, and you'll be okay. There are good people in that school. I'll introduce you."

She turned her eyes back to him. Why was he being so nice to her? Was it a Jesus thing? Or did he feel sorry for her?

"The only other thing they said is that you fell pretty hard walking up the hill." He forced a smile. "But I guess you weren't in too bad a shape, because you made it home."

Had she made it home, though? Hadn't she had some help?

"Do you know anything about that moonshine? Does it make you hallucinate?"

The horror on his face made her talk faster.

"I've drank *a lot*, but drinking has never made me see something that wasn't there."

"What did you see?" he asked slowly.

"Nothing. Never mind. I was probably dreaming."

Chapter 35
Esther

When Zoe came into the apartment, Esther looked up from the television. "Hi, honey."

Zoe gave her a weak smile and then came and sat down beside her. She seemed to be favoring her sore leg.

"Are you all right?"

"So, I'm not very good at this," Zoe said without looking at her. "So I'll probably butcher it, but I need to tell you that I'm sorry. Like, really, *really* sorry. I don't know why I did what I did, and I shouldn't have. Obviously. I didn't mean to get as drunk as I was. I was only going to have one little drink, but they tricked me into drinking moonshine." Her whole body tightened in anger as she spoke.

At first Esther didn't say anything. She hadn't been expecting an immediate confession and apology, and she was encouraged by it. But wasn't there something dangerous lurking just beneath the surface of this confession? She thought so, but she couldn't quite put a finger on it.

Zoe wouldn't look at her.

Esther tried to think of something to say. "I wish you'd answered your phone. It would have been much better if you had told me you were all right. I was scared to death." She wished Cathy were there. She would know what to say. Maybe she should pack Zoe into the car and go over to Cathy's house for this conversation.

"I'm sorry. I thought that if I answered the phone that you would come get me. And I didn't even know how many times you called until today when I saw the missed calls. I must not have heard it ring some of the time." She wrung her hands. "Or I don't remember," she said more quietly.

This child was in pain. What was causing all this pain?

"Zoe, can we talk about it? I want to understand."

"We are talking about it," she said brusquely.

Esther didn't appreciate her tone. "Fine. Well, actions need to have consequences, and I've come up with some."

Zoe's face snapped toward hers. She obviously hadn't been expecting that. "But I apologized."

"Yes," Esther said slowly, trying to be gentle, even though her sympathy was fading. It occurred to her then what had bothered her about Zoe's initial confession. "You say they tricked you into drinking moonshine."

Zoe nodded.

"So, are you saying that this is all their fault?"

Zoe's mouth fell open. "I didn't know it was moonshine! If I had, I never would have drunk it. Those guys were crazy! And they wanted to hurt me. They hate me. Everybody hates me!" She stood up as if she meant to stomp off, but the tiny apartment offered nowhere to go. She stormed into the kitchen and ripped the fridge open.

Esther got up and followed her, stopping in the narrow entryway to the kitchen. Now Zoe was trapped in the kitchen.

"Don't eat anything. I've got a boiled dinner in the oven. Look, I'm sorry that they were dishonest with you. That was horrible of them. But you need to take responsibility for what *you* did. You chose to go to this party, and you chose to drink a mystery beverage."

She snorted. "Mystery beverage. Whatever." She slammed the fridge door shut.

"Please don't break my fridge."

"Are we done?" She put her hands on her hips.

"Not even close."

Zoe's eyes flitted around the kitchen, looking for an escape.

"I still need to tell you your consequences. But first, why don't you tell me who these kids were. I should probably contact their parents."

Zoe's eyes grew huge. "You can't be serious."

Esther didn't say anything.

"No. You are most definitely not contacting their *parents*."

Esther took a long breath, trying to stay calm. "Please think about that. If you change your mind, let me know. I'm sure they don't know how dangerous their moonshine is, and I don't want them hurting someone else."

Zoe's face twisted up into a rage that also managed to be patronizing. "They don't *know*?" she said with too much volume? "They don't *know*? Are you kidding me? No, Gramma, you're the one who doesn't know anything. These aren't some church kids out having harmless fun. Maybe that's how it was in the sixties, but these people don't even have parents to call. They're animals. They were trying to *hurt* me."

Esther waited a beat and then, trying to keep her voice even, said, "And yet you drank their moonshine."

Zoe let out a loud, frustrated grunt and stomped toward her as if she were going to push her out of the way. For a second, Esther was scared, but Zoe stopped. "Would you please move?"

"Not yet. Consequences."

Zoe whirled around and leaned against the wall. "What?" Her jaw was hard as a rock.

"You're going to do ten hours of community service."

Zoe's head fell.

"With Rachel. At the church."

A tear squeezed out through Zoe's closed eyes. "You can't be serious." She slowly turned her face up and toward Esther, and something about her expression, coupled with this movement, sent a chill down Esther's spine. Something was really wrong, here. For a second there, Zoe had looked almost malicious.

As soon as she had the thought, she pushed it down. It wasn't malice. Zoe was just a teenager, out of her mind with hormones and the aftereffects of alcohol.

"Zoe, sweetie, I'm one hundred percent serious. You broke our window. Do you know how much money—"

"Window?" Zoe screamed. "I didn't break your window!" She reached up with both hands and grabbed at her hair as if she meant to pull it out. "Are you crazy? Why would I break your window? Are you seriously"—

Esther tried to interrupt, but Zoe only grew louder.

—"that out of touch with reality? I'm not a bad person. I'm not a criminal! I only went to a party, which is something *every single kid* in America does, except for maybe your precious Jason!" She spat out Jason's name as if that would somehow injure Esther.

It didn't. Esther thought maybe Jason DeGrave was their only hope at this point.

"What I was going to say is, I started this church with six of my friends—"

"I don't need a history lesson!"

Esther lost it. "Let me finish!" she hollered, and the action felt foreign to her throat. She hadn't hollered in decades.

Zoe stopped, surprised.

"And we poured everything we have into that church!" She was still louder than she wanted to be and tried to temper her voice. "We don't have anything more to give. So the fact that you broke our window hurts more than you can know."

Zoe looked at the floor, but her hands balled into fists. Slowly, as if every word were its own sentence, she said, "I didn't break your window."

This refusal to admit it hurt Esther more than the broken glass.

"You will do ten hours with Rachel, cleaning and repairing the church."

"Or what?" Zoe growled.

Esther wasn't prepared for this, didn't have an answer. She said the first thing that came into her mind. "Or you go back to Missouri."

Chapter 36
Zoe

Physically, Zoe felt a thousand times better when she woke up on Wednesday morning. Yes, her grandmother was still crazy, and yes, she still had to go hang out at church with another crazy old lady, but her head didn't hurt anymore, her stomach felt great, and her thoughts were clear.

"Do you want a ride?" Gramma asked when she headed toward the door.

"No thanks. I like walking."

"All right. Please come straight home after school. Rachel is expecting you at three-thirty."

Zoe suppressed a groan. Had she really needed to bring that up? Didn't she know that mentioning it would upset Zoe right before she started her day, which was sure to be upsetting enough?

"Yes, I know." She stopped. Did she know? What was the plan, exactly?

"We're meeting at the church?"

"Yes."

"And which one's Rachel again?" She thought she knew the answer to this, but she hoped she was mistaken.

Gramma didn't answer at first, so Zoe looked at her. She appeared to be stymied by the question. "She's the tall one."

Not mistaken. "The one who wears the crazy hats?"

Gramma nodded.

Zoe's hand fell off the doorknob. "Gramma, please. I don't need a babysitter. That lady is super weird. I don't want to hang around with her. Can't you just give me a list and I'll work on my own?"

Something flickered across Gramma's face and then she chewed on her bottom lip. She looked like she was trying to keep a secret. But what secret?

"I think you'll like her."

"Like her? Gramma, come on." She waited for her to see reason.

Nothing happened.

"I mean no disrespect, but anyone who wears hats like hers has to have a screw loose. I really don't want to be alone with her."

The smile fell off Gramma's face. "That's the deal, Zoe. Take it or leave it."

Her good mood and hope for the day vanished. Without saying anything more, she ripped the door open, went through it, and then started to slam it shut. At the last second, she decided maybe she didn't want to slam the door and tried to stop it. She partially succeeded. The door shut with a bang, but it didn't shake the wall.

Down the hall she went and out the door to find Jason sitting in front of her grandmother's building, his car idling.

He was alone.

"Want a ride?"

"What?" she said stupidly. Again she checked the car for passengers. Surely he wasn't picking her up alone? Was some scary jack-in-the-box clown going to jump out at her the minute she opened the door?

"I'm picking Alita up, and you were on the way," he said slowly. "Would you like a ride?"

Not a jack-in-the-box clown. Something worse.

"Sure," she said because she didn't know what else to say. She opened the door and gingerly climbed inside.

"Good morning," he said and then yawned.

"Morning," she admitted. It was, indeed, morning. "Did you just get up?" she asked because she felt like she had to make conversation and he had just yawned.

"Oh no. I've been up for hours. Had weightlifting this morning."

Oh, of course he had.

"But I didn't get much sleep last night."

He hadn't? Why? Was she supposed to ask?

"How did it go with Esther?"

It took her brain a second to register who Esther was. So, no, apparently she wasn't supposed to ask why he hadn't gotten much sleep.

"Not good. She's punishing me with community service at the church. She thinks I broke the window and she thinks I'm lying about it."

He looked over at her. "But you're not?"

"What? No!"

"Okay. Because if you did break the window, I wouldn't judge you. But you don't have to lie to me. I'm your friend."

"I'm not lying," she said through a clenched jaw. Why did everyone in this town assume she was a liar?

He pulled onto Battle Ave, the treacherously long road that had taken her to Hill Street, which had taken her to Moonshine Cove. Battle Ave didn't feel so long now, zipping along in a car. Her eyes scanned the side of the road, looking for the small church where she'd taken her little nap and had her little hallucination. *Dream*, she told herself. It hadn't been a hallucination. Moonshine didn't give people hallucinations. She'd looked it up online. It had been a dream. But it had sure felt real. And when was the last time she'd remembered a drunken dream? When was the last time *anyone* remembered a drunken dream?

They were nearing the stop sign, but she still hadn't seen it. "Does Alita live on this road?"

"No. She's on Richie's Head Road."

Who was Richie? And why was a road named after his head?

"She lives almost all the way out on Richie's Head. One of the last houses."

Zoe didn't understand Maine.

"Why do you ask?"

"Because ..."

He rolled to a stop.

"The road we're on right now, I thought it had a little church on it? Like not a real church, but it looked like an old church. It sort of reminded me of a museum, like a little old-fashioned church that no one used anymore, but is still being kept up."

He looked intrigued. "Reminded you? So you saw this church?"

She'd done more than see it. She'd lain on its porch.

"Yeah. I thought it was on this road." If it wasn't, then where was it? Where had she gone that night?

He still wasn't driving away, and another car was coming up behind them.

"Never mind. I don't know what I'm talking about."

He glanced in his rearview mirror and then gave it some gas. She was disappointed to not have the mystery solved, but then he blew a u-ie and crept back up the street. "What are you not telling me?"

"Huh? Nothing."

He looked at her. "Tell me the story, and I'll help you find it."

"What makes you think there's a story?"

"I can tell." He pulled the car over and stopped. "You don't have to tell me, but I *really* really want to know." His eyes sparkled with a dangerous charm.

It occurred to her that sharing at least part of her story would make them late for Alita. This would be a good thing. She took a deep breath. "Promise not to tell anyone?"

"Promise."

"So, I don't have a clear memory." This was an understatement. "But on the way home from the Cove on Monday, I sort of took a nap on some church steps." She started to feel foolish and then embarrassed, so she talked faster. "I was really grateful for them. They were clean, and there was a porch light, and I just wanted to see the church again, because I feel like we have this bond."

Jason furrowed his brows. "A small, clean museum church with a porch light?"

"Yes. It was white. Right on the edge of the road."

"Did it have a steeple?"

She closed her eyes, trying to remember. "Yes, a little one."

He leaned back. "Zoe, I have lived here for my whole life, and I promise you, there is nothing like that in Carver Harbor."

Was he sure? Not even out on Richie's Head? "Oh." She believed him, but she wasn't satisfied. "I must be remembering it wrong." She waved her hand. "We can go." Not only had she hallucinated an invisible man, she'd imaged the church too. Awesome.

"So you left the Cove and you went up Hill Street until you hit Battle Ave."

"Yes, and then I took Battle Ave all the way to Main Street." This wasn't exactly true. She'd not been in charge of the situation when she'd reached Main Street. "And then Main Street back to Gramma's."

He frowned. Then he looked at his phone. "We've got time. Let's retrace your path."

"What about Alita?"

"I'll call." He typed in his unlock code and then stabbed at his screen. "Hey, I've got to help someone. Can you get your mum to bring you in?"

Zoe heard a squeaking voice complaining on the other end.

"I'll explain later," he said, interrupting the squeaking. "But it's important."

Zoe's heart soared. She was important! To Jason!

"I love you."

Zoe's heart came crashing back down and smashed into the asphalt beneath them.

"See you in a few." He hung up. "All right." He turned the car around again. "To the Cove we go."

Chapter 37
Zoe

The Cove was breathtakingly beautiful at this time of day. It was hard to believe anything sinister had ever happened here. Of course, if Nelson had a habit of bringing new girls here, giving them moonshine, and then trying to get them into the woods, probably lots of sinister things had happened here.

Jason turned the car around for the third time. Zoe sensed that Jason *liked* driving around in circles. Maybe he wasn't interested in helping her so much as he was interested in driving around instead of going to school. Or maybe he was trying to get out of picking up his obnoxious girlfriend. Wishful thinking.

"Then you turned here." He slowed at the end of Battle Ave, where they'd just come from.

"I think so."

He looked at her. "You think so?"

"Jason, have you ever been drunk?" She knew the answer to this question.

He didn't answer.

"It's like trying to remember through mud. Like there's mud in my brain, and I'm trying to push it out of the way, but it's thick and it keeps sliding back into the path."

His eyes made it clear that he was trying to understand. They also made it clear that he didn't. But how sweet of him to try. She realized then that she was falling in love with Jason.

Awesome.

"I'm pretty sure I turned here." She ripped her eyes away from him and looked up the hill. That area also looked familiar. Had she gone further up the hill? "Or maybe I went straight."

He chuckled. "Okay, we'll do both." He continued straight, but not only were there no small museum churches up there, there were no buildings at all. He came to another stop sign. "Does this look familiar?"

"No. I really don't think I came this way." If she had, she'd done a *lot* more walking than she'd thought she had.

"All right. Let's go back to Battle Ave." He sped down Hill Street, but when he turned back onto Battle, he slowed to a crawl.

He was right. There were no churches. Then she saw a house that looked familiar. Again, she was looking at it through a layer of mud. It was a nondescript yellow house, but she thought she recognized it. Then her eyes landed on the small shack beside it. She gasped. When she'd lain down, she'd stared at the yellow house. Her eyes studied the abandoned shack in front of her.

"What is it?"

"That's it," she said and then wished she hadn't.

Jason leaned toward the windshield. "That's what?"

The tiny house's porch was the same shape and size as the one she remembered. But there was no light over it. The house had been painted white once upon a time, but the paint had now mostly flaked off. It looked terrible.

"Tell me," Jason said gently. "What is it?"

She felt sick. What was going on here? "I think there was more than moonshine in that moonshine."

"What do you mean?"

"I mean that they gave me something that made me hallucinate."

He scrunched his eyes together. "Like what?"

"I don't know, bath salts, Ecstasy, or roofies, or something?"

"Do roofies make you hallucinate?"

"I don't know!" she snapped and instantly felt guilty. "Sorry," she said meekly. "I don't know."

"I have not heard of anyone in Carver Harbor having any of those things, and if someone did, I doubt it would be Nelson. He's too poor to have any of that stuff." He sounded super snobby when he said this, but she wasn't about to defend Nelson—for any reason.

"Yeah." She studied the weird little house. The more she looked at it, the more she knew that they'd found the spot. "I did Ecstasy back in Missouri. And it didn't feel like I felt on Monday."

"How did it feel?" He sounded genuinely curious, and she felt like she was taking him over to the dark side.

"It made me really happy and like, in love with everyone. I was *not* happy on Monday. I wanted to die. And I'm grateful I wasn't in love with everyone, because I don't want to ever feel affection for Nelson." She leaned back against the seat. "We can go. Sorry for the wild goose chase. I don't know why I thought this was a church."

He hesitated.

She waited a moment and then opened her eyes. "Are we ditching school altogether?"

He laughed tentatively. "No. Definitely not. But it seems like you're still not telling me everything."

She wasn't. But she'd told him enough. He already thought she was a whack job. She wasn't about to add that a strong, gentle, invisible man had carried her home in his arms. "Nope. You know the whole stupid story."

Jason was quiet the rest of the way to school.

They were definitely late. "Do you know of a way to sneak in?"

He snickered. "No need. You're with me. Come on." He parked and got out of the car, and then waited for her to join him.

She hoped people were looking out the window and seeing this: her and Jason DeGrave casually arriving to school together, late.

He sauntered in through the front door and straight toward the office. This is not the way she usually handled being late to school. "Hey, Linda. Sorry we're late. I had to help Zoe find something." He flashed a dazzling smile at her.

It worked. "That's all right. You want a late pass?" She smiled a wide smile that revealed she once again had lipstick on her teeth.

Someone should really tell her about that habit and how to avoid it.

"Yes, please," Jason said charmingly. "That would be great. Thank you." Then he leaned on the counter, looked at Zoe, and winked.

Chapter 38
Zoe

Zoe's dread grew with every step she took toward New Beginnings Church. Then, when the church came into view and she saw Rachel standing by the sign wearing a hat the size of Utah, her dread quadrupled. She had to get out of this. How was she going to get out of this? She didn't want to go back to Missouri.

Maine was no picnic, but Missouri was worse. Trace was in Missouri. And Jason was in Maine.

She scolded herself for having the thought. Jason didn't like her. The likes of him could *never* like the likes of her. But did that matter? Maybe she could just love him without anything in return.

"Well, hello there!" Rachel cried when Zoe was still very far away. She was entirely too excited about this. "I thought we'd start with the sign!" She stood with her hands on her hips, staring at the sign in front of her as if it was her greatest love.

Zoe dropped her backpack and checked her phone. It was only a few minutes past three. She had planned to go to Gramma's first. Why was Rachel already out here working?

"I'm not sure how to go about this. If I use paint thinner, it will take all the paint of the actual sign off. And we paid a pretty penny for that paint!" She tittered.

Was she nervous? If so, what on earth for?

She glanced at Zoe. "We could rent a power washer, but I have the same fear. I don't want to ruin the paint underneath the paint." She seemed to be waiting for Zoe to chime in.

Zoe wasn't used to this. An adult wanted her input? She shrugged. "We could just paint over it."

Rachel's eyes grew wide. "I don't know. It looked so professional before." She looked at the sign. "I don't want to make things worse."

Zoe stepped in for a closer look. "It won't. It's not that big. If we can't match the paint exactly, we can just repaint the whole thing." She looked at Rachel, who still looked hesitant. "I'm pretty artistic." At least, she thought so. She got good grades in art, and she was really good at drawing. She'd never painted a church sign before.

"All right. Let's go paint shopping!"

Zoe's stomach turned. She had to *go* somewhere with this nut?

"Can you take a picture with your phone, and then we'll go look at paint?

This was a bad idea, and Zoe was loath to admit a better one, but she didn't want to chase her tail. "It would be better to go get a zillion paint swatches, and then we come back here and try to match it. We'll need a dark foresty green; a bright yellow; and a mauve."

"You know your colors!"

Hardly.

"All right. Let's go for a walk."

A walk? Wouldn't it be easier and faster to drive? But Rachel was sprier than she looked, and Zoe had to hustle to catch up. Rachel's long legs took long strides, and her oversized silk shawl sailed in her wake like a cape. What a spectacle. Zoe was so thrilled to be seen beside her, walking down Main Street.

"The hardware store is just up ahead." Rachel pointed with her chin. "See it?"

Yes, she saw it. She wasn't sure this point was worth discussing. "Yep."

They breezed inside, and someone kindly asked them what they needed.

"We need to take some graffiti off a painted wooden sign."

The worker flinched. "I'm not sure that's possible."

No, probably not, which was why Zoe had suggested painting over it. And she wasn't sure that Rachel should give that stupid childish tag the honor of being called *graffiti*. It was a thin, nearly illegible scribble.

Who would do that to a new church sign? What a loser.

"Then we need some paint samples."

"Right this way." He led them to the swatch wall.

"It just occurred to me," Zoe said when the employee had walked away. "Who did we hire to paint the sign? Could they tell us what colors to use?"

Rachel's eyes widened in unbridled joy. "Yes! That's brilliant!" She whipped a cell phone out of her oversized purse, and Zoe was impressed with the model. The phone was huge, had a fancy case, and looked brand-new. Maybe Rachel wasn't such a cluck after all.

Rachel quickly got in touch with the painter and was promptly put on hold, leaving Zoe to stare at all of the swatches for no reason. It seemed like every shade of the rainbow. It was beautiful. She wished she had a swatch wall in her room. Well, if she *had* a room, she would wish for a swatch display in it. What a glorious color pallet God created. This thought made her cold all over. God? When had God come into this? Why was she thinking about God? God hadn't done this. He hadn't made the paint or brought her to the hardware store. She shook the argument out of her mind.

Rachel pointed toward the greens. "Blarney Stone."

Quickly, Zoe's eyes scanned the cards for this name. She found it and plucked it out.

"And then ..." Her pointing finger swung toward the yellows. "Unmellow yellow."

What a terrible name.

"And finally ... Ballerina Tutu."

Zoe looked at her. Was she serious? Apparently, yes, she was, so Zoe searched for Ballerina Tutu and then plucked it from its spot.

"Thank you so much." She hung up. "We need a sealer too. He recommended a spray one." She called the employee back over as if she were hailing a cab and asked him where the sealers were.

They were right behind them.

Zoe was embarrassed. She was embarrassed that she was dealing with a church sign, and she was embarrassed to be seen with this woman in public.

"Would you like any snacks?"

"Huh?" Zoe hadn't been expecting that.

Rachel swung an arm toward a large display of old-fashioned candy. "My kids always came home from school hungry. I thought you might like a snack."

Before she could stop it, the question flew out of her mouth: "You have kids?"

Rachel tittered. "Of course I do. What, did you think I was too ugly to procreate? Go ahead, pick a snack or two."

Rachel's sentence made Zoe stand up straight. Rachel was talking to her as though she were an adult. She liked it. She grabbed a bag of maple nut goodies.

"Oh, those are my favorite. Grab two bags."

Chapter 39
Zoe

Zoe's mind settled into a comfortable peace as she painted. At first, she'd been annoyed that she would have to stand for the hours it would take to fix this thing, but her legs weren't bothering her. She would never admit it to anyone, ever, but she was having *fun*. The painting was incredibly soothing, and she was sad that she was already half-done.

Rachel, for the most part, was ignoring her. Telling her that she was "the artistic one" so therefore should do most of the work, Rachel had dragged a folding chair out of the church and now sat with her eyes closed. It almost looked as though she were sunning herself, but the sun was rapidly sinking toward the horizon.

Zoe was just over half done when it became too dark to do more. If she'd hurried, she probably could've gotten the thing done, but she'd begun to take a strange pride in the task and wanted to get it right. She bent to tap the cover of the paint can back into place.

The noise prompted Rachel to open her eyes. "Aho!" she cried.

What did that mean?

Rachel sat up straight. "Wow, Zoe, that looks great!"

Zoe stepped back and looked at it. Yes, it did look great, didn't it? She felt something odd in her chest, something puffy and pleasant. Was that pride? Had she actually done something worth being proud of? Figures, she'd find her true gift in painting the vandalized sign of an old lady church.

"So, am I done?"

Rachel frowned. "The sign's only half-fixed!" she cried indignantly.

"I know, but I mean, am I done for today? Gramma said I have to do ten hours. Do I have to do them all today?"

Rachel shrugged. "That's between you and Gramma, but I suspect the scheduling is flexible. What do you say I order us some takeout? We can run a little more time off the clock." Without waiting for an answer, she stood and folded up her chair.

The truth was Zoe was starving. But knowing Gramma, she had already cooked her some big meal that consisted mostly of beef and potatoes. "I should call Gramma, make sure it's all right."

"I've already cleared it with her," Rachel cried while walking away. "Come on in. Bring the paint."

Zoe picked up some of the paint and brushes. She was going to have to make two trips. She set the first load down just inside the front door. "I'll be right back." She went for her second trip. When she returned, Rachel had four paper menus spread out in front of her. "What kind of food would you like? I'd offer to cook for you, but I don't cook."

This surprised Zoe. She thought all old ladies cooked. "I don't cook either." She sank into a comfy chair, and only then did she realize her legs were tired. "Though I suppose I don't need to know yet, since I'm only sixteen."

"You might not need to know ever."

"Really?" She raised an eyebrow in surprise. She thought any old lady would tell her she had to learn to cook so she could win a man, especially because she wasn't going to win one with her looks.

Rachel shrugged. "I've lived a good life without ever cooking a good thing." She held up a hand. "Now, if the good Lord tells you to learn to cook, don't quote me as your argument. Who am I to know what he has planned?"

Zoe concentrated on not rolling her eyes. Here we go. The God talk.

"All I know is, there is more to life than cooking." She slapped her thighs. "Now, what kind of food do you want? This is all that Carver Harbor has to offer: a pizza place; a cold sandwich shop that makes gourmet sandwiches on homemade bread—that would be my vote, but it's up to you; a diner; and a fancy-schmancy seafood place."

Zoe was overwhelmed. "The sandwich shop is fine."

"Great." Rachel handed her a menu, and Zoe examined it. Her stomach rumbled. She scanned the offerings, became even more overwhelmed, and handed it back. "Turkey and cheese, I guess."

"Good choice. All the veggies?" Rachel took out her phone.

Zoe scrunched up her nose. "Do they have black olives?"

"I highly doubt it."

"Then sure. Veggies are okay."

Chapter 40
Zoe

Rachel drove Zoe to the sandwich shop, which was an old house. The smell of bread hit her like a rambunctious hug.

"Go ahead and pick out a drink." Rachel pointed her chin at a drink cooler. "Wait, are you allowed to have soda?"

Zoe almost laughed. Gramma was far too worried about moonshine consumption to worry about sugar. "As far as I know."

"Great. Grab whatever you want and then get me a Moxie."

Zoe vaguely remembered having Moxie when she was little, but she couldn't remember what it tasted like. She seemed to remember that she hadn't liked it, but what had her younger self known about the finer things in life? If Rachel liked it, maybe it was worth trying. She grabbed two.

"Ah, Moxie. Excellent choice." Rachel made pleasant conversation with the woman behind the counter, and Zoe wasn't even embarrassed—until Rachel invited her to church. Then Zoe wanted to sink into the floor.

The woman politely declined. Sunday was her only day off.

"I understand. Well, if you ever need us, we'll be there." Rachel took the bag of sandwiches and thanked the woman. Then they returned to the car.

"Do you invite everyone you meet to church?"

Rachel laughed. "Definitely not."

Zoe waited for her to elaborate, her mouth watering now that the smell of fresh bread had entered Rachel's car.

"I try to wait for the prompting of the Holy Ghost. I say, "Do you want me to invite this person to church?"

Zoe remembered those strong invisible arms, how they had felt around her body. "And that works?"

"Honestly?" Rachel snapped her seatbelt into place. "Buckle up, buttercup." She put the car in reverse. "Honestly, usually nothing happens. But somethings, I get a little nudge."

"Nudge?"

"Yeah. It's like a good feeling, a comfort and an excitement about the idea, and it comes with a little burst of courage."

"And that just happened to you, in there?" This woman was nuts. Of course, how nuts was being carried home by an invisible man?

You *weren't* carried home by anyone, Zoe reminded herself. You were only dreaming.

"Yes, and sometimes, I get a firm no, like a solid wall appears between me and the person."

"A no? Like God doesn't want someone going to church?"

"I don't know about that. Maybe it's just that he doesn't want that person at *our* church. Maybe we're not ready for him or something."

"Were you guys ready for that homeless man who sits in the back?"

"I'm not sure, and I don't know who invited him."

They returned to the church, and Rachel carried the food inside. Zoe checked her phone. It was getting late. She needed to eat and then fly. She hoped this eating time was counting toward her ten hours, but she wasn't sure how to ask without sounding like a snot.

When they'd both sat and started in on their sandwiches, Rachel said, "So, tell me about Monday night."

Zoe stopped chewing. "What?"

Nonchalantly, Rachel said, "I like a good story. Tell me the story of Monday night."

Instead, Zoe unscrewed the top of her Moxie and took a long drink. It was wonderfully refreshing. Like Coke with a kick.

It gave her a little buzz. Her younger self had been dead wrong about the stuff. She swallowed and looked at Rachel. "I don't know. There's not much to tell."

"Baloney," Rachel said matter-of-factly. "You can tell me that it's none of my business, but don't tell me there's nothing to tell."

Zoe studied her. What had she heard? And why on earth was Zoe having the urge to share with her? Maybe because she'd had the urge to share with Jason earlier and hadn't? Maybe because an old lady in a peaceful church felt like the most trustworthy confidant in the world? She swallowed. Was she really going to do this? Was she really going to tell someone the whole story? She put her sandwich down.

She was.

She was going to tell this woman her story.

And she had no idea why.

"So, I went to a party. You know Jason, right?"

Rachel nodded with no expression on her face other than polite interest.

"Well, he's like my only friend here. And he's not really my friend yet. Well, maybe he is. I don't know. Anyway, I went to this party because I thought he was going to be there."

She wasn't sure this was entirely accurate, but she didn't really understand her other motivations. "So I walked there, and there was this total slimeball jerk, and he tricked me into drinking moonshine ..." She paused to give Rachel time to judge her and to jump on her the way her grandmother had.

But Rachel took another bite of her sandwich and then looked at Zoe, waiting for her to continue.

"So obviously, I got really drunk really fast because, *moonshine.* I've never had moonshine before." She paused. Dare she ask the question that had just popped into her brain? "Have you?"

Rachel smiled widely and then wiped her mouth with a napkin. It almost looked as though she were wiping the smile off. "I have, but this is your story, so please, continue."

She had! Zoe had had a feeling. "So I got really drunk, and I don't remember much, but I remember standing by the water, and the guy who gave me the moonshine came really close to me and asked me to go into the woods."

Any hint of joy slid off Rachel's face. Now she looked scared.

"I didn't go," Zoe said quickly. "Instead, I just left. I don't know what happened. I think I walked back to the street, and then Jason says I turned and hollered at them and swore and stuff, but that doesn't sound like me. I mean, the swearing part does, but I don't think I would have hollered at a whole crowd I don't know. I think they're lying, but ..." She shrugged. "I guess I'll never know." She took another bite of her sandwich. It was the best sandwich she'd ever had. The bread tasted like molasses, and there were a bunch of sprouts that gave the sandwich a good crunch and a fresh taste.

"Jason told you? Jason was there?"

Zoe shook her head. "No." She covered her mouth as she chewed. "Someone told him that, and he told me."

"So then what?"

"So then I walked home." She considered stopping the story there, but part of her really wanted to continue.

Chapter 41
Rachel

"And?" Don't push, Rachel reminded herself. Be patient.

Zoe leaned back in her chair. There was more to the story, and from the looks of things, it was juicy stuff. Rachel *really* hoped it didn't involve the moonshine boy. She had enough information to know already that he was dangerous.

"You won't tell my grandmother?"

It had occurred to Rachel that, once they got talking, this question would come up. But she hadn't thought it would come up on their first day together, and she hadn't come up with an answer yet. She took a deep breath. She didn't want to lie to the girl. She leaned forward and tried to convey with her eyes the love she felt in her heart. "If you need help—"

"I don't need help."

Rachel held up a hand. "Please, let me finish. If, at any time, you need help, and I am not able to give it, then I will probably ask for other help."

Zoe looked confused.

"I can't promise I will keep all your secrets. I will try, and I would never gossip for the sake of it, but if you are ever in trouble, I will move heaven and earth to help you, and if that means spilling a secret or two, then yes, I will."

She still looked confused. "Why on earth would you be so motivated to help me?"

"Jesus. Now tell your story." She leaned back and picked the sandwich up from her lap. It was delicious.

"So …" She still sounded tentative.

Rachel looked her in the eye, trying to will her to be courageous.

"I was in bad shape. I had trouble walking. I fell down and skinned up my knee. I ripped my pants and was bleeding, and I was partway home when I just sort of ran out of gas." She averted her eyes and stared at the walls. "And that's when it gets weird."

Good. "I am quite comfortable with weird. Sometimes I think I was born for it."

Zoe glanced at the hat she was wearing and then returned to staring at the wall. "Does moonshine make you hallucinate?"

"Not that I know of. What did you see?"

"See, heard, felt." She took a long breath. "I saw a small, old church. It had a porch light on." She sounded as if she was tired of telling the story. Had she told it to someone else? Or had she simply been over and over it in her own head? "I thought it looked like a good place to rest. So I literally went and lay down on its little porch." She shook her head. "So weird. Anyway, I was resting there, and then, and this part is super hazy, but a man's voice said, 'You know better than this.'"

Oh boy. This *was* good.

"But there was no one there. He said some other stuff too, but that's all I really remember. And then ..." She looked at Rachel.

"I believe you," Rachel said softly.

"And then he carried me home." Her voice cracked on the word *home*. "He talked to me, my brain can't remember his words, but I felt him carry me home. I passed out and woke up, a few times I think, and then we were home, and he disappeared." She laughed. "Actually, he didn't disappear, because he never actually appeared. I never actually saw him. But I felt him. His arms and his chest. And I saw my own feet swinging in the air with the ground moving beneath us. Beneath *me*, I mean." She gulped for air. "So, I'd like to believe it was a hallucination, but now that I'm telling the story, I'm thinking that maybe, without that hallucination, I wouldn't have been able to get home. And if so, then it wasn't really a hallucination."

Rachel's brain searched for words. She had plenty she wanted to say, but she didn't want to scare the child off. The man, of course, had been Jesus. And this was such good news! Jesus had his hand on her already!

"And that's not even the weird part."

You're kidding. "All right."

"So, the church isn't there. I can remember it, but Jason drove me all over this town, and it doesn't exist. But I figured out where I was, because I remember the big yellow house beside the supposed church. And that church? It's not a church at all. I thought it was like some weird museum thing, but it isn't. It's just a shack. I *saw* a steeple. There is no steeple. I *saw* the porch light. It was so bright that I had to shield my eyes. But there was no porch light."

Rachel gave her several seconds, to make sure her story was over. "And then this man left you to crawl through a window into your grandmother's building?"

A hint of a smile played on Zoe's lips. "I don't think we should call it a man."

"What would you call it?"

"You know, you sound like a shrink."

Rachel laughed. "I am definitely not a shrink. I think most of that stuff is quackery." Oh no. She shouldn't have said that. "Why, have you been to a therapist? I didn't mean to offend—"

"Yes. My mom made me go to counseling. A fat load of good that did."

They fell into silence. Should she tell Zoe who the man was? Or should she let her figure it out? "I wish you could remember more of what he said."

"To tell you the truth, I've tried not to think about it. The whole thing freaks me out." She closed her eyes.

Rachel tried to be patient.

"Wait! I remember. He said something like, 'This is not who you are.'"

Yes. That made perfect sense. "What else?"

She scrunched up her face. "This is not where you're supposed to be? Or something like that. And then when we got back to Gramma's building, he said again, 'You know better than this.' I think. That might not be his exact words, but it's close. I think."

"I believe you. That makes perfect sense."

Zoe's head snapped back. "It does?"

Rachel nodded. "It does." She wanted to tell Zoe that Jesus, or that an angel of Jesus, had carried her home, but she was going to try not to—unless she asked. She didn't want this to turn into a preacher-audience situation. She waited for her to ask, but she didn't.

Zoe took another bite, swallowed, and then took a long drink of Moxie. "This is a really good dinner. Thank you."

"You're very welcome."

Chapter 42
Zoe

Zoe couldn't believe it, but she was actually a little *excited* to get back to that church sign. Painting it had been fun. As she daydreamed about it during math class, she realized she probably shouldn't hurry to get the sign done. She still had about six hours of service left. She didn't know what came after the sign. Probably something far less soothing.

The day dragged by, but eventually she was outside in the fresh air and then she was walking down Providence Ave. toward her grandmother's building. When she couldn't see Rachel outside this time, she was disappointed. They *had* said three-thirty again, hadn't they? It wasn't three-thirty yet, but Rachel had been early last time.

The homeless man sat on the church steps singing. This wasn't good.

Zoe had decided to just pass the church on by and maybe come back after three-thirty, but Rachel stepped outside just as Zoe was in front of the building.

"Yoo-hoo!" Rachel waved, looking like a lunatic. This time she wore a brown hat with hideous purple fringe dripping off it. The hat had been designed by a drunken cowgirl in the Wild West. "Do you need to go home first?"

Zoe glanced toward her grandmother's building longingly and then headed across the church's lawn. "No, I'm okay."

Rachel came down the steps and met her in the grass. "Would you like to continue painting?" she asked as if this whole thing had been Zoe's idea.

"Sure." Zoe looked over her shoulder. "Is he going to be a problem?"

Rachel didn't look. "I don't think so. He's not a problem until he's a problem, right?"

Zoe had no idea what that meant, and she wasn't excited about walking past the man to get her paint and brushes.

"I'll go get your things." Rachel waved toward the sign. "You go get emotionally prepared."

Zoe laughed. She didn't think she needed to get emotionally prepared to paint a church sign, but okay. She went to the sign, dropped her backpack in the dead grass, and rolled up her sleeves. Yesterday's paint had dried and blended nicely with the original. She wasn't going to have to repaint the whole sign. Bummer.

Rachel appeared beside her and set the paint down. "I'll be right back. I need my chair."

Zoe took a long breath. What an odd predicament she'd found herself in. Doing community service—that she didn't hate— with a crazy old woman—whom she didn't hate. Life was full of surprises.

Zoe took one of the paintbrushes out of the plastic baggie and then opened a paint can. She dipped the brush into the sunny yellow color, which deserved a better name than Unmellow Yellow. "I will call you Splashing Sunshine," Zoe whispered.

Rachel reappeared as Zoe scraped the excess paint off the brush. "How was school?"

Zoe straightened and shrugged. "I don't know. School was school, I guess."

"Did you get to talk to Jason?"

Zoe frowned. "Uh, yeah. I talk to him every day."

"Cool." Rachel cracked open a soda and took a long drink.

She hadn't offered Zoe any. Zoe expected more probing questions, but Rachel was apparently out of them and was instead content to stare off into the distance as Zoe worked. The silence went on for so long that

Zoe started trying to think of something to say. "I think this sign's almost done."

Rachel didn't answer, so Zoe looked at her to make sure she wasn't dead. She could hardly see her eyes because the brim of her floppy hat drooped down over her face.

"So what do we do next?"

"We fix the window." A question lurked beneath her words.

Zoe stopped painting and looked at her. "I didn't break it."

Rachel pushed the brim of her hat up and studied Zoe. "I believe you."

Zoe exhaled. "Thank you. I wish my grandmother did."

"I'll tell her."

She went back to painting, trying to act as though she cared less than she did. "Tell her what?"

"I'll tell her to believe you. I'll tell her that you're telling the truth."

Zoe was touched by this. "How do you know I'm telling the truth?"

She took another drink of her root beer. "I guess I don't *know*, but you told me that you drank moonshine and then hitched a ride with an invisible angel, so I doubt you'd lie about the church window."

Zoe stopped painting and looked at her again. "You think there was an *angel*?"

Rachel hesitated. "No, actually, I don't. I think it was Jesus himself, but I didn't want to freak you out."

Zoe snorted. Yeah, right. With an entire planet to take care of, like Jesus would show up to carry *her* home. "I doubt it," she mumbled, but Rachel didn't say anything, so Zoe didn't know if she'd heard her. "I don't know how to fix a window," she said more loudly.

"That's all right. I do."

"Really?"

"Yep. I can fix just about anything."

Zoe stared at her. Was she kidding? An old lady who could fix anything? Was there any such thing? "Why?"

"Why what?"

"How are you able to fix anything? Isn't that usually a dude thing?"

Rachel shrugged and took another swig. "I had a great dad. He taught me things. But also, it came naturally to me. And then I worked in a shoe factory for twenty-five years."

Really? Rachel had worked in a factory? "You were a working mom?"

"Yes. There weren't a lot of them back then, but I was one of them. But my children still turned out just fine. They live nearby. We are very close."

"Girls?"

"One of each."

"Do they go to church?" Again she was surprised by her own question. Why was she so interested in Rachel all of a sudden? *Because she's the only one here*, she told herself.

"They do. They are strong in the Lord. So, your grandmother, myself, and the rest of the women used to go to a different church. My children grew up there, but when my children had children, they wanted to go to a church that had programs for little ones. Our church was a dying one by then, and now it's a dead one. But they go to great churches. I visit on occasion."

"Cool."

Rachel snickered at her. It *was* a little strange that she'd just called that story *cool*. "I'm tempted to ask you if you want children, but you're probably too young to think of it."

Zoe thought carefully. She appreciated Rachel asking intelligent questions and wanted to give an intelligent answer. "I don't think I'll have kids."

"Why not?"

Zoe was done with Splashing Sunshine. She tapped its lid back into place and opened the Blarney Stone. "I don't know. I don't think I'm very maternal. And I doubt I'll ever get married." She laughed. "I know you can have babies without a husband but that sounds even worse than having some with one."

"Why do you doubt you'll get married?"

The real reason? Because she didn't think anyone would marry her. She was too ugly. "I watched my mother's marriage fall apart. I watched her go through the divorce. It all seemed more trouble than it was worth."

Rachel didn't say anything and Zoe glanced at her to see if she'd heard her. It seemed she had, but she had this amused, curious expression on her face, as if she was waiting for Zoe to say more, as if she didn't quite believe her. "Divorce is awful," she finally said, "and while I know sometimes it's the only option, I think most of the time people pull that particular trigger too quickly. Every marriage goes through ups and downs, and you've got to ride through the downs to get to the ups. Too many people jump off at the downs." Rachel pointed at the sign. "You missed a spot."

Annoyed with the micromanaging, Zoe stepped back to see where she'd missed. Then she stepped forward again to fix her error. She might as well tell Rachel the truth, right? They were trapped there together with nothing else to do, and Rachel was the first person to really listen to her, ever. Even her therapist back in Missouri had sort of stared at her with this glazed expression on her face, and Zoe had known she was just waiting for the clock to run out.

This wasn't the case with Rachel. Zoe couldn't imagine *why*, but it seemed Rachel actually cared about her.

"I also highly doubt that anyone will ever want to marry me."

She expected Rachel to say something obnoxious like, "Oh, you don't know that" or "There's someone for everyone." But she didn't. She just sat there staring at her.

And though Rachel hadn't argued with her, still Zoe felt the need to defend herself. She pivoted so that Rachel could get a good look at her. "Look at me. I look like a horse. I'm six foot two. *Six foot two*. What guy is going to want a girl who is six foot two? And then I'm ugly. And then I'm fat." Tears sprang to her eyes so she spun back to her work. Part of her desperately hoped Rachel would argue with her. The rest of her thought that, if Rachel *did* argue, then Rachel would lose all credibility as a counselor.

There was a painfully long pause. Good. She wasn't going to argue with her. But that meant that all of what she'd just said was true.

"Do you know how tall I am?"

What? *That* was her response? Zoe turned to look at her. She remembered being folded up with her in the back seat of Gramma's car. She'd been pretty tall. "I don't know, maybe six foot?"

Rachel smiled. "I'm about six foot one now, but at my prime, I was six foot two. Six foot six when I wore heels."

Why on *earth* would she wear heels?

"Keep painting. I want to show you something." Slowly, she set her soda can down in the dead grass and then got up and went inside.

Zoe watched her go, but then looked away quickly when Derek waved to her.

Chapter 43
Rachel

Rachel brought the photo album out into the sunlight and flipped it open. This felt both terrifying and liberating. The sunshine was *so* bright. Nothing could hide in it. "Here I am at twenty-five."

Zoe gasped.

Perfect. That's exactly the reaction Rachel had hoped for: horror. The picture showed her in the factory, in her work boots, which made her two inches taller, and her dirty work clothes. Her hair was pulled back, making the miserable expression on her face even more pronounced. Her cheekbones looked like blades trying to cut through her skin.

"I was a looker, wasn't I?"

Zoe looked at her wide-eyed.

This was wonderful. She smiled at Zoe, trying to convey everything she felt in her heart with that smile.

Zoe looked away, went back to her painting.

"The truth was, I was *not* a looker. I was an ugly duckling. And I was very hard on myself because of it. I was big and strong and ugly, and none of the boys wanted anything to do with me. Well, that's not quite true. They were fine with being my buddy. But they certainly weren't lining up to be my husband." She couldn't see Zoe's face, yet she felt Zoe was listening closely. "And Zoe ..." She softened her voice. "I have lived the fullest, best life. I don't have words to tell you how much joy and fun I've experienced."

Zoe's arm dropped to her side. She still didn't look at her, but Rachel could hear tears in her voice. "But you *did* get married, right?"

"Yes."

"Then things must have been different back then. Nowadays, guys see the movie stars and the models, and a girl like me doesn't stand a chance."

Rachel hadn't anticipated this argument and took her time countering it. "Things have certainly changed. I don't know much about your generation, I'll admit. But let me tell you about mine. You're right, there weren't as many movie stars and models. But girls were *skinny*. And I wasn't. I was thick like a beef stick."

Zoe giggled.

"And girls were feminine. And I wasn't. I've never had breasts big enough to notice, and my voice has always been as deep as a canyon."

Zoe giggled again.

Rachel found this incredibly rewarding. This was working. This was actually working. God was so good. "And in a way, girls in my generation had it a bit harder even. Girls back then knew their way around a household. They could all sew, cook, and clean because their mothers had taught them to. I didn't know how to do any of that." She slowly returned to her chair. "My mother died when I was young. I was raised by my father. Wonderful man, but he didn't know how to cook, and even if he *had* known how to boil an egg, I wouldn't have cared to learn. I had no interest and no ability in any of that stuff. Zoe, do you know what home ec class is?"

Zoe scrunched up her face. "Like they used to teach you how to cook and stuff in school?"

"Right. Easiest class ever. And I *failed* it. The teacher hated me. I almost burned the school down."

Zoe finally looked at her. "You seriously don't know how to boil an egg?"

Rachel didn't appreciate the patronizing expression on the kid's face. Rachel highly doubted that Zoe knew how to boil an egg either and was tempted to quiz her on it, but she had bigger fish to fry. She forced a smile. "I do *now*—sort of. But I didn't back then. My point is, I had *nothing* that men were looking for. I wasn't pretty. I wasn't good with kids. I was a disaster in the kitchen."

Zoe looked skeptical.

"I was smart as a whip, I was great at fixing cars, and I could make the men laugh, but none of them wanted to take me out to the movies."

Zoe nodded, but Rachel sensed she was tired of this conversation. Then Zoe surprised her with a question. "So how did you find your husband?"

Rachel smiled at the memory. "It was a tent revival. He was an usher. He showed me to my seat. I didn't even notice him at first, but he kept smiling at me."

"Why?"

"Why what?"

"Why did he keep smiling at you?"

Rachel thought about it. "I don't know. He saw something in me. By then, I was going on thirty, nearly an old maid. He was twenty-eight. And he was handsome as all get out. So don't buy the lie that us plain Janes only get to marry ugly men."

Zoe's face fell.

"What?"

Zoe looked down.

"What is it? Do you not believe me?"

Zoe shook her head and then spoke almost too quietly to hear. "I think calling me a plain Jane is generous."

Rachel leaned forward and lowered her voice as well, something that didn't come easily to her. "Look at me."

After a hesitation, Zoe did.

"You are your harshest critic. No one looks at you the way you look at yourself. You want to know what I see? I see a lively, strong young woman who no one wants to mess with. I see a tough, healthy woman with great hips. I see beauty, Zoe. No, you're right. Not the conventional beauty that Hollywood tells you is in style right now, but a deeper, God-given beauty that is uniquely yours." Rachel was impressed with herself. She wasn't usually this articulate. God must be helping. "Zoe, you *are* beautiful. And you need to claim it, own it, walk in that beauty."

Zoe studied the sign, her body as stiff as a board.

"I am confident that God has a husband in store for you, and if he doesn't, then he's got something even better. Zoe, God *made* you who you are. He has—"

Zoe's head snapped in her direction. "*If* there's a God, and that's a big *if*, then he is a *huge* jerk for making me like this." She dropped her brush into the can, and paint splashed onto the grass. "I'm going home." She stooped, picked up her backpack, slung it over her shoulder, and started to stomp away.

But then she stopped. Without turning back, she let the backpack slide off her shoulder and drop to the ground. Then she slowly turned. "I'm sorry." Leaving the bag behind, she headed back toward the paint. She knelt beside the cans, gently removed the brush, and started to scrape all the excess paint off it. "I didn't mean to be a ... you know. But can we please not talk about this anymore?"

Relieved she hadn't left, Rachel sat back in her chair. "Sure. What do you want to talk about instead?"

"I don't know. Let's try and figure out who broke the window."

Chapter 44
Zoe

If it weren't for Jason, Zoe thought she might give up and go back to Missouri, even if it meant Reboot. Jason was the *only* one who would speak to her. Everyone else avoided her like the plague. Even the teachers were standoffish.

No one was outright *mean* to her, and she figured she owed this to Jason. Why was he being so nice to her? She didn't know, and she was both annoyed by it and grateful for it. She wasn't sure how much worse these kids would be if he wasn't there.

She was walking home from school, trying to decide if she would stop at the church or if she would go to see Gramma first, when a car pulled up alongside her. Out of the corner of her eye, she saw that it wasn't Jason's car and she braced herself for something terrible: rotten eggs, rocks, or a barrage of verbal abuse. The situation wasn't good if she was hoping for the rotten eggs.

"Hey, Zoe." It was Alita.

Oh no. Zoe looked at her. "Hey."

The car stopped. Alita wasn't smiling, but neither did she look menacing. There were three other girls in the car. Zoe knew them by sight, but didn't know anything about them. The two in the back were looking at their phones. The one up front stared out the windshield, a vacant expression on her face.

"Hop in." Alita swung her head over her shoulder. "We're going to the boat landing. Having a little TGIF celebration."

"No thanks. I have somewhere to be." Zoe hadn't stopped walking, so Alita rolled the car ahead a few feet and stopped again.

"Look, I'm not excited about it either, but Jason is there, and he said to pick you up if we saw you."

Zoe glanced at the others again. They were all still ignoring her. If this was a trap, none of them were very into it. Instead, it seemed they didn't really *want* her to get in the car. "Jason doesn't drink."

Alita rolled her eyes. "Nobody said anything about drinking. You know, people *can* celebrate without booze, Zoe. Geesh." She put the car in park. "Will you wait a second? I don't want to have to keep chasing you." She reached between the seats for something. "Here. Look."

Zoe stopped, thought about fleeing, and then backpedaled slowly. Alita was holding her phone out. Zoe stepped closer. Still ready for one of them to fling something at her, she leaned slightly toward the phone, squinting, trying to see the dark screen in the sunlight.

"Oh my word, just take it. You are such a weirdo."

She took the phone, thinking that this must be for real. If Alita was trying to trick her, then she would be nicer. She looked down at the screen. It said Jason on the top, and the last message was, "I'm getting some guys. Meet at the boat landing. If you see Zoe, grab her."

Huh. Zoe handed the phone back. She could walk to the boat landing. It would probably be safer. But that would take a while. They might be gone by the time she got there.

"Look, get in if you're going to get in. I'm not going to wait forever."

This might be her chance. She knew she'd never be *popular*, but maybe she was about to break into the popular circles.

She got in.

"Good decision." Alita pulled a u-turn right there in the street and headed toward the river.

Zoe forced herself to breathe. The two girls beside her still ignored her.

Yes, this definitely wasn't a trap. If it was, they'd be nicer.

Alita yanked the car around a corner, and Zoe grabbed the door handle. Was the plan to crash the car and kill them all? With a struggle, she managed to slide her phone out of her back pocket, earning a dirty look from the girl beside her, whose kidney she had to elbow. Then she texted her grandmother, "Going to boat landing with Jason and some kids. I'll be home soon." She held onto the phone, thinking it was too much trouble to put it back.

She realized she was excited and tried to temper it. Stupid to get excited until she knew this wasn't some elaborate prank. It would be too bad to get excited and then get thrown into the river. She imagined the Bagaduce was a bit chilly this time of year.

Alita pulled the car into the empty parking lot and slammed on the brakes. Had she even taken driver's ed? Zoe looked around. No Jason.

The girls spilled out of the car. They went to a stone bench by the shore and sat down. Zoe slowly followed, determined to keep a few grabbable trees between her and the water.

One of the girls reached into her backpack and pulled out a bottle of wine. She unscrewed the top, and Zoe perched on the end of a nearby picnic table, trying to appear relaxed, trying to pretend she didn't feel like a big buck on the first day of hunting season. The nameless girl took a long drink and then passed the bottle to the girl beside her, who also took a long drink. Then this girl held the bottle out toward Zoe.

Zoe hesitated.

The girl raised an eyebrow at her. "You don't have to take it."

But Zoe wanted to take it. She wanted to feel the wine slide down her throat. She wanted the warm numbness that this wine would bring. And at least this time, she knew it wasn't moonshine. She'd seen the girl open it. She stretched out and took the bottle. She lifted it to her lips, saw that no one was watching, and took an extra-long haul. She wasn't sure she'd get another turn and wanted to make it count.

Chapter 45
Zoe

Zoe held the wine bottle out to the girl on her right, who took a tiny sip and then handed it off to Alita.

"Holy cow, you guzzle guts!" Alita cried. "Leave some for me!"

"It's okay," backpack girl said. "I've got another."

"When's Jason coming?" Zoe asked. She could already feel the alcohol doing its job.

Alita and backpack girl exchanged a look that made Zoe think this was a prank after all.

"He'll be here," Alita said without looking at her. She tipped the wine bottle up, polished it off, and then looked at her friend. "Open number two."

The girl giggled and pulled out another bottle. One of them started some music on her phone. Another pulled out a bag of weed and some rolling papers.

Zoe's mouth watered at the sight of it. "I thought people around here didn't smoke pot."

Alita laughed. "Who told you that?"

Zoe wasn't about to admit that she was quoting Nelson. She imagined these girls didn't even know who Nelson was. Actually, they probably did because their school was so small. But she'd bet they pretended they didn't know who he was. Zoe shrugged. "I dunno."

"Yeah, this is a respectable town." Alita said the word *respectable* with a good dose of irony, and a few of her friends giggled. "But some of us are still cool." She took the joint and lighter out of the roller's hand before she could light it. Then Alita did the honors and took a long pull. When she'd exhaled, she smiled at Zoe and strode toward her. "This is the *best* stuff. Try it. I'm curious how it compares to the stuff in Mississippi."

"Missouri," Zoe said, taking the lit joint from between Alita's manicured nails.

"Whatever." Alita giggled.

Zoe took a long drag and within seconds felt the first inklings of a good high. She closed her eyes and exhaled slowly, so happy to finally have some pot.

But then something unexpected happened. It felt as though a giant black umbrella was being lowered over her. She was tempted to look up, but she knew she wouldn't be able to see anything. Yet, it was there. She had to move. The umbrella was about to cover her, and she had to move, or she would be trapped. But if she jumped to the side, they would all think she was nuts. There is no umbrella, she told herself. She needed to get out of the way. She couldn't. She needed to get out of—and then it was too late. She was trapped. And she could hear the tee-heeing of the creatures who had lowered the umbrella. What had they given her? Had the joint been laced with something? No, because Alita had smoked it too. So what was going on?

Something bumped into her arm. She opened her eyes to see someone was handing her another wine bottle. Hoping that more wine would dampen the effects of the pot, she took the bottle and chugged it.

Alita laughed. "Woah, take it easy, Missouri."

Tires crunched on gravel, and Zoe turned to see a small red Dodge had arrived. Jason. Thank God. So it hadn't been a trick. They really did want to hang out with her.

Jason got out of the car. Something wasn't right. He looked furious. "Zoe, get in."

What? She looked around for clues.

"Calm down, Jas," Alita said. "We're just having a little fun."

"Zoe," Jason said, "get in the car."

While Zoe normally didn't like being bossed around, something in Jason's voice scared her. She looked at Alita, who was red with fury. A few of the other girls were giggling.

Zoe started toward Jason's car and found that more difficult than it should have been. Her legs were thick and heavy. She tried to go faster, and she could feel the eyes of a thousand critics boring into her back. The umbrella was gone, but she could still hear the tee-heeing. She opened the car door and fell into the front seat. She closed her eyes. The effects were still coming on, but they didn't feel as good as usual.

"I'll call you, Alita," Jason said. "Don't call me." Wait, what had that meant? Was he going to break up with her?

He got behind the wheel, and Zoe opened her eyes. "What's wrong?"

He gave her a dirty look and then stomped on the gas, spraying chunks of dirt behind him as they took off. "What is wrong with you?"

"Huh?" Why was he mad at *her*? Tears burned at her eyes. "They told me you would be there," she said weakly.

Now out of sight of the others, Jason pulled the car over and looked at her. His face fell, and he looked away. "I'm sorry. I didn't mean to make you cry. Look, Zoe, if anyone tells you that I will be somewhere drinking, it is never true."

"She didn't say you'd be drinking," Zoe said. She tried to say it quickly, but she didn't think she'd managed. Her words drifted out of her and seemed to hover between her mouth and Jason's ears.

"Whatever. Let's get you home. I'm sorry they did that to you."

"Did what ..." She thought there was more to that question, but it didn't come.

"I don't know exactly what they had planned, but it wasn't good."

Her heart sank. So it *had* been a prank. But it hadn't happened yet. Jason had intervened.

"Why are you so nice to me?"

He laughed.

"It's not a joke. I'm serious."

He shrugged. Both hands had a tight grip on the wheel, and he wouldn't look at her. "I don't know. I'm nice to everyone, I guess. Always have been. I guess I want people to like me, so I'm nice to them." He glanced at her. "But with you, it's even more than that. I think you're interesting. You're new, from away." He stopped at a stop sign and took a deep breath. "And I guess that you're Esther's granddaughter, so I want to help you."

"So you don't like me."

He looked at her. "What? I didn't say that."

Her eyelids felt heavy. "But you don't."

"Oh." He caught her meaning. "No, Zoe. Sorry, I don't think of you in that way."

"Don't be sorry," she tried to spit out. "I didn't say I was in love with you or anything. Aren't you worried about what being nice to me will do to your rep?"

He laughed. "Not at all. This is a small town. I'm nice to everyone, so most people like me. And it doesn't matter what my family does to embarrass themselves, people will still like me. Believe me, my mother has already test-driven that theory."

She didn't know what that meant. "Where are we going?"

He gave her an incredulous look that made her feel small. "I'm taking you home."

"I don't want to go home. Can you drop me off at the church?"

He looked at her again. "Why do you like hanging out alone at church so much?"

"No, I won't be alone. I'm helping Rachel with stuff there."

"Oh." He actually sounded impressed. "Sure, I can take you there. She won't care that you're drunk?"

"I'm not drunk."

"Sure."

They said nothing else until he pulled up in front of the church. "Thank you, Jason. I'm sorry I made your life more complicated."

He sighed. "You're welcome. And you didn't. Don't worry, once you've been here a while, things will settle down, and people will leave you alone."

She believed that. People would leave her alone. They would forget she existed. She slammed his car door shut and started across the lawn as Jason drove away.

Rachel came down the front steps and met her halfway. "You're drunk."

"I'm not drunk."

Rachel grabbed Zoe's chin and turned her face up to meet hers. She studied her for what felt like a long time and then let go. "Come inside."

Slowly, Zoe followed Rachel inside, glad that Derek wasn't sitting on the front steps this time.

Rachel pointed to a chair. "Sit." She grabbed her phone and dialed.

Was she calling the police? Zoe's chest tightened in panic. "Please, don't ..."

"Delivery, please."

Zoe relaxed—a little.

"Large pepperoni and a two-liter of coke." She rattled off the church's address. Then she hung up the phone and turned to glare at Zoe, who slid down in her chair.

Rachel moved a chair so she could sit opposite her. "Tell me what happened."

"Alita, that's Jason's girlfriend, told me that Jason had told her to pick me up and take me to the boat landing." She remembered the text. "Jason acted like I was stupid for believing her, but she had a text message from him. She showed me!" When she said it out loud, her story sounded pathetic.

"So she took Jason's phone and sent a text with it?"

Zoe looked at her hands. "I guess."

"But Jason's the one who dropped you off, so he *was* there?"

"No, he only came at the end." Suddenly, Zoe's mouth was so dry it hurt. She tried to swallow. "To get me."

"Well that was nice of him."

Yes, it was *so* nice of him. Because Jason was a saint, and she was such a charity case. "I didn't do anything that bad."

Rachel scooted her chair closer to Zoe's. "Remember the tent revival I mentioned, where I met my husband?"

Something about Rachel's voice made Zoe focus. She sat up a little. She'd never seen Rachel look so serious.

"I'm about to tell you something that my own daughter doesn't know. I want to trust you with it. Can I do that?"

Zoe didn't know what to say. Of course Rachel could trust her. But she was a little scared of what Rachel was about to say. This didn't make any sense. A secret that Rachel's daughter didn't know was also a secret that Rachel thought Zoe needed to know? What on earth? "Yes. You can do that."

"What I didn't tell you about the tent revival is ... I didn't go there alone."

Chapter 46
Rachel

A large part of Rachel's brain was screaming at her to slam on the brakes. Was she really about to tell this teenager she hardly knew her biggest secret, a secret that Esther and the others didn't even know?

Yes. She told herself to calm down. God allowed people to go through things so that they could then help others through those things. If she kept her past to herself, she couldn't help Zoe.

"I was there with my daughter."

Zoe didn't react. She didn't get it yet.

Slowly, Rachel said, "I met my daughter's father while holding my daughter in my arms."

"Oh," Zoe said slowly.

"No one knows that. I don't want my daughter to ever know. My Andrew was her father in every sense of the word. Genetics don't matter."

Zoe tilted her head to the side a little. "Rachel, don't be so hard on yourself. Lots of people get—"

"Stop." Rachel tried to reel in her irritation with Zoe's response. "I didn't say anything about being hard on myself. I'm not being hard on anyone. I'm not keeping this secret because I'm ashamed. I'm keeping it for the good of my daughter. I'm only telling you right now because I think … I *hope* that my story might help you make better decisions, decisions that will keep you safe."

Zoe furrowed her brow.

Rachel slid closer still, till she was barely on the chair at all. "Zoe, the night that my daughter was conceived, I went to a party with a bunch of guys from work. I used to drink a lot back then. I wanted to fit in. I wanted to be one of the guys. I wanted their respect. So I drank a lot. And one night, someone took advantage of that."

Zoe gasped. "Oh, Rachel. I'm so sorry."

Rachel held up a hand. "Don't be. I'm fine." She lowered her hand and forced her heart to go back there, just for a minute. "I'm fine now, but I wasn't. I wasn't fine for years and years. Zoe, it was horrible. It was a nightmare. I was so powerless. I knew what was happening, and I couldn't stop it. He hurt me, Zoe. I remember thinking that he was going to kill me. And it took me years to recover." She swallowed. Enough of that. God had healed her, but it still wasn't comfortable revisiting the occasion.

"Rachel, it's not your fault."

"I know that," Rachel snapped. This child was being thick. "I never said it was my fault, and if it happens to another young woman, I wouldn't say it was her fault either. Heaven forbid, if it happened to you, I wouldn't blame you for a single second. But still, Zoe, we can take steps to stay safe. And the biggest step we can take? Not drinking and doing drugs with a bunch of strangers."

Zoe flinched. "They weren't strangers."

"Maybe not this time. Maybe this time they were worse. Maybe this time they were people who were actually intent on doing you harm."

Someone rapped on the church door, and Rachel stood. "Hang on." She grabbed her purse and headed toward the door. What was wrong with her? Why was she butchering this? *Father, help me do better*, she prayed silently. *Give me the words.* She had to be more gentle, yet still persuasive. She opened the door to a pizza delivery boy with bloodshot eyes. Of course. She paid him, tipped him, and took the pizza and soda back inside. "Now, this is really bad for us, but I'm hoping it will sober you up some."

Slowly, Zoe pushed herself up from the chair. "I'm sober."

"So you keep saying." Rachel went to the corner of the sanctuary, where they kept their kitchen supplies and grabbed two plates. Then she returned to the pizza box and slid three slices of pizza onto one of the plates. She handed it to Zoe.

Zoe looked at her questioningly. "Three slices? What do I look like, a horse?"

"No. For the last time, you do not look like a horse. But I don't know how much you drank, and I want your belly full of beer-absorbing bread."

Zoe took the plate. "I didn't drink beer." She went back to her seat.

Rachel poured her a glass of soda and then slid a small table over next to her chair. "Here. Not exactly hydrating, but yummy nonetheless." Rachel returned to the pizza, filled her own plate and cup, and then joined Zoe.

They ate in silence.

Zoe was halfway through her third slice when she rubbed her belly. "Okay, I don't think I can finish this."

"That's fine." Rachel wiped at her lips. "How are you feeling?"

Zoe shrugged. "Mostly sober. Very tired." She looked at Rachel sheepishly. "I'm sorry. I shouldn't have gone with them."

Rachel shook her head. "Going with them was probably not a good decision, but that's not the decision that scares me. Zoe, you are a young woman. It's not safe to be drinking and doing drugs."

"It was just pot."

Part of Rachel wanted to give up then. "Fine. Honestly, I could care less about the pot. That's your grandmother's job. All I want, Zoe, is for you to understand what I'm saying to you." She took a deep breath. "Your future is so bright. I can see it. I can feel it. I *know* that this is true. But your future cannot happen if you won't let it."

Chapter 47
Zoe

Zoe stared at Rachel blankly. She was making more sense than Zoe wanted to admit. But Zoe didn't believe that there was some sparkly, magical future waiting for her. She looked around the sanctuary. She was too full to move and wanted to do nothing but go to sleep.

She was desperate for her couch, but she didn't want to face her grandmother. Her eyes landed on Rachel's. "Are you going to tell Gramma?"

Rachel hesitated. "I'm not sure. I'm tempted not to, but I'm still struggling with whether that's dishonest."

Zoe managed to not roll her eyes. "It's not dishonest."

"All right."

"Do you think I could take a nap on a pew?"

Rachel sighed. "Sure. But we're not counting these hours."

Of course not. Did Rachel think she was an idiot? "Thank you. If you can, I'd love it if you'd wake me up in a few hours." Zoe got up and was headed toward the closest pew when she saw the expression on Rachel's face. Suddenly, a nap seemed shameful. She stretched and tried to open her eyes wider. "What were we supposed to accomplish today?"

"I'm sorry?"

"I'm supposed to be doing my community service, right? But the sign's done. What were we supposed to do next?"

Rachel folded her arms across her chest. "I was hoping to get started on cleaning out the basement."

Oh no. Images of the basement flashed through her mind. "That's going to take forever."

"That's why I wanted to get started."

Zoe took a long breath. She didn't know long she'd last, but she didn't want to further disappoint Rachel. "All right. Let's go then."

"Really?"

"Yep." She headed toward the stairs.

"Wait!" She heard Rachel hurrying after her. "Watch out for the third step. It's broken."

Zoe's foot hovered over the third step, and she grabbed the railing to steady herself. The railing was not as firm as she'd expected, and she started to pitch forward. It occurred to her that this was the fall that was going to kill her, but Rachel's strong hands grabbed her from behind.

"Easy, girl."

Despite her thick misery, Zoe chuckled. "Thank you."

"Maybe I should have gone first."

"No, it's okay." Gingerly, Zoe continued down. "Just stay close."

"That's my intention."

They made it safely to the basement floor, and Rachel flipped on the lights.

Zoe groaned. "Why is there so much *stuff* down here?"

Rachel stepped around her, and Zoe saw for the first time that she had a roll of giant black trash bags stuck under one arm. "I imagine that there was quite a bit of stuff in the basement when it was a church. Then it was bought by a woman who wanted to open an antique store." She looked around, her face twisted up in disgust. "I'm guessing that she was planning to sell some of this stuff."

Zoe guffawed. "I don't think this stuff is sellable."

Rachel picked up a ceramic rabbit, looked it over, and then set it back down. "Maybe that's why she never hung the open sign." She pulled the trash bags out of her armpit, ripped one off the roll, and shook it out. "We're going to throw most of it away. But if you see anything that someone might want, we'll just put it out on the lawn."

"And then what?"

"And then we hope that someone who wants it takes it." She handed Zoe a trash bag and then started to rip off another one.

"I think we need to find someone with a truck."

"I've already got one lined up for tomorrow." She pointed toward the opposite wall. "Things that are supposed to go into the pickup truck, we put right there against that wall."

Zoe looked at the wall. "There's no room to put anything against that wall."

"Exactly. That's why we start there."

Chapter 48
Zoe

When Zoe woke up on Saturday, the room was warm and the sunlight was strong through the window. What time was it? She groped around on the floor till she found her phone. Nine-thirty. She sat up. Whoa, Gramma had let her sleep late. She looked around the apartment. Where *was* Gramma?

"Hello?"

No answer.

She got up and went to Gramma's open bedroom door. Her bed was empty and neatly made. She turned to go to the kitchen and realized she was sore. Not hungover sore, not fell-down-and-smashed-her-knee-into-the-tar sore, but cleaned-out-a-church-basement-for-hours sore. Her back was tender, her quad muscles were tight as a drum from going up and down those stupid stairs, and her arms were killing her.

Yet, she felt great. She had worked extra hard and extra long the night before. Her motivation had begun as a way of trying to make up for her mistakes, trying to redeem herself in Rachel's eyes, but the more she worked, the better she felt, and the more she wanted to work. She'd continue pitching, lugging, bagging, sorting, and stacking until Rachel had forced her to quit at ten o'clock.

Gramma had left a note on the fridge. Zoe plucked it off. "Good morning, honey. Thought I'd let you sleep. Rachel told me how hard you worked, and I am so, so proud of you! Roderick is at the church with the pickup, so I'm heading over to help. Come when you want, if you want. Love you!"

Who was Roderick?

Zoe leaned ahead and rested her head on the fridge. Rachel hadn't tattled. That was amazing. She owed Rachel big time—in so many ways. It occurred to her that if Rachel hadn't force-fed her pizza, then she wouldn't have gone on her big cleaning spree and then she wouldn't be feeling so good right now.

She decided she wanted this good feeling to continue. She swigged some orange juice and then hurried to get clothes changed, face washed, teeth and hair brushed, and feet dressed. Then she headed outside.

Brr. It was cold out this morning. She could see her breath. The church lawn was bustling with activity. A man stood in the back of a pickup, and she recognized him immediately. Oh, that guy. The one with all the kids. His name must be Roderick. Several of those kids were helping to hoist what looked like a broken dresser into the back of said pickup, which was almost full.

By the time Zoe got there, the dresser was loaded, and Roderick had hopped out and was slamming the tailgate shut. Sure enough, his bed was chock-full of junk. Yet there was still a neat row of furniture along the sidewalk. A few people stood examining the offerings as if they were at a yard sale. She supposed, in a way, they were. A yard sale where everything was free.

"Good morning, Zoe," Roderick said, surprising her that he knew her name. "I'll be back soon for another load." He looked at the closest boy. "Jump in, Peter." The boy jumped into the truck.

Zoe looked around for someone she knew, and her eyes landed on Emma. "Where's Rachel?"

"In the basement. Come on, I'll show you."

Zoe followed Emma back into the church and down the stairs. Someone—presumably Roderick—had fixed the third step, so it was no longer a deathtrap.

The basement was packed full of people. Zoe found her grandmother and had an urge to hug her. Instead, she said, "I didn't know we were having an official workday."

"I didn't either. I came to help because Rachel had asked the Puddys for help. Vicky must have caught wind of it somehow and sent Emma and her mom."

Emma overheard her. "No, it wasn't Vicky this time. Mary Sue invited me." She grinned.

"Oh." Zoe looked around the large room. They had cleared out a lot of space. "What do you want me to do?"

Gramma shrugged. "You know more about this process than I do. Just do what you've been doing."

"Okay." Zoe turned to Emma. "Let's find something to lug."

Chapter 49
Zoe

Zoe wasn't even dreading church this time. She wasn't exactly excited about it, but she no longer wished for death instead. By the time she was up and ready, Gramma was gone already, of course, so Zoe headed across her grandmother's small parking lot alone. She'd just stepped onto the church lawn when she noticed people clustered around the church sign.

She smiled, imagining that they were all admiring her painting job. Why hadn't they noticed that yesterday? They'd had all day to admire it then. Then she got a bad feeling. They didn't look like people who were admiring something. They looked like people who were upset about something.

Then she noticed a giant goofy hat rising about the small crowd. Rachel. She definitely wouldn't be standing around in the cold admiring Zoe's handiwork.

Something was wrong.

Zoe broke through the small crowd to see that someone had once again defaced their church sign. Only this time it was even worse. In the same untalented scrawl, someone had painted a curse word across the whole sign. Zoe's face grew hot.

"It's all right, Zoe," Rachel said. "We can paint it again."

"It's not all right," Zoe said. None of this was all right. All of her work had given her a sense of ownership over this little church. She didn't have to agree with the place's religion to be fond of the physical place. The building, the lawn, and definitely the sign. She'd spent hours on that sign. She caught Emma looking at her, but returned her glare to the sign.

Suddenly, Jason was standing beside her. "I'm sorry," he whispered.

"It's okay," she said, even though it wasn't.

"I can help you repaint it."

She gave him a sheepish smile. "Thanks." She looked for Gramma to make sure she was out of earshot. Then she lowered her voice. "Thanks for Friday. Sorry I was … awkward."

"Don't mention it."

"And my grandmother doesn't know so …"

"I don't know what you're talking about." He winked at her, and she thought her knees might give out.

She tore her eyes away from him. No use being in love with someone she could never have.

"Maybe we need to take it down," one of Gramma's old friends said. "We don't really need a sign. We could put it back up later when our vandal has lost interest."

"No," Vicky said. "We can't give them the satisfaction."

"Come on," Rachel said, tugging on one of the kids' arms. "It's time to ring the bells."

"Come on, everyone," one of the other women said. "Let's have church."

Zoe didn't move, though. She waited while everyone but Jason, Emma, and Mary Sue drifted inside. Then she looked at Emma. "The last time this happened, you had a theory?"

Emma nodded slowly.

"Tell me about this suspect of yours."

Emma and Mary Sue exchanged a look.

"Come on, tell me."

"Her name is Isabelle Martin," Mary Sue said, "and she is evil."

"Maybe not evil," Emma said quickly, "but close."

"And you think she would do this?"

They both nodded.

"Why?"

Emma shrugged. "She likes to cause trouble. She hates me, and—"

"She hates us both," Mary Sue jumped in, as if she didn't want to be left out.

"Why does she hate you?" Zoe couldn't imagine anyone hating these two. They were like innocent little doves.

Mary Sue smirked. "We ganged up on her once."

Nice. Maybe not so innocent. "Okay, so this chick is a kid?"

Mary Sue scrunched her face up. "She's in eighth grade, like us."

Emma looked nervous. "We don't know it was her, Mary Sue. Maybe we shouldn't do anything till we have some proof."

"I bet it was her," Jason said.

Zoe looked at him. "You know this chick too?"

"It's Carver Harbor. Everyone knows everyone." He sighed. "I don't *know* that she would do this, but she is a little puke. It could definitely be her. I know someone called her mother last time, and the mother denied it, but I still think it's her."

"Does this girl have long dark hair?"

All four of them turned toward the deep male voice. Derek strode toward them.

"Yes," Emma said.

"It's big." He held his hands on either side of his head to indicate big hair. "Poofy ... and curly?"

"Yes," Emma said again.

"She wore Adidas pants and an L. L. Bean jacket."

This guy had an eye for detail.

Emma gasped. "Was the jacket pink?"

Derek nodded. "Painfully pink."

Zoe looked at the girls. "So, it's her?"

Emma nodded, her eyes wide. Then she looked at Derek. "Where were you that you saw her?"

He looked toward the church. "Sittin' on the porch steps. About midnight. She was with another girl, but the other one never got close. She was watching for cars while the pink girl painted. Took her forever."

"You sat there and *watched* her paint the sign?" Zoe asked, growing angry.

Derek shrugged and started to hum a tune.

"And she didn't see you?" Mary Sue asked.

He stopped humming. "Most people don't."

Chapter 50
Zoe

The church service was lasting forever, and Zoe couldn't focus on any of it. All she could think about was that slimy Isabelle Martin. She and the two eighth graders had tried to tell Esther what they'd figured out, but she'd shushed them because church was already starting. So now Zoe sat waiting for it to end, so she could tell her grandmother what they knew. But Derek, for some reason, had grown bored with the whole thing and left in the middle of the service. Their tale wasn't going to be nearly as captivating without testimony from their eyewitness.

Finally, the talented organ player finished the final song with a flourish, and everyone got to their feet and started to chitchat.

"Gramma." Zoe grabbed her arm before she could go in the wrong direction. She motioned for Emma and Mary Sue to join her, and they came running. "We know who painted the sign, and she's probably also the one who broke the window." She had no idea if this Isabelle was also a window-breaker, but she was desperate to clear her name.

Gramma looked skeptical.

"Her name is Isabelle Martin," Emma said confidently. Then she waved to her mother, who also headed their way. "I've known her my whole life, and she is awful. She goes to my old church, and she was always vandalizing things there." This last part didn't sound convincing.

"*Vandalizing* might be a strong word," Emma's mother said, "but she is a troublemaker."

"Do you think she's capable of painting obscenities on our church sign?" Esther asked the woman, ignoring the three girls who'd brought her the information.

Zoe tried not to be annoyed.

Emma's mom looked contemplative. "Yes." She sighed. "Probably. But I'm not sure what we can do about it. Her parents will never hold her accountable."

Mary Sue groaned. "But we have an eyewitness."

"Who?" Gramma and Emma's mom asked in unison.

"Derek," Zoe said, and both of their faces fell.

"Are you *sure* he saw it happen?" Esther asked. "Derek is not the most reliable witness."

"He described her coat perfectly," Emma said, sounding a little desperate.

Zoe wasn't sure that saying it was an L. L. Bean coat and that it was painfully pink counted as describing it perfectly, but she wasn't going to argue.

"So, he saw Isabelle," Esther said. "Doesn't mean he saw her paint the sign."

"He *said* he saw her paint it. Why would he lie?" Zoe said.

"I don't know if he would," Esther said, "but he says things all the time that don't make sense. Maybe he wanted to please you guys and tried to contribute to your little investigation. And maybe he did see something, but we can't exactly take his story to the police. They won't believe him. And why would Isabelle commit a crime while someone was watching her?"

"He says she didn't see him." Zoe scanned the adults' faces and realized they were never going to accept Derek's eyewitness account. She looked at Emma. "We need to catch her in the act."

"In what act?"

"I don't know yet. But if we all witness it, then they'll believe us."

Mary Sue gasped. "We should video her!" She looked at Emma. "Can we use your phone?"

Zoe waited for one of the adults to argue, but neither did. She looked at her two new eighth-grade friends. "First, we need to paint the sign. I'll go get the paint." For the thousandth time that weekend, Zoe headed into the basement.

Chapter 51
Esther

It was Esther's and Rachel's turn to count tithes and offerings. They sequestered themselves into their makeshift office and dug out the calculator. This was a tiresome little chore, but it never took long.

Rachel unfolded a check and gasped.

The first thing to occur to Esther was that she'd discovered more vandalism. Then she decided that it was unlikely someone had violated the collection plate. "What is it?"

Rachel flipped the check toward her so she could see it.

Esther's hand went to her chest. "Oh my."

"Do you know what this means?"

It meant all sorts of things. Which of these things was Rachel thinking of?

"I think it means that Walter is coming around," Rachel explained.

"Coming around?"

Rachel lowered the check to the desk. "We all like the man. Maybe not as much as *you* do, but we all like him."

"Oh, stop it."

"But he's made it clear that he's not buying into all this Jesus stuff."

Esther looked at her sharply.

"His words, not mine," she said defensively. "Anyway, if he's decided to tithe, then maybe he's coming around to Jesus."

"We don't know that this is a tithe," Esther said.

"True."

"It could be a one-time gift. Maybe he just feels sorry for us."

Rachel snickered. "Maybe, but I doubt it. And you're right, if this is a tithe ..."

"Then he makes a *lot* of money," Esther finished.

"Well, he *is* a lawyer."

"But he's a lawyer in Carver Harbor," Esther said. "How much could he make?"

"Esther, he's the *only* lawyer in Carver Harbor. I've seen his house. I'm guessing he makes enough."

Esther had seen his house too. It had an ocean view. It was a nice house, but it wasn't a mansion or anything. Esther shook her head. She didn't want to know how much he made. It felt like violating his privacy. She grabbed the bills out of the basket. "You count the change."

It was the highest offering to date, and they zipped it into a bank deposit envelope that Esther forced into her oversized purse. Then she left the office with her head down, so in a hurry to get to the bank's overnight dropbox that she almost smashed right into the only lawyer in town.

"Ah!" she cried out. "Sorry about that!"

"That's all right. I was … are you busy? You seem in a hurry."

"No, no, not a hurry. Not in a hurry or anything." Her cheeks were on fire. She backed up a step.

"Great. So, I was wondering if … there's a new place in Hill Blue, I mean, Blue Hill." He laughed.

Was he nervous? She'd never seen a nervous Walter Rainwater before.

"New place in Blue Hill called Pie in the Sky, and I was wondering … I was thinking about going to try it out and thought maybe you'd like to come along?" He stopped talking.

She stared at him, unable to make her mouth answer him. Finally, after a mighty struggle, "That would be lovely."

He smiled broadly. "Great. Tomorrow? I could pick you up around four?"

"Sure. That'd be great."

His smile widened. "Great. I'll see you then."

Esther watched him walk away. What had just happened? What had she just agreed to?

"Aha!" Rachel called from behind. "Now, *that* is the kind of church fellowship I like to see!"

Esther slowly turned toward her friend. "Rachel," she said weakly. "What am I going to do?"

Rachel laughed. "Do? You're going to take a lovely leaf-peeping drive to Hill Blue, I mean Blue Hill, and then you're going to eat pizza."

Esther thought she was going to faint. "I think it's a date, Rachel. I can't go on a *date*." She hadn't been on a date in nearly sixty years.

Rachel took both her hands and squeezed them. "It is definitely a date, and you can definitely do it. It's going to be *great*."

Chapter 52
Zoe

It was so cold that her fingers were numb around the paintbrush handle. The wind was blowing in off the ocean as if it was trying to sweep them off their feet. "Here." She handed the brush to Jason. "Your turn. I can't feel my fingers."

He started to take the brush, but Mary Sue yanked it away from them. "I'll do it. Girls are better painters than boys." Emma was already happily painting away with the other brush.

Jason smiled at Zoe. "Oh they are, are they?"

"Yes," Mary Sue said matter-of-factly. "They are better at paying attention to detail."

Zoe shoved her hands in her pockets, willing them to warm up. She would have to take back over soon. Girls might pay better attention to detail than boys, but these two particular girls were making a lot of mistakes.

Suddenly, Emma stopped painting and held her brush out toward Jason. "Actually, you do need to take a turn. I need to use the bathroom."

Laughing, Jason took the brush and dipped it in the paint.

"I'll go with you," Zoe said, not because she had to go to the bathroom, but because she thought her fingers would warm up faster inside.

Once they'd stepped inside, Emma flashed her a knowing smile. "So, Jason ... pretty awesome, right?"

Zoe nodded. She didn't want to have this conversation with an eighth grader. "Yeah, he's great."

"Every girl in town is in love with him."

"Sure." Zoe looked toward the bathroom. "You can go first."

"Okay." She bounced into the room.

Every girl in town? Every girl was in love with him and he picked *Alita*? Sure, she was pretty, but surely there had to be a better option. And Zoe wasn't even thinking she should be that option. She knew Jason would never pick her, but she cared enough about him to want better for him than Alita.

When Emma came out of the bathroom, Zoe went in and ran her hands under hot water for a few minutes. Then she came out, surprised to find that Emma had waited for her. "Let's get back to work." Zoe smiled. It was nice to have a mission. It was even better to share that mission with others.

Oh no. She hurried toward the sign. Jason was making a total mess of things. "Give me that." She took the brush from his hand.

He stepped back laughing and rubbed his hands together. "Just as I planned it."

"Planned what?" she asked without turning around.

"I knew if I did a terrible job, you'd take back over."

She doubted that this had been his plan, but given how truly *bad* a job he'd done, it was possible.

Mary Sue gasped beside her. "Oh my word, here she comes."

Zoe peeked around the sign to see two girls bouncing down the street toward them. One of them wore the brightest pink she'd ever seen. "Don't let them know we know," Zoe said through closed teeth.

"Of course not," Emma said.

"We're not stupid," Mary Sue added.

Zoe focused on her painting.

"Nice sign, Emma," the pink girl called out, and the other girl laughed.

"Thanks," Emma called back.

"Nice church," the pink girl called, and then both girls laughed as though that were the funniest thing that had ever been said.

"Thanks," Emma said again. "You're welcome to join us any Sunday at ten-thirty."

Zoe bit back a laugh.

Giggling, the two girls continued by.

"That was a nice touch, Emma," Zoe muttered.

"Thanks."

"If she doesn't spray paint the sign again," Jason said thoughtfully, "she's going to get away with it."

"She'll do it again," Emma said confidently. "Don't worry. She can't help herself."

Chapter 53
Zoe

"So," Emma said, looking around the now mostly empty church basement. "What are we going to do for the next four hours?"

Zoe dragged a chair over to the broken window. "We wait."

"I wish this little brat wasn't such a night owl," Jason said, looking out the window. "I have to get up early tomorrow for weightlifting."

"You don't have to stay," Zoe said, though she very much wanted him to stay. "Emma and I can handle videotaping the world's worst most unartistic tagger."

Jason snickered. "I can't believe we have a tagger in Carver Harbor."

"You don't," Zoe said quickly. "I shouldn't have called her that. She doesn't deserve the title."

Jason stood up straighter. "I'll stay. I don't want to leave you two unprotected."

Zoe and Emma exchanged a look. Did he really think that the two of them couldn't handle an eighth grader?

"I'm sorry Mary Sue couldn't stay," Zoe said to Emma.

"That's okay," Emma said. "Jason is like my back up best friend."

Zoe expected Jason to bristle at this claim from a junior high girl, but he laughed. "Yep. We've already been through war together." He rolled his neck. "I'm definitely going to get tired of standing here. Can we go hang out in the bell tower instead? We'd have a better view."

Emma gasped. "I hadn't thought of that! That's a great idea."

Jason stepped back from the window. "Great! To the bell tower we go!"

Zoe was a little disappointed. She'd grown attached to the basement, but Jason had a point. They would have a much better view up there. She picked up her blanket and pillow and followed them up the stairs.

Jason gave her pillow a look. "Are you planning on spending the night here?"

"No, but I might as well be comfortable while we wait."

Emma was the first one up the stairs. "Brr, it's getting cold."

She was right. Zoe was glad she'd brought a blanket.

They stepped out into the small bell chamber.

"Oh wow," Jason said, pulling up his collar. "I'm glad she didn't paint the sign in January."

Zoe giggled. "Who wishes they'd brought a blanket now? And won't the sign be buried in snow in January?"

"You'll be surprised," Jason said. "We don't get much snow here. Well, it snows all the time, but it doesn't stick much. I think we're too close to the ocean." He looked at Zoe and then at Emma. "I'll take the first watch, but it's going to be a lot easier now. He sat on the floor and peered out through the slats in the woodwork. "Shoot. I can't see the sign from here. Maybe not so easy." He pulled himself back to his feet.

Zoe had just started to sit down, but now she stopped. "I'll go get you a chair." She went back down the stairs, grabbed a folding metal chair, and then headed back up to find he'd wrapped himself in her blanket with just his face poking out.

Emma was giggling.

He started to take the blanket off. She protested, but he still handed it over to her. "I was just kidding. Just trying to get a laugh out of you."

Now she felt bad for not laughing. He was going to think she had no sense of humor.

She tried to remember the last time she'd laughed. Maybe she didn't have a sense of humor. "I'm going to get another chair." She looked at Emma. "You want one?"

"I'll come too." Emma followed her back down the stairs.

They each grabbed a folding metal chair, and then Zoe headed for the stairs again.

"You like him, don't you?" Emma whispered.

Of course she did. But did she want to admit that to Emma? It was so ridiculous, like a toad having a crush on Bob Morley. "We're just friends," she said in a monotone voice. Then she hurried up the stairs.

Embarrassed to be out of breath, she tried to keep her panting quiet as she unfolded the chair. Then she picked up her blanket, plopped down into the chair, and covered herself up. Realizing Jason was looking at her, she avoided his gaze and looked out at the sign. "We should probably stop moving around so much. We'll make too much noise and scare her off."

"You give her far too much credit," Emma said, and Zoe could sense serious disdain in her voice. This chick did *not* like this wannabe tagger, and Zoe thought this dislike was about more than the tagging.

"What did she do to you?" Zoe asked.

Emma and Jason exchanged a look. "She's just awful," Emma said, which told Zoe exactly nothing.

Annoyed that they apparently weren't going to share the story, she settled in to stare at Jason, and unpleasant thoughts began to chase one another around her head. He was so gorgeous. He was so nice. She had been worried that she was falling in love with him, but it was too late for that: she *was* in love with him. And this made her angry. With herself, mostly. Why had she done that? Why had she allowed her heart to do that? But she was also angry with Jason. Why was he so unreasonably nice to her? Now, seeing how kind he was to an eighth grader, she thought he was probably this nice to everyone. Hadn't he said something like that on Friday? That he was nice to everyone because he wanted to be liked? But it was still obnoxious. And thirdly, she was mad at God. If there was a God, he had brought her here to Carver Harbor to give her a fresh start, a clean slate, and he'd plopped her right down beside a guy she couldn't help but fall in love with, a guy she could never, ever have.

God did have a sense of humor, and it was a cruel one.

Chapter 54
Zoe

"Is that her?" Jason whispered, jolting Zoe out of her drooly almost-sleep.

She sat up straight and looked over the railing. Painfully pink. Yes. That was Isabelle.

"No one else would wear that coat," Emma whispered.

Jason turned on his camera and slowly stood, aiming the phone up the street, where two girls were tiptoeing down the street. Zoe almost laughed. If they walked normally, most people wouldn't have given them a second look. But with them acting like gumshoes in some cheesy play, anyone who might see them would certainly be suspicious.

"Oh no," Jason said.

Zoe pulled her eyes away from the tiptoeing teenyboppers to look at him.

"I've got them on film, but I don't think we can tell for sure that it's them. If I zoom in, they get all blurry."

"No one else in the whole town has that coat," Emma said. "This doesn't have to stand up in court."

Jason looked at Zoe nervously.

"Keep filming," Zoe said. "I'll try to get closer and get more footage."

Emma snickered. "You guys are taking this really seriously."

"I painted that sign!" Zoe said, probably too loudly.

Emma's face fell. "Sorry."

"No, you don't need to be sorry ..." Zoe gave up. She had to get filming. She took her own phone out and stood. The blanket fell away from her, and her whole body caught a chill. Why were her legs so stiff? How long had she been sitting in that chair? She looked down at her phone. It was almost one in the morning. This chick was definitely a night owl. She started down the stairs, hoping her legs would warm up. It seemed to get colder as she descended, but the blood was starting to move through her body. She got to the sanctuary and stopped. Now what? She could go to a first-floor window, but that wouldn't get her much closer than Jason was. If she went out the front door, though, Isabelle would definitely hear her, no matter how unobservant Emma claimed she was. She could go into the basement and climb out the window, but she feared they would see her. She turned and headed for the back door. She'd never seen it open and didn't even know if it *would* open. Had it been opened in the last thirty years? It was worth a shot.

She unlocked the door and tugged on it. Yes, it opened. Excellent. She slid out through the opening, not wanting to shut the door behind her, in case it made a sound. She started down the back steps, tripped over something invisible, and almost fell on her face, but she caught herself. She put a hand against the cool wall to steady herself and then picked up speed while still trying to be quiet. If she didn't hurry up, they would be all done painting before she reached the front lawn.

She reached the corner and peeked around.

There she was, already painting. The other brat stood up the street, looking around like a trapped rabbit and bouncing from one foot to the other. Zoe held up her phone and pressed record. Then she started across the lawn. At first, she tried to look confident, but as she got closer, she started to *feel* confident. It was weird being on the right side of the law.

Isabelle *was* incredibly unobservant. Or she had earplugs in. And her lookout was useless. Granted, she was stationed up the street, on the opposite side of the sign from Zoe, but still. A lookout is a lookout, and this one was failing. She was so close she could smell the spray paint when she said, "Hey!"

Isabelle jumped nearly a foot in the air, spun around, let out a weird little cry that sounded like it should have come from a toddler, and then took off running. Zoe glanced up into the belfry and then took off after her.

Zoe wasn't much of a runner. Thankfully, neither was Isabelle, but Isabelle was a smidge better than Zoe, and the gap widened. At first Zoe tried to keep filming, but holding the phone up in the air slowed her down, so she turned off her screen, shoved the phone in her back pocket, and started pumping her arms.

She heard some chaos behind her that she hoped was Jason and/or Emma joining the chase, but she didn't dare look back for fear of losing her balance. Isabelle turned onto a side street, and, huffing and puffing, Zoe followed. Thank goodness for the bright pink coat, or she might have lost her. There were no lights on this street, and Zoe was plunging through the dark with every step.

A shadow darted away from her to her right, and she would've screamed if she'd had the breath. She hoped it was a cat. Not a skunk. The lookout was nowhere in sight.

Where had she gone? Maybe she'd ducked into someone's yard to hide. If Isabelle had any sense, that is what she would do. Zoe would never be able to find her if she just hid somewhere. Isabelle was a terrible criminal.

Zoe's legs were tired, but she could now clearly hear Jason's voice. And he was gaining on her. Not wanting him to think she was fat and out of shape, she pushed herself harder. She needed to catch the little brat before Jason caught them both—or worse, before Jason passed her and did the honors himself.

Chapter 55
Zoe

Isabelle *did* duck into a yard, but Zoe saw which one. That was lucky. She didn't know where Isabelle lived and hoped this wasn't her house. It might be hard to chase her through a locked door.

But she wasn't behaving as if this were her house. Zoe slowed to a stop at the end of the driveway and tried to quiet her breathing so she could hear. But then Jason and Emma sounded like a herd of elephants coming up behind her, so she didn't think her breathing noise was making much difference and allowed herself to resume panting.

She heard a small squeaking sound. Was that Isabelle? Was she crying? A flash of pink darted through Zoe's peripheral vision, and she looked to see that Isabelle had jumped up and was running again. But she was only feet away.

Not this time, you little brat. Zoe was tired of running, and she knew that this was her last chance to be a hero before Jason would take over the honors. Zoe pushed her legs into action—they were no longer cold or stiff— and pumped her arms for all she was worth. Isabelle had almost made it to the fence in this unsuspecting person's backyard. Then where did she plan to go? She had run herself into a dead end. More evidence of what a terrible criminal she was.

But then Zoe saw the hole in the fence. Shoot.

She was almost in reach. Isabelle turned sideways to slide through the crack. If she got through that, the chase was over. Zoe wouldn't even be able to slide her arm through a hole that size. Isabelle stuck one leg through the gap and then started with the rest of her. Zoe wasn't there yet, but she was out of time. With arms outstretched, she dove forward like a baseball player trying to tag home plate, desperate to get a piece of that pink coat.

And she did. She got more than a piece. Zoe overshot her goal, and her upper body slammed into Isabelle's shoulder. The fence abruptly halted Zoe's progress but then made an eerie cracking sound as it gave way, and then they were falling. Zoe grabbed at Isabelle's coat, just in case she was planning to get up and run again, and the coat made a loud ripping sound as some part of it caught on some part of the fence. Oh no. They'd torn Miss Isabelle's fancy L. L. Bean Pink Panther coat. Isabelle cried out in terror as Jason yelled something unintelligible from behind.

Zoe rolled away from Isabelle just in case she was crushing her and then pushed herself up to get a look at the kid. Too late she realized the little highbrow thug still had the spray paint, and now she pointed it at Zoe's face like a pepper spray canister. Zoe yanked her hand up to shield her face, but it was too late—Isabelle had depressed the button.

But nothing happened. Isabelle looked at the can in her hand in horror, shook it, and then tried again.

Still nothing.

Zoe slapped it out of her hand. "I think you're all out."

Isabelle burst into tears, and snot bubbled out of her nose. Gross. "You're breaking my arm!"

"No, she's not," Emma said. "Don't be a baby."

Zoe turned to see that Jason and Emma had joined them. Neither of them appeared winded. Jason grinned from ear to ear. Emma whipped out her phone.

"Are you calling the cops?" She eased her weight off Isabelle's arm, just in case she really was breaking it. She wouldn't be super sad if she broke the kid's arm, but she would be super sad to get in trouble for it.

"No, my mom," Emma said. "She's really going to want to be a part of this."

Jason stepped closer. "You can probably let her up. I don't think she's going to run."

Zoe didn't want to let her up. She found sitting on her arm incredibly satisfying. Grudgingly, she got to her feet; she didn't let go of the precious coat, though.

"Hey, Mom! We've got her! Yeah, we're in somebody's backyard, but we'll get her out to the street for you if you want to come. We're on Ingalls Street … yep … yep … okay." She hung up.

Zoe looked at her, incredulous. "Your mother is *coming*?"

Isabelle cried out. Zoe didn't know if the cry represented pain, frustration, or fear of Emma's mother.

"Yeah," Emma said as if this were a stupid question. "What do you think we're going to do with her?"

Jason reached down to help Isabelle up. Argh. He was trying to *comfort* this little brat? He was *obnoxiously* nice. "It's all right. You won't be in that much trouble."

This attempt to calm her down elicited another wail of sorrow.

Zoe rolled her eyes. Emma had made a good point, though. What *did* they plan to do with her next? She'd thought they were going to video her in her crime and then post it all over social media, shaming her into repentance. She didn't think they would chase her halfway across town, knock down a rotten fence, and then stand around in the dark listening to her cry. "So ... what is the plan exactly?"

Jason laughed, which sounded super weird layered over Isabelle's continued sobbing.

"Oh, will you stop crying?" Zoe's voice sounded heartless, and she liked it.

"I have a plan," Emma said matter-of-factly. "Let's get her out to the street."

"Come on." Jason gently tugged on the pink sleeve that Zoe wasn't hanging onto.

Isabelle wailed again. "No ... please ... let me go. I won't do it again, I promise."

Jason kept tugging, but Isabelle's feet didn't move and she almost pitched forward.

"Walk, or I'll carry you," Zoe said. She didn't know if she could sling Isabelle over her shoulder, but she'd be willing to try.

Isabelle's feet promptly started moving. She cried out again. She sounded a little like a pig. "I'll pay for the sign. I'm sorrrry! Please, let me go! I said I was sorry!"

Light flooded the yard, instantly making it feel smaller.

"Who's out there?" a man's voice boomed.

Chapter 56
Zoe

Of course. The man whose yard Isabelle had chosen had slept through the high-speed chase and the crashing down of his fence, so Isabelle had seen fit to squawk like a soap opera actress until he woke up.

Zoe looked up to see a man in his underwear had emerged onto his back steps. It took Zoe a second to realize what she was looking at. He was holding a shotgun. Zoe's blood ran cold.

Jason let go of Isabelle, and Zoe tightened her grip. He threw both of his hands into the air. "Sorry, sir! I'm Jason DeGrave, and someone vandalized my church, so I chased after her."

He had chased after *her*? What a glory glutton.

"And she ran into your yard. We've caught her now, though, and we're leaving. She broke your fence, and I'll"—

"I didn't break the fence!" Isabelle screeched. "She did!"

Jason raised her voice to talk over her. — "be sure to let her parents know that she broke it. I hope they'll pay for it. If not, I'm sure my church can help."

Was Jason really that wholesome, or was he acting that wholesome to avoid being shot?

The man came down off the steps, and Zoe pulled her captive toward the street nervously. Maybe she should let go of her and run for her life. Jason didn't seem scared, though. Did that mean that they weren't in danger, or did that mean that Jason wasn't smart enough to know when they were in danger?

In Missouri, if someone came outside with a shotgun, that meant danger. Unequivocally.

"Jason DeGrave, you say?"

"Yes, sir."

Zoe rolled her eyes. Oh yeah, she'd forgotten that Jason was a local hero.

"You guys getting a new basketball coach this year?"

"Yes, sir."

"Heard you might be going Class D, seeings how enrollment's down."

"I hope not, sir. Don't want to have to play Piercehaven."

The man guffawed. "Can't blame you there. All right, well, don't worry about the fence. 'Tsnot mine. 'Ts the neighbor's."

"All right, sir. Thank you very much." Jason was using an entirely different voice with this man. Maybe Jason had politics in his future. "You have a good night."

"You too, son." The man turned and headed back inside. Then he stopped and turned back. "Do you want me to call the cops?"

Jason looked at Zoe, and she shook her head. She never wanted to deal with the cops. Jason turned back to the man with no name, and Zoe got a little thrill that Jason had turned to her for any guidance, no matter how small. "No, sir. I think we can handle it."

"Yeah," Emma said. "My mom wants to bring her to her parents."

Zoe decided then that Emma's mom must be a complete nut.

The man went inside, and Zoe got Isabelle to the sidewalk. There, her sobs slowed and quieted.

She sniffed. "Please, guys. Let me go. I'll pay you."

Emma laughed. "Stop begging, Isabelle. I'm not letting you go, and you should know that. This has been a long time coming."

Isabelle's head fell.

"How long before your mom gets here?" Zoe asked.

Emma glanced up and down the street as if her mom might already be approaching. Not seeing her, she said, "We live outside of town. And I think she was sleeping, so probably be a few minutes."

Zoe tapped her foot. She didn't want to hang out on this sidewalk. "Maybe we should walk toward her?"

"Nah, I told her we were on Ingalls."

"Yeah, but I think she'd find us. It's not like there are a lot of streets or a lot of people to get lost among."

Emma and Jason both ignored her.

Fine. She would wait on this godforsaken sidewalk in this godforsaken town. Actually, now that she'd had the thought, she realized the town wasn't really all that godforsaken, was it? She didn't even hate it anymore. Sure, she hated the fact that she'd fallen in love with a guy she could never, ever have, but the rest of it wasn't so bad.

"Did you know that guy?"

Jason looked surprised that she'd spoken, as if he'd been in deep thought. Maybe he was analyzing whether he hated the town. She doubted that. He didn't hate Craver Harbor. He *was* Carver Harbor. "He looked familiar, but no, I have no idea who he is."

"He was in his *underwear*," Isabelle said, managing to sound disgusted through her snot and tears.

"Right," Jason said slowly. "Like you're in a position to be judging anyone."

Oh good. Maybe he wasn't *always* nice.

Chapter 57
Zoe

Emma's mother pulled her car up alongside the sidewalk, and Emma ripped the front door open. "Does Vicky know you took her car?"

"Get in," the woman said, not answering Emma's question. "I already called Isabelle's mother and told her we were coming."

Emma looked at Jason deferentially and then stepped back. "Do you want the front?"

"Nah." He started around the back of the car. "Go ahead." He opened the door.

Still holding onto Isabelle's sleeve, Zoe opened the other back door. She considered going in first so that she could the one sitting next to Jason, but she thought that was a bit obvious. So, she nudged Isabelle toward the car. "Watch your head," she said, trying to make a *Law & Order* joke, but no one laughed.

Isabelle ducked and climbed into the car, where Jason had already settled.

It occurred to Zoe that she did not need to continue on this journey. She could just go home and get some sleep. But she didn't want to do that. Oddly enough, she was sort of enjoying herself. It wasn't *fun* exactly, but she felt happy. Though she couldn't quite remember the last time she'd had fun, so maybe this was what fun felt like. She shut the door behind her.

"No," Emma's mother finally answered. "I was not going to wake a senior saint in the middle of the night to ask if I could borrow her car when she's made it clear I can borrow it anytime I want."

Why did they need to borrow Vicky's car? Did they not have a car of their own? Was Emma like super poor or something? For some reason, this made Zoe like her even more. She didn't want her first female friend in Carver Harbor to be an eighth grader, but that might be the case.

"Was Mrs. Martin excited to hear from you?" Emma snickered.

"No, and I didn't even pretend that I wasn't thrilled to be calling her. I made it clear I was delighted." She adjusted the rearview mirror so she could look at Isabelle, but Zoe couldn't tell if Isabelle was looking back. "Young lady, I don't wish you any harm, but I know you've been getting away with mean, cruel, expensive pranks for years, and I'm glad you've finally got caught so that you can face some consequences."

Isabelle let out a low, guttural laugh that sounded more like a snarl. "My parents aren't going to do anything."

Emma's mom looked at her daughter. "You have footage, right?"

Zoe fished out her phone.

"We've got two different videos," Emma said proudly.

Zoe opened her camera and started playing the video. She held it up so Isabelle could see it. Zoe didn't know if she was looking, of course, but she didn't think she'd be able to help herself. It bounced around like a pogo stick, but it was still easy to see what she'd filmed: a girl in a pink coat spray painting a church sign. Then, thirty seconds in, the girl turns and looks right at the camera. Clear as day. The great innocent Isabelle Martin.

"Oh wow," Jason said, sounding smug. "That's not good."

"So there's video evidence," Emma's mom said. "If your parents don't do anything, and I doubt that will be the case, then we will go to the police. You won't go to jail or anything, but I doubt the police *won't do anything.* At the very least, you'll have to repaint the sign."

Isabelle groaned. "My parents will just pay for it."

Was she serious? Were her parents really this ridiculous?

"Good," Zoe said. "While they're at it, they can pay for the new basement window."

Isabelle's head snapped toward her.

"*You're* the one who broke the window?" Emma's mom said, sounding appalled.

"It was an accident," Isabelle said weakly.

Sure.

Emma's mother pulled Vicky's old car up a long, winding driveway, and a giant house came into view. The whole building was lit up like some kind of government facility. No way. This chick was rich.

"Are your parents criminals too?" Zoe asked.

Isabelle gasped. "No! My dad's a dentist!"

Zoe almost laughed at the preposterousness of this. Of course. It was the dentist's kid.

Emma's mom stopped the car and quickly climbed out. She was certainly excited. More slowly, Zoe got out and then looked back at Isabelle, who hadn't moved.

"Please don't do this," she said in a pathetic voice.

"Pretty sure it's already done. Come on, get out."

She still didn't move.

Jason hadn't moved either, so she couldn't escape, but she wasn't trying to. She wasn't trying to do anything. She was just sitting there like a frozen popsicle.

Zoe leaned down and forced eye contact. "Have a little pride. Get out of the car and walk to your house." Zoe knew a little something about getting in trouble. You might as well hold your head up.

Slowly, Isabelle extricated herself from the car, and the front door of her mansion opened.

A woman appeared completely dressed with good hair and makeup. That was weird. Zoe looked back, and Jason still hadn't gotten out of the car. That was also weird. Didn't the glory glutton want to share in the glory?

Emma's mother greeted Isabelle's mother, managing to sound civil.

Isabelle's mother did not return the civility. She came running toward Isabelle, wrapped her arms around her. "Did they hurt you?"

Zoe laughed.

"No one hurt Isabelle," Emma's mom said. "Obviously. But we have video of her vandalism, so if you don't do anything about it, we will take it to the authorities."

"Don't forget the fence!" Jason called from the car.

"What?" Emma's mom said.

Emma turned toward Isabelle's mom, who was still bear-hugging her thirteen-year-old as if she were some kind of prodigal son. "Oh yeah. Isabelle smashed down a fence at 16 Ingalls Street. We told the owner that you guys would pay for it."

Isabelle's mom let go of her with one hand so she could put that hand on her hip. She kept the other arm wrapped protectively around Isabelle's shoulders. "I am *certain* that Isabelle did not *break* anyone's fence. And we won't be paying for—"

Isabelle shrugged away from her a little. "Actually, Mom ... I'm sorry."

Isabelle's mother stood up straighter. "Get inside," she said, in a whole new tone of voice. "We will talk about this in private."

Isabelle obediently headed toward her front door. Her mother spared Emma's mother another unpleasant glance and then followed her.

"Would you like me to forward the video to you?" she called after her.

Isabelle's mother didn't answer.

"I think you still should," Emma said.

"Oh yeah, I was going to no matter what." She stood there for another satisfied moment and then looked at Zoe. She clapped her hands together. "All right, who needs a ride home?"

"That would be great," Zoe said. "Thanks." She went back to the car, excited to rejoin Jason in the back seat.

"Why didn't you get out?" she asked quietly, once she'd shut the door.

"Honestly? I'm a little tired."

He was lying. She didn't know him that well, but she'd been lied to enough to recognize when it was happening. "No. Really."

He looked at her sheepishly. "Isabelle's father is in the running to be the next basketball coach. I forgot the connection until she said her dad was a dentist."

"Oh. I'm sorry to hear that."

"Yeah, me too." He looked out the window. "Me too."

Chapter 58
Esther

Esther woke up on Monday with her stomach in knots. At first she couldn't remember why she was in such a tizzy. Then it came flooding back to her: the date. Oh no. She had a date. Was it a date? Maybe, if she could convince herself that it wasn't a date, she wouldn't be so terrified.

She puttered around the apartment, trying to make enough noise to wake Zoe, but Zoe didn't wake up. She knew she'd stayed out late the night before, but she didn't know how late. She hadn't heard her come in. She was a little worried that Zoe had made some bad decisions again.

When it was so late that Zoe would be hard-pressed to get to school on time, Esther gently shook her foot. "Zoe, honey? It's time to get up."

Zoe moaned and rolled over. "Nooo."

Oh no. Maybe she was hungover. She shook her foot again. "Zoe? You okay? Are you not feeling well?"

Zoe's eyes cracked open, and she gave her a small smile. "Don't worry. I didn't drink last night. I was too busy catching criminals."

Esther laughed. "Really? You caught her?"

"Yep. And we've got it all on tape." Zoe sat up and rubbed her eyes. She looked exhausted, but did she also look happy? How terrific was that?

Esther knew she was beaming and tried to control it. She didn't want to frighten the child. She was so enjoying having her around. Maybe she should get her a real bed. Even if they had to put it in the living room, Zoe should have a bed. She added that to her mental to-do list.

Zoe leaned back into the couch and closed her eyes.

"Unless you're planning on being late, you really need to get moving."

Zoe opened her eyes again, reached for her phone, and checked the time. "Oh no." She stood up, and the covers fell away. She headed toward the bathroom.

"So was it the kid you guys thought it was?"

"Yep," she said without turning around. "Isabelle Martin. A real piece of work." She stopped in the bathroom doorway and turned to face her. "Also, she admitted to breaking the basement window."

Esther gasped. Some stranger had broken the church window? And she'd blamed her granddaughter? This wasn't good. "Oh, honey, I'm so sorry." She wished she had more to say, but she couldn't think of anything.

Zoe gave her a small smile. "It's okay. If I were you, I would have suspected me too. But, officially, I didn't do it. Do you believe me?"

Esther nodded quickly. Rachel had been right. It hadn't been Zoe. "Yes, of course."

Zoe's smile widened a little. "Good." She stepped back and shut the bathroom door.

She was so much prettier when she smiled. Esther wished she would do it more often.

Esther went into the kitchen to toast some bread for Zoe. She didn't know if she could get her to eat it—Zoe wasn't big on breakfast—but she hoped the gesture would make her feel loved.

"I don't have time for breakfast," she said when she saw the toast, all ready with butter and jam. But she looked happy to see it.

"You can take it with you. And let me give you a ride this time, so you're not late."

Zoe hesitated. "Are you going out anyway?"

"No, but it's not like I have a lot to do today. I'm just going to sit around and twiddle my thumbs worrying about tonight."

Zoe's eyes widened. "Oh yeah! That's right! Gramma has a date!" She looked her up and down. "We're going to have to find you something to wear."

Esther faked a scowl. "Grab your toast and your bag and let's go."

Zoe reached toward the floor by the foot of the couch and then cried out.

Esther looked up, assuming she'd injured herself. "What's wrong?"

"My bag."

Esther waited for her to elaborate.

"Um … I think I left my bag in Alita's car." There was panic in her eyes.

"Alita? Who's Alita?"

"Uh … you know what? It's not a big deal." It was obviously a bigger deal than she was making it. "I'm sure she'll bring it to school." She didn't sound sure at all.

"Who's Alita?" she repeated, genuinely worried now.

"No one." She sounded disgusted. "I mean, she's just a girl from school. She gave me a ride home Friday."

Oh! Was Zoe making more friends? How lovely! "I can't believe you didn't notice your bag was missing till now."

"Yeah." She chuckled. "I don't think much about schoolwork, even when I'm in school. I def don't think about it on the weekends."

Esther thought she should probably think about her schoolwork a bit more, but she also thought it was valuable to choose one's battles. "All right, then. Let's get you to school." She left the apartment, not entirely sure Zoe would follow, but she did. "You know," she said when they stepped into the elevator. "I'm going to try to get you a real bed."

Zoe looked up, obviously surprised. "You don't have to do that."

"You're planning on staying a while, aren't you?"

"Yeah, if that's okay."

"Of course it's okay. You can stay forever. And I'm going to try to get you a real bed." It felt good to make this promise. She wasn't sure how she was going to pay for this bed, but how expensive could it be?

"Is my community service done?"

It took Esther a minute to figure out what she was talking about. Oh yeah, her Rachel time. "Yes. I think so."

"Okay." Zoe looked down, and if Esther didn't know better, she'd think she was almost disappointed.

Chapter 59
Zoe

When Zoe and her grandmother stepped outside, Jason was waiting beside the building.

"Holy moly, slowpoke. You're going to make us late."

Zoe looked at her grandmother nervously. She wasn't sure what to do. She felt bad just ditching her.

Gramma waved at the car. "Go ahead, honey. Have a good day." She smiled at Jason and waved. "Good morning, Jason."

He waved back. "Good morning, Esther."

"Did you stay last night till the vandal was caught?" She was talking really loudly, and Zoe thought about how ridiculous that must have sounded to anyone within earshot.

"I sure did."

"Well, thank you for your service."

Zoe got into the front seat, her stomach full of butterflies. Her backpack sat on the floor by her feet. "Hey, how'd you—"

"Alita gave it to me. She acted all disgusted that you'd left it in her car, as if she wasn't the one who'd tricked you into getting into her car in the first place." He looked at her. "Sorry about that."

She buckled up. "Why? You didn't do anything."

He shrugged and pulled the car out onto the street. "I know, but I don't think she would have messed with you if I hadn't tried to be your friend. Anyway, we broke up." He said this as if he *hadn't* made a major announcement.

"What?" Zoe cried and then mentally kicked herself. If he was trying not to make a big deal of it, she should follow his lead.

"Yeah. Whatever. I probably should have done it a long time ago." His tone made it clear that he didn't want to talk about it, and she didn't know what else to say.

"Well, thank you for getting my backpack."

"You're welcome. And I thought about going through it to make sure it's not full of itching powder or snakes, but I thought that would violate your privacy." He looked at her. "So you might want to look for itching powder or snakes before you go reaching in there."

She thought itching powder and snakes seemed a bit subtle for Alita. She'd probably filled her bag full of anthrax. Or she'd planted some crystal meth, and the cops were waiting for her at school. She picked up the bag and gingerly unzipped it.

The silence felt awkward. "So, how tired are you?"

He exhaled so dramatically that his lips vibrated. "I am *so* tired. I had weightlifting this morning."

"You didn't have to come pick me up!"

"No, that's okay. It's getting cold. I'd hate for you to have to walk." He acted like a boy who liked a girl.

But she knew that this boy definitely did not like this girl, and she needed to stop thinking thoughts like that. They were depressing and dangerous.

"You could join us anytime, you know."

She laughed. "Yeah, right."

"You might like it. It's good for mental health." He looked at her quickly. "Not that you have mental health problems."

She laughed. She knew he hadn't meant to imply that, and yet she *wasn't* the most mentally stable kid on the block.

"Besides, I am going to convince you to play basketball this year, so you might want to start weightlifting."

"I'm *not* playing basketball, Jason."

"Not even for me?"

"Not even for you." Although, if he really kept at her, she thought she probably *would* play for him. She thought she'd probably do anything for him.

He parked in the school lot, and they got out of the car and walked toward the building, side by side. Several people stood outside staring at them. This was unusual behavior, even with her.

"They might think we're together," she mumbled.

He laughed. "No, they don't think that."

And just like that, all the good mood she'd been building up over the last twenty-four hours of spending time with Jason dissipated so fast it was as if it had never been there. She was back to the lonely darkness.

She should get used to it. This was where she belonged.

Chapter 60
Esther

Esther stood staring into her closet. All her clothes looked the same. Zoe was right. She did have a wardrobe problem, and she wasn't sure how to fix it.

She thought back to how she'd used to dress prettily for Russell. She'd been good at it then. She'd known what colors looked good on her, what cuts flattered her figure. But clothes were different now. *She* was different now.

She didn't really have the gumption to go clothes shopping. She hadn't been in a fitting room in over a decade. She couldn't afford new clothes, either, and even if she could, she wasn't going to find anything suitable in Carver Harbor. She'd have to go all the way to Ellsworth or Bangor. She didn't have time for that. And so it was back to surveying the same ten outfits in her closet.

She heard Zoe come in and glanced at the clock. It felt early, because Zoe had been going to church after school for the last several days, but it wasn't that early. Zoe was just home on time.

"Hi, honey."

Zoe stepped into the bedroom. "What are you ..." Her backpack was slung over her shoulder.

"Oh good, you got it back."

"Yep," she mumbled, "and there wasn't even any anthrax in it."

"What?"

She shook her head. "Nothing."

Esther frowned. Kids these days had the strangest sense of humor. "Speaking of lost bags, your luggage showed up."

Zoe laughed. "What?"

Esther nodded toward the front door. "Yeah. A carrier dropped it off today. Better late than never, I guess?"

Zoe looked at the bag, seemed excited, but then turned her attention back to the closet, as if she had to deal with her grandmother's crisis first.

Esther was touched.

Zoe whistled. "Gramma, did I inherit my fashion capabilities from you?"

"What do you mean?"

"I mean that we're both terrible at it." She looked at her. "Your clothes are all blue." She looked into the closet. "Multiple shades of blue, but all still blue. You must really like blue."

Esther stood up straighter, feeling defensive. "I do like blue. And if everything is blue, then everything matches."

Zoe grimaced. "What time is he picking you up?"

"Around four."

Zoe snickered. "Old people dinner time."

"Hey!" Esther cried. "We're going all the way to Blue Hill!"

"I'm just teasing you." She looked toward the door. "I think we need some help."

"Like who? Rachel?"

Zoe let out a strangled cry. "No! Are you joking?"

Esther laughed. No, she hadn't been joking, but now that she'd thought about it, Rachel probably wasn't the best one to call for fashion help.

"I said you shouldn't wear blue polyester pants with a clashing blue t-shirt. I didn't say you should wear a bright yellow out of season dress with a giant orange hat plopped on top."

This description brought such a vivid image to Esther's mind that she barked out a laugh that was probably too close to being critical of Rachel.

Zoe started laughing too, and Esther didn't know if she was laughing at their conversation or at the sound that Esther had just made laughing. Ultimately, Esther decided it didn't matter. The sight and sound of Zoe laughing was so beautiful and it brought her such joy that she laughed even louder.

Zoe gasped for air. "I'm sorry," she said in a squeaky voice. "I didn't mean to be mean to Rachel."

Esther waved a limp hand at her. The other hand was on her chest, as if clutching her chest could help her catch her breath. "No, no, it's all right." She tried to stop laughing and mostly managed. She took a long shaky breath and wiped at her eyes, which she hadn't realized were as wet as they were. "But we must never tell Rachel."

Zoe wiped at her eyes too. "I *love* Rachel. I really do. But those dresses! What on earth? And those hats? Where do you even get a hat like those? In comparison, the dresses aren't so bad."

Esther had mostly calmed down, but she still didn't dare meet Zoe's eyes for fear of going off again. "I don't know, but I can tell you that she has been wearing those getups for *years*. So maybe you can't buy a hat like that anymore." She took a long breath and returned her eyes to her closet. "What am I going to do?" Most of her nerves had abated, probably thanks to the laughter, but she was still facing the same problems.

"We don't have time to go shopping, probably?"

"No. And we don't have the money."

"Is there anyone else? Anyone from church who might loan you something, someone who doesn't dress like Rachel?"

Esther thought about it. Most of the people in Carver Harbor dressed the way she did: drab. And some dressed even worse than her. A slew of people wore nothing but stained blue jeans and ripped flannel shirts. "I can't think of anyone."

Zoe stepped closer to the closet. "All right then. He's only ever seen you in these clothes, and he likes you enough to ask you out, so let's pick the best blue pants and the best blue shirt you have."

Chapter 61
Esther

Esther stood in the common room, looking out the window. She was a nervous wreck. She was sweating, couldn't breathe correctly, and was on the verge of tears.

Zoe stood right beside her in stalwart companionship.

If Zoe hadn't stopped her, Esther would have canceled this date over an hour ago. This had been a crazy idea. Why had she agreed to it? She was a widow who still loved her late husband very much. She was still grieving. And she was also quite content to live out the rest of her life on her own. She liked her own company. So why had she said yes?

"This was a mistake."

"No, it wasn't."

Milton walked into the room and jumped at the sight of them. He looked Esther up and down. "You look nice."

Esther was certain this compliment wouldn't have been given if she hadn't let Zoe run to the drugstore for some mascara and lip gloss. "Thank you." She leaned closer to Zoe. "What good can possibly come from this?"

Zoe looked at her. "You're just going to have a nice dinner that a handsome man is going to pay for. That's all. Doesn't have to mean anything."

Oh, this generation. Nothing meant anything. "I'm not so sure about that."

"Well, be sure. He didn't ask you to marry him or anything."

Esther gasped in terror.

"Sorry," Zoe said quickly. "I shouldn't have said that. Really, we don't know that he's thinking about anything long term. It's just dinner. Maybe he's just lonely. Maybe he just wants a friend, someone to talk to, a reason to go to nice restaurants. Just try to enjoy yourself." She stopped. "And get dessert. Maybe even bring me home one. There he is!" She sounded so excited. It was cute.

Esther thought she might faint. She imagined that she was pale as a ghost. "Are you sure—"

"Yes," Zoe said emphatically. "I'm sure about everything." Then, to Esther's complete shock, Zoe wrapped her arms around her and squeezed. She held on for several seconds and then let go. "You're going to do great. You *are* great. Just relax and be yourself. And please try to have fun." She started toward the door, and for a second, Esther wondered if Zoe planned to come along, but then Zoe opened the door and stepped back to make room for her to exit the building.

Exit the building.

She needed to leave the building.

Her legs needed to move. She begged them to do so. Then they were so shaky that she asked for some divine assistance. "Please let me get through this evening without making a fool of myself and without making Walter regret the whole thing." She stopped in front of Zoe and squeezed her hand. "No parties while I'm gone."

Zoe laughed again. "Yeah, cause your apartment is so party-friendly." She waved toward the car. "Go. I'll be fine. There's a TV dinner up there with my name on it."

"No. I made you meatloaf. It's in the oven."

Zoe didn't respond, so, after taking a deep breath, Esther walked away from her granddaughter and toward the waiting car.

Walter got out and came to open the door for her. This was so silly. She wasn't a teenager anymore. She smiled at him. "Thank you."

"You're very welcome." He tucked her into the car and then went around the front of his car to slide behind the wheel. He put the car in drive and slowly pulled into the street. "Esther, at the risk of lowering your opinion of me, I feel it is safer to just come clean and admit I am a nervous wreck."

She almost barked out another ridiculous laugh but managed to hold it in. Good thing she'd gotten it out of her system with Zoe. "I'm fairly nervous myself," she managed.

"Oh good. I mean, it's not good that you're not nervous ... I mean, it's good that you're not nervous. Ahh! Do you know what I'm trying to say?"

She tried to keep her laughter at a reasonable volume. "Yes. Definitely."

"Oh good. I don't *want* you to be nervous, but it makes me feel better about being nervous knowing that you are too." He rubbed furiously at his jaw. "I can't believe how hard this is. I mean, it's not hard. I want to do it. I just can't believe how nerve-racking it is. So ... I got us reservations."

She smiled. "Good." She couldn't imagine eating under the circumstances. Her stomach was far too tied up to manage digestion, but it was probably too late to say she wasn't interested in supper.

"So, how is the new granddaughter going? I mean, obviously, she's not a new

granddaughter, but her living with you is new."
This was adorable. He was usually so well-spoken.

"It's going great actually. There have been a few bumps in the road, but I think she's settling in nicely. I really like having her around. In fact, I'm going to get her a bed." As soon as she'd said the words, she realized how stupid they sounded. "I mean, she's had a bed. I have a hide-a-bed couch, and she hasn't complained. But I want to get her a real bed."

"That's really kind of you. And I didn't think that you didn't give her anything to sleep on." He chuckled, and they fell into an awkward silence.

"Last night she stayed up into the wee hours of the morning catching the sign vandal."

"Oh, really?"

"Yep." She was prouder than she should have been about this, maybe. "She stayed in the church until the kid came back, and then she chased her all the way to Ingalls Street."

"So it *was* a kid? I'd heard that rumor."

"Yes, she's a kid. Eighth grader. But don't let that fool you. I hear she's quite the troublemaker."

Walter laughed. "Well, I'm glad she caught her. We've got enough to do at church without repainting the same sign over and over."

We. He'd said *we*.

Chapter 62
Esther

Pie in the Sky was the weirdest little restaurant. It had been a house in its previous life, and the remodelers hadn't bothered to change the layout. The rooms were small, and the candlelight made them feel intimate. Esther was grateful for the dim lighting, but she wondered if the ambiance wasn't a bit too romantic.

A server delivered giant menus, and Esther was grateful for something to hide behind.

"Would you like to try our house wine?"

"Actually, can you bring us some of your best chardonnay? Oh wait, do Christians drink wine?"

Esther peeked out over the top of her menu. "Many of them do, yes."

He chuckled awkwardly. "Would *you* like a glass of chardonnay?"

She had no theological stance against wine, but she hadn't drank any in years. She didn't want it to make her silly. "Sure. I'll have a taste."

His smile broadened and looked more sincere. "Great." He looked at the server. "Chardonnay, please."

Esther ducked behind her menu again. He had called this place a pizza joint, hadn't he? Or was that only what she'd heard? It wasn't a pizza joint. It was an Italian restaurant with exorbitant prices. She was horrified. He was buying, right? If not, she was going to have to call someone to bring her money. And she didn't know anyone with any money.

Seeming to read her mind, he said, "This is a special occasion, so the sky's the limit." He laughed at his own joke. "You see what I did there? The sky's the limit at Pie in the Sky?"

Esther forced herself to lower her menu a little so that he could see that she was smiling. "Yes, I see what you did there."

He looked quite proud of himself. "But really, get whatever you want."

She wanted to know how and why this was a special occasion, but first, she had to figure out what she was going to eat. She really just wanted pizza. Would it be too simple to order pepperoni pizza at a place this fancy? She decided she didn't care. It was what she wanted. She closed the menu and laid it beside her plate. He still studied his, so she busied herself with staring at the walls, which were painted sky blue. She was excited to tell Zoe that the expensive Italian restaurant agreed with her color palette. On these sky blue walls were painted clouds of various shapes. Each of these clouds had eyes, a nose, and a smile painted on them. Mixed among the clouds were painted pizzas. Each of these also bore a smiley face. The floor to ceiling murals reminded her of a Sunday school classroom—one in which the intent was to get the children hungry.

The server returned with a bottle of wine and bent to pour her a glass.

Walter snapped his menu shut and laid it on the table. She poured him a glass as well, and he thanked her charmingly. Had he always been this magnetic?

"Have you decided what you would like for dinner?" the server asked.

Walter smiled. It seemed he was relaxing. "I'm ready. Are you?"

"Yes." The word came out shaky.

Walter waved at her. "Ladies first."

She looked at the server and swallowed hard. Her mouth was suddenly as dry as a bone that had been left out in the sun. "I'll have the personal pepperoni pizza."

"Excellent choice. That comes with a side salad. Would you like garden or Caesar?"

Esther froze. Decisions were hard enough when she was prepared for them. "Caesar," she said quickly.

The server turned to Walter, who gave her an even broader smile. "I'll have the same thing."

She smiled, jotted something down on her pad, and then left.

Esther narrowed her eyes. "Did you plan on that or were you copying me to make me feel better?"

He tipped his head to the side, looking a bit like a curious puppy. "Make you feel better? Why would you feel bad about ordering a pepperoni pizza?"

Her face got hot. "Nothing. I don't." She returned her attention to the cartoon clouds on the wall.

Walter leaned forward. "So, I wanted to talk to you." He cleared his throat. "And I'm sorry I'm making this so awkward. I don't know why it's so hard for me. It shouldn't be. Anyway, I wanted to talk to you about all this Jesus stuff."

Esther was swarmed with conflicting emotions. Part of her heart soared to hear these words. Walter was interested in Jesus? But another big part of her heart sank to her knees. So this wasn't a date after all. He just wanted to talk about Jesus. Good thing she hadn't bought a dress. She forced a smile.

He cleared his throat again. "I've decided ... well, it's been made clear to me that this Jesus stuff is real." He looked down at the cream-colored tablecloth. "I always thought religion was something for old people." He laughed. "But now I'm thinking that Jesus himself doesn't really have much to do with religion. I mean, I'm no theology professor, so I have no idea what I'm saying, and if I say something offensive, please forgive me." He looked up at her, and his eyes looked so young.

She forced another smile. "Sure. Of course."

"But you ladies got me thinking, and I did some research, and the evidence is fairly overwhelming. Jesus of Nazareth was a real man, and he really was crucified, and then his body really did disappear."

Esther nodded.

"And so, if that's all true, then I had some decision making to do. And ..." He took a deep breath. "And I've decided that if Jesus Christ died for my sins, then the least I can do is follow him for the rest of my life. I've already wasted enough of my life acting like I was too good for God. Now I understand that I've never been anywhere near good enough."

Esther nodded. She didn't know what to say.

"So, would you mind if I asked you the occasional theological question? There's so much I don't understand."

Esther struggled to find her voice. "Of course not. I'll help when I can. You might also want to talk to Cathy. She understands the Bible really well."

He smiled. "I've noticed that. She's a smart lady. But I like you better."

Wait, what?

He leaned back in his chair. "Thank you. I feel so much better now that I shared that. I don't know why I was so nervous, but I had to tell you. Firstly, because I have some questions for you, and secondly, because I didn't think you'd consider a real relationship with me unless you knew that I was a believer too."

Wait, *what?*

He stared at her. Was he waiting for her to say something?

She was tongue-tied. A *relationship*?

"Sorry, did I scare you with the word relationship?" His smile was gone now. "I'm sorry. Please don't be alarmed. I know you had a great husband, and I assume you are in no hurry to get serious with anyone." He stared at her again.

She opened her mouth, but no words came out.

He reached across the table and touched her hand so gently that he almost didn't touch it at all. "For now, I would just like to spend time with you, have fun with you, and get to know you. Would that be all right?"

Still tongue-tied, she managed to nod.

The server arrived with their salads. Thank God.

Chapter 63
Zoe

Zoe stood on the sidewalk shivering. Jason was late. He'd been picking her up every morning to drive her to school, and it was wonderful. She wasn't feeling ungrateful, only cold. She was finally wearing something other than sweatpants to school. She was so excited to have her world-traveling suitcase back in her possession and was wearing her favorite ripped jeans. So her knees were really cold.

It was almost November, and she hadn't packed a winter coat, but she couldn't ask her grandmother to spend more money on her. She'd already bought her a brand-new bed with brand-new mattress and box spring. She'd gotten home on Wednesday to find it plopped down on the edge of the living room. Gramma had already made it up with new flannel sheets, fluffy pillows, and a sweet comforter. Zoe had no idea where she'd gotten the money and felt bad that she'd spent so much on her. She also felt bad that her bed now took up literally half the living room.

Despite all her guilt, the bed was *amazing*. She'd never felt uncomfortable on the couch, and she certainly wouldn't have complained, but now that she had that new bed, she knew how lumpy the couch had been.

Where on earth was Jason?

And then she saw him, and her stomach turned. He wasn't alone. Alita was sitting in the front seat.

Calm down, she told herself. This doesn't necessarily mean anything. Maybe she just really needed a ride to school. But as he stopped in front of the building, Zoe saw that they were holding hands, and the storm in her stomach intensified.

She considered running away. No matter the direction, just run. She considered lying. She wasn't feeling well, was going to stay home today. She considered pulling Alita out of the car by her hair and reclaiming her seat in the front.

She did none of these things, of course. Like an obedient puppy, she pulled her gangly limbs into the back seat and stayed quiet, even though Jason greeted her jovially.

She realized she was crying. Oh no. She couldn't let either of them see that. This was so ridiculous. Why was she crying because her completely platonic friend had gotten back together with his girlfriend? Why was she crying over a guy she couldn't have? Even if she were the only female left on the planet, he still wouldn't be attracted to her, which is why it was so, so ridiculous that she was crying. She had to stop. She studied her phone, trying so hard to get a grip. But the more she tried not to cry, the more she cried, and by the time they got to school, she knew she wouldn't be able to hide it. She knew her eyes were beyond red by then, so she jumped out of the car without saying anything.

Just barely, she heard Alita say, "She doesn't talk much" in her obnoxious cheerleader voice.

Zoe kept her head down and walked inside. She needed to never talk to Jason again. That would make her life easier. Avoiding eye contact with everyone, she made it to homeroom, where her teacher asked if she was okay. No, she was most definitely not okay. She told the teacher she was fine.

She tried to focus on her classes, but the material seemed even more useless than usual. When was she ever going to need to know how many electrons an iron atom has? When was she ever going to need to know how to use a semicolon? Periods had been working just fine for her since she'd learned about them in first grade.

Jason kept texting. "What's wrong?" and "Are you okay?" and "I'm here if you need me."

She blocked his number.

She considered ditching school but where would she go? It was too cold out to wander, and she had no friends except for the eighth graders from church. She almost smiled at the idea of busting them out of junior high.

Lunch eventually came and she went through the line, got her tray filled with greasy carbs, and then went and sat down. Usually, she found comfort in food, but she had no appetite. Usually, Jason sat with her, and she didn't know if he would today. The thought of him *not* sitting with her made her sad. She would miss him. The thought of him sitting with her made her want to sob. Surely Alita would be with him.

And then there he was, coming toward her. He paused a few feet away, though, and looked at her. She tried not to return his gaze, but he was just standing there silently, so she finally looked up.

"Would you rather I didn't sit with you today?" he said quietly.

How was she supposed to answer that? He knew how she felt. He was trying to be sensitive, but she found it the most obnoxious thing in the world. "I would rather you never sat with me again."

Chapter 64
Zoe

Though she still had nowhere to go, Zoe slipped out of school before the last period started, just so she could have the satisfaction of ditching school. Then, even though it was chilly out, she took her time walking home. She didn't want to get there too early and make Gramma suspicious, although when she told Gramma why she was upset, she didn't think she'd be too hard on her.

Then she saw Derek sitting on the front steps of the church, and she had an idea. Slowly, she approached. She was feeling self-destructive and didn't care if Derek murdered her, but she was still nervous about talking to him.

He stopped singing and gave her a broad smile. "Hey, Chloe, how's it going?"

Her name wasn't Chloe, but she let that slide. "Hey. If I give you some money, will you go get me a bottle of vodka at Irving?" She pointed her chin toward the gas station.

The smile slid off his face. "No."

She snickered. "Are you serious? I'll give you enough so you can get a bottle too."

He studied her, and for a minute he looked almost sane. "Does your grandmother know you're asking me this?"

Of course not. "Look, I'll give you twenty bucks, enough for two bottles. You can keep one. Do you want the twenty bucks or not?"

It took him a long time to answer. "I would be happy to take your twenty bucks, but I'm not going to go buy you booze."

She rolled her eyes. "Fine. Enjoy your high horse." She walked away, keeping her chin up even though it weighed a ton. She didn't need him. She'd stolen booze before and she could do it again.

She passed her grandmother's building and kept walking, heading for the gas station. It was really busy. Good. She went inside and made a beeline for the bathroom because it was right beside the liquor section.

When she came out, she casually grabbed a pint of vodka and slipped it into her backpack. If anyone looked closely at security tapes, they'd probably be able to see what she'd done, but she didn't think anyone would look.

With her bag zipped up, she headed toward the warm two-liter soda bottles. She preferred her mixers cold, but warm was so much cheaper. She grabbed a bottle of Mountain Dew and then headed for the coffee. She didn't want coffee, but she'd learned long ago that buying cups and Mountain Dew made people suspicious. She filled the biggest cup up with coffee, added a lid for show, and then headed toward the checkout.

"Wow, you need some caffeine?" It was the same creepy clerk who'd given her directions to the Cove.

"Yeah." She didn't look at him. "Got a lot of studying to do."

He hesitated. "On a Friday night?"

Oops. "Yeah. All weekend long." *Just sell me the stupid soda already. What do you care?*

He took her money, and then she was out in the world. Free.

But where was she going to go? It was too cold to drink outside.

The church. It was weird how happy the idea made her. Yes, the church. It felt safe and familiar. She liked the basement.

She didn't want to get caught by Derek, though, so she slipped around the back of the building. When she crept around the front of the church, she couldn't see Derek's legs. She stopped and listened. She didn't hear singing. He must have left. Good. She looked both ways to make sure no one was watching, and then she slipped in through the broken window. If anybody ever fixed this window, she was going to have a much harder time at life.

Once inside the dim light of the basement, a weird contented peace filled her. She didn't know why she felt so at home here, but she'd take it. She went to the bathroom, dumped the coffee down the sink, and then found a chair. She sat down and opened the soda. She poured an inch of vodka into the coffee cup and then added a good dose of Mountain Dew. She drank the first half of the drink in one long guzzle.

Then she tipped her head back and waited for the relaxation to hit.

It didn't take long. She hadn't eaten anything all day, and the calmness flooded through her like a welcome shot of novocaine. Alone in the darkness, she grinned.

Jason might never love her, but Zoe could take care of herself. She didn't need anyone else. She was content to hang out in a dark basement with her cheap vodka. She took another drink, wishing she had some ice. Oh well, soon she wouldn't be able to taste it anyway.

Something banged upstairs, and she quickly polished off her drink and then looked around for a place to hide. Too bad that they'd done such a thorough job of cleaning the basement out.

A long folding table was set up against the wall, and chairs were stacked up in front of it. It wouldn't provide complete cover, but she couldn't think of any other ideas. She heard footsteps. She hurried to the table and slid under it. This was ridiculous. Only a third of her body was covered. This hiding spot would only work if no one came downstairs.

She heard footsteps on the stairs. She peeked out around the chairs, holding her breath. It wouldn't be the end of the world if she got caught in here. It wasn't like she was going to get away with this little bender anyway, but she didn't want to get caught *yet*. She wasn't even drunk yet. She was still in a lot of pain. She didn't want to get caught until the pain was gone.

She saw feet. And they were unmistakably her grandmother's feet. She squeezed her eyes shut, and it occurred to her to pray that she wouldn't be found, but she stopped herself just short of that absurdity. God, if he was real, probably wouldn't be on her side with this.

She opened her eyes. The feet held perfectly still. What was Gramma doing? Zoe's lungs were starting to hurt. She would need to exhale soon, and she thought Gramma would probably hear that.

The white sneakers at the bottom of the stairs turned and started back up. Zoe counted steps, *one, two, three* ... *six* and then exhaled.

A door clicked shut. More footsteps. It sounded as though her grandmother was alone up there. But why was she there at all? It's not like she would be worried that Zoe hadn't gotten home from school yet. She wasn't even late yet. Close, but not yet. Maybe Gramma had come into the church for some other reason. Maybe it had nothing to do with Zoe. Yes, that was probably it. And then she'd heard something in the basement and come to investigate. Zoe relaxed. This was a good theory. But she had to hurry up and drink her vodka before she *was* late getting home and her grandmother did start looking for her.

She wanted to get drunk, but she didn't want to torture her grandmother.

She slid out from under the table, but then she didn't even bother to get up. She mixed another drink right there on the floor and started drinking. Then she took out her phone and looked up Jason's social media profile. Yep. "In a relationship." She brought the cup to her lips. Down the hatch.

Chapter 65
Zoe

The bottle of vodka was almost gone. Her pain wasn't, but she hesitated to polish off the booze. If she drank the whole pint, she might not be able to make it home.

She looked around the room. Would that be so bad? No, it wouldn't. She poured her last drink.

Then she heard footsteps again. This time it was more than one set of feet, and there were voices to go with them.

Gramma again. And Rachel.

Fluorescent lights flooded the basement.

Zoe looked to her left and decided to hide under the table again, but the women arrived in front of her before she could make that happen.

Rachel reached down and grabbed the cup from her hand. She smelled its contents. "Oh, Zoe."

Shut up, Zoe thought. "You don't understand," she said. "I've had a hard day."

"Get up," Rachel said.

Gramma didn't say anything, and Zoe couldn't bear to look at her. She tried to get up, but her legs felt like the trunks of two dead trees. Rachel grabbed her arm and helped her up.

Rachel handed the cup to Gramma. "Dump that evil out." Then she stooped and picked up Zoe's backpack.

Zoe felt bad. It was a really heavy backpack.

"Come on." Rachel tugged her toward the stairs.

Zoe staggered a little but then found her footing. Then she decided she didn't want to leave. She yanked her arm away. "Just leave me here."

Rachel grabbed her arm more firmly. "Absolutely not. This is a house of God."

Zoe tried to yank her arm away again, but Rachel's fingertips sank into her flesh. Zoe expected it to hurt, but it didn't. Why did Rachel have such strong hands?

"I don't want to go ..."

"Don't care." Rachel pulled her toward the stairs. "Upsy-daisy."

Despite her anguish, Zoe laughed at this, and this little flicker of joy propelled her up the stairs. Toward the top she got tired and thought about stopping, but Rachel was right behind her, and Zoe was a little scared of what she would do if she stopped.

They arrived in the sanctuary, and it was almost dark. How long had she been in the basement? "How did you find me?" she asked, slurring her words.

"God," Rachel said.

That wasn't much of an answer. "Where are we going?"

"Home," Gramma said from somewhere behind her.

Rachel gave her another little shove toward the door.

It wasn't worth resisting. Her little party was over. Might as well go home and go to bed. She remembered her new bed and got excited. It was so comfy. She couldn't wait to pull the blankets up over her head and slip into oblivion.

Rachel stayed uncomfortably close to her across the lawn. Was she worried she might run away? Her foot hit a hole and she staggered sideways. Rachel caught her arm and steadied her. Oh. Maybe *that's* why she was so close.

By the time they arrived at Gramma's front door, Zoe was exhausted. She couldn't wait to hit that bed.

Rachel had other ideas. Once in the apartment, Zoe tried to get to the bed, but

Rachel guided her to the couch. Zoe sat and looked up at her. She looked so tall.

"Bad day?" Rachel didn't sound concerned.

Gramma went into the kitchen.

Zoe nodded. "Jason is back together with Alita."

She expected Rachel's expression to soften, but it didn't.

Gramma grabbed her purse off the kitchen table. "I'm going to the grocery store. I'll be back."

"I'm sorry, Gramma," Zoe called out weakly.

Her grandmother ignored her.

"I love you," she called after her, but again—ignored.

Rachel watched Gramma leave and then turned her eyes back on Zoe, and she shrank under the weight of her gaze.

"Can I just go to bed?"

"Who cares?"

Zoe looked up, confused. "Huh?"

"Who cares about Jason?" She threw her arms up in the air, and one of her hands hit her enormous yellow hat, knocking it askew. "He's a stupid boy!"

Zoe almost laughed at the crooked hat, but Rachel's words took away the funniness. "He's not stupid. He's perfect."

Rachel laughed derisively. "Oh, I assure you, he's not. And even if he was, I repeat, *so what*?"

What was the point of this? She was tired. She started to tip over and lie down. She could sleep on the couch too.

Rachel grabbed her shoulders and sat her upright. "No. We're going to talk. You were doing so well! Why did you decide to get drunk in a church?"

I had nowhere else to get drunk, she thought but did not say aloud. "I told you. Jason got back to—"

"Ahh!" Rachel cried dramatically. "I don't care one iota about Jason!"

Zoe shrugged. "But I do."

"No. You don't get to use him as an excuse for this. This is about you, not him. You need to take responsibility for your actions."

All right. Enough of the lecture.

Rachel stepped closer and lowered her voice, but only a little. "So, I repeat, why did you decide to get drunk?"

She'd just answered this question. Maybe if she didn't participate in this interrogation, it would go faster. She folded her arms across her chest, accidentally clawing herself on the chin in the process.

"You've changed since you got here, Zoe. You've had a direct encounter with the God of the universe. That's something that a lot of people never get to experience. And then you just threw away all that progress because a boy made you sad? Why are you kicking against the goads? Why are you trying to hurt yourself? I know you've got lots of hormones swirling around inside you right now, but that's still no excuse for choosing death! Come on! Don't you know? Haven't you learned in the past few weeks that life is worth living? You have such a wonderful life, Zoe! Your future is so bright! Why are you trying to throw it all away? Why are you trying to die?"

She'd stopped talking. Zoe was confused. That had been *so* many words. "What's a goad?"

Chapter 66
Rachel

What's a goad? That's what this child in front of her had just asked. And despite all her righteous indignation, this softened Rachel's heart. This young woman was as clueless as Rachel had been at her age. Why had she expected anything different?

She took a deep breath and sat down beside Zoe on the couch. "Do you know who Paul was in the Bible?"

Predictably, Zoe shook her head.

"Well, Paul was one of the greatest men of the Bible. He wrote many books of the New Testament and helped to spread the Gospel all over the world."

She could see that Zoe's eyes were glazing over.

"Paul changed the world. But he started out as kind of a jerk. He did a lot of bad things. And then, and this was *after* Jesus died on the cross and came back to life, Jesus appeared to Paul on a road. Sound familiar?"

Zoe's eyes did not register any connection.

Rachel reached out and took her hand. "Jesus doesn't appear to many people the way he appeared to you."

"Jesus ... he didn't appear to me."

"Zoe, *Jesus* is the one who carried you home that night."

She didn't argue. Her face was impassive. How drunk was she?

"You know what? Hang on a second." She got up and went toward the kitchen. Then she stopped and turned back. "Don't you dare lie down." Once she was encouraged that Zoe would at least try to remain upright, Rachel continued into the kitchen and ripped open the fridge. There was precious little in it, and she didn't want to prepare anything. A box of cheese crackers on top of the fridge caught her eye. Perfect. She brought them to Zoe. "Eat these."

She expected an argument, but she didn't get one. Zoe opened the box and shoved a handful into her mouth.

Rachel sat back down. "So, Jesus appeared to Paul in the road, and he said, 'Paul, you idiot, why are kicking against the goads?' A *goad* is a sharp stick that people use to direct cattle. If the cow goes where it's supposed to, all is well, but if she doesn't, then she gets stabbed with a sharp stick. Sometimes Jesus carries a sharp stick, which doesn't hurt us at all if we walk straight, but when we don't, we get jabbed. And when we *kick* against the goads, then we experience *real* pain. You don't even know what real pain is yet, Zoe, and I don't want you to."

Zoe's face was still blank.

Rachel had an idea. She took her phone out of her pocket, did a quick search, and held the phone out so Zoe could see its screen.

The video showed a handsome young rancher following a cow around with a stick. Rachel realized too late that this particular stick was the electrified version. She didn't even know they made such a thing. What would the Apostle Paul think of that—an electric goad? Oh well. The metaphor still worked.

The young rancher poked the cow. The cow's back legs spun at the ground for a second, but then the cow moved forward.

"See? Just a little jab, and the cow moves. The cow's not stupid enough to stand there and kick against the stick."

Zoe slowly turned her head toward Rachel. "It's a cattle prod."

Rachel snickered. "Yes. A cattle prod."

"So why didn't you just say that in the first place?"

Rachel sighed. "The King James calls it a goad. Anyway, do you get the point I'm trying to make?"

Zoe nodded slowly, and the expression on her face gave Rachel hope that she really did get it.

"I'm not supposed to kick a cattle prod."

Rachel snickered. "Right."

"If God is real, then he's trying to force me where he wants me to go, and I don't want to go there."

Oh boy. "Yes, something like that. God *is* real, and the fact that he's pursuing you like this means you are *very* special, Zoe."

Zoe's eyes filled with tears. "I'm not special. Well, I might be special, but in the wrong way."

Rachel tried to understand that but didn't. "What do you mean?"

She shook her head. "I'm hideous. No one is ever going to love me."

Rachel's heart cracked. "Zoe, you are *not* hideous. You are a beautiful child of God. You might not be Hollywood beautiful, but you are still beautiful because you're *you*. You're the only one of you there is."

Zoe studied the box of crackers in her hand. "I used to try, you know? I used to try to look good. Wear good clothes. Makeup. Not wear my hair like this." She reached up and raked a hand through her short hair, which was now growing out and showing dark blond roots.

When she didn't continue, Rachel asked, "Why'd you stop trying?"

She shrugged. "Way better to act like you don't care than to try and fail."

Rachel could definitely relate to this. "Who said you were failing?"

She shrugged again. "Everybody ... my mom."

"What did your mom say?" Rachel asked softly.

Zoe didn't answer at first. "She didn't have to say it. She was thinking it."

Rachel took a long breath. "Eat some more crackers."

Zoe did.

Rachel got up to get her a glass of water. When she returned, she said, "Zoe, I don't know everything, but I think it's important to be who God made you to be. If you want to wear sweatpants and black hair, then okay. But if you don't, then don't."

Zoe looked confused.

"You may not have noticed, but I don't exactly dress like everyone else."

Zoe's eyes drifted to the hat on her head. It was one of her favorites. It was made with actual peacock feathers. "Really? I hadn't noticed."

"You know why I wear this hat? Because I used to do the same thing you're doing. I wasn't good at looking like a lady, so I dressed like a man. I acted like a man. I wanted them to like me and the only way I thought I could accomplish that was to be one of them. But you know what? That failed miserably because that's not really who I was. So I decided that I would just be me and not worry about who liked me. I started buying bright, bold, colorful clothing because I thought it was fun. Bright colors make me happy. I was so full of Jesus that I was full of joy, and I wanted that joy to show. I was tired of hiding."

Zoe gave her a disgusted look. "Was this before or after your handsome husband came to save you? I'm guessing it was after? So you had the confidence to dress crazy?"

Rachel flinched. "My husband didn't save me. Jesus did that. And I suppose my husband did give me more confidence, but I already had a lot of confidence because of Jesus."

Zoe tipped her head back. She was obviously disgusted, and Rachel wasn't sure where the conversation had gone off the tracks. She'd thought they were making good headway. "You said you were a single mom and then your husband came along and made everything okay."

"I never said that. I was a single mom, yes, but I was a single mom depending wholly on Jesus. Life wasn't perfect, but I was content, and I was filled up with him. When my husband came along, he was just icing on the cake of my life. He wasn't the cake. I already had cake." She scooted closer to Zoe and forced eye contact. "Zoe, no boy and no man will ever be the cake. That's not what they're designed for, and if you have that expectation, you will always be disappointed. And it's not fair to the man. If you're expecting him to fix all your problems, then he'll fail. A man is just a man. But God is God. If you get right with God, you *will* be okay, whether or not you have a man."

Zoe broke eye contact, and tears slid down her cheek.

Rachel reached out and gently wiped them away. "It's going to be okay, Zoe. God's got you. I have a feeling he's had his hand on you for a long time." She leaned back into the couch and pressed play on her phone. That was enough lecturing for now. Might as well watch the rest of the cow video. "Finish your crackers. Then get some sleep. I'm glad you're home and safe. I was really scared."

Chapter 67
Zoe

Zoe slept straight through until Saturday morning. When she woke up, both Rachel and her grandmother were sitting at the tiny kitchen table that people rarely sat at. "Good morning." Zoe rubbed her eyes.

"Good morning, honey."

The events of the night before came rushing back, and Zoe felt sick. She got up, and wobbly legs carried her to the bathroom. When she got to the door, she turned and looked at her grandmother. "I'm really sorry." She wanted to say more, but she didn't have the words.

"I know, honey."

She went into the bathroom. Her grandmother hadn't seemed mad. Disappointed, sad, but not mad. She thought maybe her being mad would be easier to bear than the disappointment.

When she came out of the bathroom, both women watched her walk into the kitchen. She took the jug of orange juice out of the fridge and poured herself a quart.

When she'd drunk half of it and set the glass down, Rachel said, "I owe you an apology, Zoe."

Rachel owed *her* an apology? How did that make sense?

"I threw a lot of stuff at you last night, and I'm sorry. Not only do I not want to lecture you, but I should have waited till you were sober."

Zoe pulled a stool over to the table and sat on it. "It's okay. I wasn't that drunk."

Rachel looked skeptical. "Do you remember what we talked about?"

Zoe thought about it. "I think so. Colorful hats, electric cattle prods, and men not being cake."

Gramma's eyes widened in bewilderment.

Rachel laughed. "Yes, that was pretty much it."

Zoe looked down at her glass of orange juice. "I don't even know if God is real. What if he's not? Don't really want to be making life decisions based on a fairy tale."

Her grandmother jumped as if *she'd* been the one shocked by a cattle prod, and Zoe felt guilty. She didn't want to hurt her grandmother.

"Sorry," she mumbled.

"I understand," Rachel said.

Zoe looked up. She did?

"We're going to go work at the church." She looked at Gramma. "You ready?"

Gramma nodded and stood up. "Let me know if you need anything, honey."

"Okay," she said because she didn't know what else to say.

And then they were gone, leaving her all alone. Again. Why hadn't they invited her to go with them? Maybe they didn't want her. Or maybe they'd just assumed she didn't want to go. Maybe they'd thought she was too hungover to work. She would have been if Rachel hadn't force-fed her a giant box of cheese crackers.

Zoe got dressed, wondering what she was going to do with herself. The image of that poor cow getting jabbed in the butt was fresh and vivid in her mind. Was that what this move to Maine had been? God jabbing her in the butt? And then everything since then? More little jabs? And she still wasn't going in the direction he wanted her to go, apparently. What direction was that, exactly?

She shook her head. Why was she trying to figure all this out when she didn't even know if God was real? All old people believed in God, right? It was a generational thing. She liked Rachel, and she loved her grandmother, but that didn't mean they were right about the meaning of life.

She tried not to think about it as she got dressed. But her mind kept coming back to that poor cow. So funny that Rachel had shown her a *video* of it.

Fully dressed and partially rehydrated, Zoe sat down on the couch. What was she going to do with herself? The very first thought that occurred to her was to find some alcohol. She couldn't believe this had popped into her head, and she tried to slap it out. What on earth was wrong with her? Her eyes rested on the window. It was super sunny out. She should go outside. And then what? She didn't know, but she should go outside, and she shouldn't bring any money with her, or any bag big enough to hide a stolen liquor bottle in.

The sunlight felt like a kiss on her forehead. Yes, this had been a good decision. She wasn't much of an outdoor girl, but the fresh air felt good this time. She started walking with no destination in mind.

Her stomach churned a little. So she hadn't *entirely* escaped without a hangover, but she was closer to healthy than she deserved.

The leaves were falling rapidly, leaving branches almost bare. It was almost winter. What was a winter in Carver Harbor going to be like? Probably unbearably boring. Maybe she *should* play basketball like Jason kept insisting.

No.

Better not to think about Jason.

She realized she was standing in front of the weird little shack that she, in her drunken stupor, had once thought was a tiny church.

Chapter 68
Zoe

Zoe looked up and down the street to see if anyone was watching. It appeared she was alone. She tentatively stepped up onto the creaky, partially rotten front porch of the small shack. She couldn't believe she'd lain down on this thing.

She stopped and turned back to the street. This vantage point felt incredibly familiar. She closed her eyes and tried to remember that night. The sound of his voice. The feel of his arms. The smell of him. She'd felt so safe in his arms. And it was unlike any safety she'd ever felt before. Not only had she felt safe from any threats around her, but she'd felt safe to be herself.

Her eyes popped open, and tears sprang into them. She grabbed a post to steady herself.

Oh no.

That hallucination had been real, hadn't it? Somehow, right then, she knew that it had been. It hadn't been the moonshine. It hadn't been a dream or a vision. It had really happened. How else could she have gotten all the way home?

She let herself slide down until she was sitting. Her breath came fast as the reality of it washed over her. If it had been real, what did that mean?

She closed her eyes again. "God, are you real?" she whispered. "Are you really out there?" She laughed at herself. This was preposterous. "If you are real, can you show me?" As soon as she whispered the words, she was embarrassed of them. He already *had* shown her. He'd picked her up and carried her home. He'd spoken to her.

You know better than this ... This is not who you are ... This is not where you're supposed to be ...

Her tears came harder and faster. She bowed her head. She was so sick of crying, and she wasn't sure she had the fluid to support another fit of it. "How do I know better than this, God? And if this isn't who I am, then who am I? Where am I supposed to be?"

And then she remembered her eighth birthday party. The crushing disappointment. The embarrassment. The loneliness that felt like drowning.

And then she remembered the hug that had come after. The presence. The peace.

"Oh my God," she whispered, and her voice didn't even sound like her own. "You're real, aren't you?" He had to be. He was real, and he'd been there all along. Hadn't Rachel said something like that? *God had had his hand on her for a long time.* She remembered knowing him when she was little. She remembered when he'd shown up after her failed birthday party. "Okay," she said aloud, "I give up. I'll stop fighting you. I'll stop kicking against the … against the whatever. I'm sorry."

A feeling settled over her then, permeating every layer of herself. She didn't know what to call it. It was warm, it was peaceful, it was real. It felt supernatural and completely natural at the same time—like she'd been waiting for that exact feeling for her entire life, and now it had come. She opened her eyes and looked up. She almost expected to see someone else there, but there was no one, and then she felt silly. Yet, weren't the falling leaves golder than they'd been before? Wasn't the sky bluer? What was happening to her? "I give up," she whispered. "But you'd better show me what to do, because I have no idea."

There was no answer, but Zoe got the idea that under the circumstances, the best place for her to be was with Gramma and Rachel.

So she got up and headed back toward the church.

She felt lighter. Walking felt easier. There was a new feeling in her heart, and it took her a second to give it a name, but then it came to her: hope.

As she approached the church, she noticed that the graffiti was gone. And as she got closer, she could see that the sign had been repainted. And whoever had done it had done a great job.

Neither Gramma nor Rachel seemed surprised to see her.

"The sign looks good. Who fixed it?"

Gramma shrugged. "That little girl's family paid someone to do it. I assume he was a professional because he was very fast."

Figures that she wouldn't have to fix the sign herself.

"Can we help you?" Rachel looked amused.

"Actually, I came to help you. So, what can I do?"

Rachel looked at her curiously. "You look good." Her words were layered with meaning.

Zoe smiled at her. "I feel pretty good." She was tempted to tell them more, to tell them everything, but she didn't know how to explain what had just happened.

Rachel returned the smile. "Good."

Gramma's eyes traveled back and forth between them. "We're tearing up these tiles."

Zoe looked at the floor. There were tiles, for sure, and some of them had been ripped up by feet from long ago or from time itself, but she didn't see any evidence that anyone had ripped up any tiles *today*.

"Well, we haven't exactly gotten started yet," Rachel admitted. She handed her a scraping tool. "Here's a spatula."

Zoe took it from her hand. "Thanks. Why are we ripping these up?" As she got down on her hands and knees, it occurred to her that she had made a mistake in coming here.

"There's a rumor that there might be mold beneath them. And either way, it would be good to get new flooring down, so Vera doesn't catch her cane in these holes anymore."

Yes, that did make sense. So, for the love of Vera, Zoe started scraping up tiles. They came more easily than she'd anticipated, and soon Rachel had appeared beside her with a spatula of her own. Gramma had disappeared.

"You know, I was thinking ..."

"Yes?" Rachel sounded intrigued.

"If you wouldn't mind supervising, I think it would help me stay out of trouble if I kept helping out around here."

She could almost feel Rachel's joy emanating off her. "Of course I wouldn't mind! I think that's a fine idea!"

Awesome. So she did have friends in Carver Harbor. A couple of eighth graders and an old woman. She grinned. She also had Jason. She should be his friend. It made no sense to give up his friendship just because he wasn't in love with her.

She stopped and sat back on her butt. Rachel raised an eyebrow at her.

"Don't worry. I'm not quitting," she said, although it felt good to get off her knees. She took out her phone, unblocked Jason's number, and then texted, "Sorry. I was having a bad day yesterday, and I shouldn't have taken it out on you. Please forgive me?"

Feeling much better, she slid the phone back into her pocket and went back to scraping.

Chapter 69
Zoe

Zoe was actually excited to go to church. It made little sense to her, but that lack of reason didn't dampen her excitement. She was so excited that she almost went to church early when her grandmother went. But then she decided she didn't want to sit around and eat doughnuts with Gramma's friends, so she stayed home and played on her phone instead. Nevertheless, her leg bounced up and down nervously, and she checked the time at least every two minutes.

Finally, it was time to go. She jumped up and headed for the door.

It was freezing outside, but Derek was still on the steps. He was singing, and she could see his breath in the cold air.

"Good morning," she said brightly.

He stopped singing. "Good morning. Hey, sorry I tattled on you. It seemed the thing to do."

She stopped. Tattled? Oh, so *that's* why her grandmother had been looking for her. The homeless guy had ratted her out. "That's okay." She didn't know what else to say. She forced another smile and then quickly went up the steps.

The sanctuary looked the same as it had looked on previous Sundays. All the same people were there. Yet, everything felt different.

When Jason walked in, Zoe's breath caught. *Stop it*, she told herself. *He's just a boy. He's not cake.* She waited for him to drift into a pew and then went to him. He'd texted her back that all was forgiven, but she still wanted to make sure.

"Hey."

He gave her a broad smile. "Hey yourself. Did you see the sign's fixed?"

She nodded. "Yeah, but Isabelle wasn't the one to fix it."

He shrugged. "We'll take what we can get. And rumor is they're going to pay to have the window fixed too."

Her first reaction to this was panic that she wouldn't be able to use the broken window to sneak in anymore, but then she thought, *Do I really need to sneak into the church anymore?* She realized she was grinning like a nut and tried to wipe the smile from her face.

"You look happy."

"Thanks. Yeah. I guess I am happy, a little. It's been a weird weekend."

Jason nodded as if he understood, which, of course, he didn't. "Yeah."

"I wanted to ask you ..." Her stomach felt like it was on a roller coaster.

"Yeah?"

"You invited me to a Bible study in the morning?"

He nodded with an eagerness that bordered on lunacy. "Thursday mornings!"

She smiled. "If that invitation still stands, I'd like to join you."

"Of course! I'll pick you up!"

"Great. Thanks." She wondered if Alita went to Bible study, but then she decided that she didn't care.

Rachel called out the two-minute warning. "I'm gonna go sit with Gramma. See you later."

"Do you want a ride to school tomorrow?"

She smiled. "Sure. That would be great. Thanks."

She returned to the second pew, where her grandmother was sitting beside Walter. In fact, they were sitting quite closely together. Almost feeling like she was intruding, she gave them a buffer.

Her grandmother completely ignored this buffer and slid closer to her. "How are you doing, honey?"

She thought about how she should answer. She almost felt *bubbly*, but she didn't know how to express bubbliness. "I'm good, Gramma. Like, really good." She paused. How could she explain what she was feeling, what she'd figured out? "I'm sorry that I acted like all the Jesus stuff wasn't real. I know now that it is."

"Oh, honey!" Her grandmother slid even closer, wrapped her arm around her shoulders, and squeezed her so tightly it hurt. "I love you so much, sugar, and I am so proud of you."

Zoe felt like beaming. Had anyone ever been proud of her? For anything? If so, they hadn't told her.

Her grandmother kissed her on the temple. "Thanks for coming to live with me, kiddo."

Yeah, like she'd had a choice. She giggled. "You're welcome."

Rachel carried her hymnal to the pulpit. "Welcome to New Beginnings Church! We're so glad you're here! Do we have any announcements?" She barely gave anyone a chance to answer before continuing, "Great. So, I know we usually start with some good old-fashioned hymns, but Fiona"—she glanced at the organist, who didn't turn to look at the congregation—"heard a new song this week that she feels led to share with us. So …" She turned to look at a mobile projector screen. Where had that come from? "We're going to try to get some lyrics up on a screen."

Nothing happened.

Rachel was staring intently at someone over Zoe's head. Zoe turned to see Cathy in a near panic, fiddling with a projector. Should she go to help? She wasn't sure she could do any better, but maybe? But then the great Jason hopped up and went to Cathy's rescue. Oh good, she wouldn't have to do it.

Within seconds, there were words on the screen. And immediately, without being told to, Fiona started to play.

"Feel free to sing along, if you know it," Rachel said.

The melody grabbed Zoe by the heart and squeezed. There hadn't even been any lyrics yet, and Zoe's eyes watered. What was going on? She gripped the pew in front of her and looked at the floor. But then the congregation started to sing the words, and Zoe had to look up in order to follow along. *I am brand-new. I am brand-new in you. When I'm feeling old, when I'm feeling worn, remind me that I'm brand-new in you.* Whoa. Zoe hadn't ever felt old, but she sure had felt worn, and she'd *never* felt brand-new. At least, not until yesterday, when whatever had happened had happened on that weird little porch, the porch on the church that wasn't even a church. Was that what she was, brand-new?

The sky might be falling. The weight might be too much for my shoulders to bear. But I have heard you calling, so take this weight, take this pain, take all my cares. She didn't know the tune yet, but she tried to sing along. *I am brand-new. I am brand-new in you. When I'm feeling old, when I'm feeling worn, remind me how I'm brand-new in you.* This song was hitting a little too close to home. Tears gushed out of her eyes. She stopped singing, stopped trying to follow along and keep up, and she simply bowed her head and listened to the others singing. *I can forget yesterday. You have erased who I used to be. All I want to do is what you say. I just want to be the me you made me.* Zoe smiled, remembering that voice, that voice that had broken through all her darkness: *This is not who you are.*

But things were different now. She could feel it. Finally, after all this time, she was becoming who she really was. She'd spent so much time hating herself, but that person she'd hated hadn't even been the real her. And the thought of discovering who she really was thrilled her. It filled her with hope. It made her excited for the days ahead.

Unfortunately, the song ended, and they went back to their usual hymns. These were boring, but her encouragement didn't dissipate. She was still on cloud nine when the final hymn ended and Cathy told them they could all sit.

Cathy was staring at the front door, which was in the back of the sanctuary. Zoe craned her head around to see that a man had entered their church. He wore jeans and a short sleeve dress shirt. He looked about twenty years old and carried a giant Bible at his hip. Who was this guy and where had he come from? Zoe turned back around. And why was Cathy staring at him like that? Zoe turned again to watch the man come down the aisle.

"Sorry to interrupt," he said, sounding nervous.

Cathy seemed to find herself. "Of course not. No interruption at all. Welcome, welcome." She put on her reading glasses and looked down at the papers on the pulpit. But she didn't start talking. This was unusual.

Cathy was always so comfortable up there, but right now, she looked distinctly uncomfortable. After a painful silence, she looked at the man again, peering out at him over her glasses. "I feel as though you have something you want to tell us."

He glanced nervously around the sanctuary. What on earth was going on? He stood up and cleared his throat. "My name is Adam Lattin, and God told me to come here and be your pastor."

For a minute, no one responded. Then Derek called out, "Well, it's about time you showed up."

***

Large Print Books by Robin Merrill

New Beginnings
Knocking
Kicking
Searching

Piercehaven Trilogy
Piercehaven
Windmills
Trespass

Shelter Trilogy
Shelter
Daniel
Revival

Gertrude, Gumshoe Cozy Mystery Series
Introducing Gertrude, Gumshoe
Gertrude, Gumshoe: Murder at Goodwill
Gertrude, Gumshoe and the VardSale Villain
Gertrude, Gumshoe: Slam Is Murder
Gertrude, Gumshoe: Gunslinger City
Gertrude, Gumshoe and the Clearwater Curse

Wing and a Prayer Mysteries
The Whistle Blower
The Showstopper
The Pinch Runner
The Prima Donna

Want the inside scoop?
Visit robinmerrill.com to join
Robin's Readers!

*Robin also writes sweet romance
as Penelope Spark:*

Sweet Country Music Romance
The Rising Star's Fake Girlfriend
The Diva's Bodyguard
The Songwriter's Rival

Clean Billionaire Romance
The Billionaire's Cure
The Billionaire's Secret Shoes
The Billionaire's Blizzard
The Billionaire's Chauffeuress
The Billionaire's Christmas

Made in the USA
Coppell, TX
18 December 2020